Phantom's Dance

LESA HOWARD

DEDICATION

For DJ, Keith, and Kaylie. The original pieces of my heart

ACKNOWLEDGMENTS

When I set out to write this story, I had no idea what it took to become a ballerina. The dedication, athleticism, and sheer passion I discovered in my research astounded me. Though many attend ballets, I'm convinced few know the extent of commitment and sacrifice the ballet dancer makes for his or her art. Only those in this small distinguished community are fully aware. To that end, I apologize for the liberties I've taken in this book. At times, I may have sacrificed the purity of the ballerina's craft to fit my own.

I'd like to thank Jennifer Sommers with the Houston Ballet. Without her help I would have stumbled, pun intended, my way through the world of ballet. Also, and enormous thank you to Hafsah at Icey Designs for the seriously fabulous cover and the patience it took for us to get there.

Chapter One

"Mom, you can't seriously be thinking of injecting poison into your face." Seated in the brocade wingback chair outside my mother's walk-in closet, I tried to process the revelation that she wanted to add Botox to her beauty regimen.

"Don't be ridiculous, Christine. It isn't poison. If it was, the government wouldn't allow it on the market." She emerged from the closet with a hanger in each hand. "Which one looks best?" Casually, she held out the dress in her right hand and then proffered the one in her left.

I pointed to the olive green belted sheath in her left hand and continued, "I don't get it. You're only thirty-eight, and you want plastic surgery?"

"I'm almost thirty-nine, and it's not plastic surgery. Only a couple of injections."

"Have you talked to Dad about this?"

To avoid my question she retreated into the closet, but I wasn't letting it go that easily. I stood and walked to the door, folded my arms across my chest, and leaned against the doorframe to wait for her reply.

Surveying the closet, my gaze landed on the row of Dad's clothes still hanging there. It had been months since he'd stepped foot inside to retrieve any, yet his scent remained, clinging to the slacks and shirts as if the fragrance itself waited for his return.

"Mom, have you discussed this with Dad?"

"You talk to your father more than I do. You tell me what he thinks."

Her biting retort made my stomach churn.

"We have a video chat scheduled Saturday," I said. "You could talk to him then."

Having slipped into the dress, she stepped closer and turned around for me to zip it up. The dress was a good choice. The fabric spread smoothly down her slender hips and accentuated her long back. Dad had always told me I should be grateful I had Mom's figure and not his thick thighs and broad shoulders.

"Benjamin knows how to call me," she said. "If he wanted to talk to me, he would. I'm not having a video chat."

I could remember almost to the day when my mother stopped calling my father Ben and started calling him Benjamin. The summer before my sixteenth birthday, Mom and I had come to Houston for a couple of months so I could attend a summer intensive hosted by the Rousseau Academy of Dance. The Rousseau Ballet Company had one of North America's premier ballet schools, and they only offered a few coveted spots every year. At the end of that summer session, I auditioned and made it into the academy. My parents had known it would mean a move from El Paso to Houston.

As far as their jobs were concerned, the change wasn't a

problem. Dad could work anywhere there was internet, and Mom had transferred to the Houston office of the finance company for which she worked. Not long after we'd moved, though, the arguing started. Then they'd stopped talking altogether. Before long, Dad relocated to Norway. He claimed the demands of the job required him to go. But I knew differently. From then on, Mom called him Benjamin.

"Mom, could you at least try?" I asked.

Sliding a silver hoop into her earlobe, she ended the conversation. "Get your things, Christine, and I'll meet you at the door."

I walked to my room to gather my dance bag and met her in the foyer.

Taking her keys from the table by the door, she looked at me and picked a piece of lint from my warm-up shrug. "Really, Christine, you couldn't have put a little more effort into your makeup this morning?"

"What's wrong with my makeup?" I raised a hand to my cheek.

"It's a bit dull, honey," she said and opened the door to walk out. "You know that looking the part is a significant aspect of your training."

"Yes, but they don't expect us to wear glitter eye shadow to class."

"There's no need to get snarky. I simply think you could do better."

Neither of us spoke after that, not on the elevator down to the parking garage nor on the ride to the school—which gave me time to stare at my reflection in the car window and ponder if she was right. With my hair swept back in the prerequisite bun, it exposed my unusually small ears, but no amount of makeup would fix that. Plus, I probably toweled the sweat from my face a dozen times a day, so what was the point? The makeup I do wear is off by midmorning anyway.

It wasn't until Mom eased the car to the curb in front of the school building that she broke the silence. "I have a meeting this afternoon, but I'll be here around five to get you."

"Okay," I replied, dragging my bag from the seat and stepping out of the car. "But I don't see why I can't walk home." I lowered my head to look in at her. "It would only take about ten-minutes. In fact, with traffic, it probably takes longer to drive it than it does to walk it."

"How would that look, though, honey?" she said. "What if one of your instructors saw you walking home? Or worse, what if Mr. Darby spotted you?"

Stifling a groan, I hoisted my bag high on my shoulder. "I don't think the school's artistic director cares much about how I get home."

"I don't have time to argue this now. Just wait for me this afternoon. Now close the door. I have to go."

Biting my lip to hold back the curse on the tip of my tongue, I slammed the door a split second before she hit the gas and the car pulled away. Then I heard someone call my name and I spun around to see Jenna down the block, wrestling with her dance bag and loose hair bun as she hurried to catch me.

"What was that about?" she asked giving up on the bun to raise the bag over her head and anchor it across her chest.

I glanced back at Mom's car, now stopped at a red light, and I couldn't help wonder why she worried so much about what other people thought. She hadn't always been that way.

But then, I knew why she was in such a foul mood today. It was because I pressed her to talk to Dad.

Dropping my bag onto the pavement, I put my hands on Jenna's shoulders to wheel her around and redo her unraveling bun. "That was Sharon Dadey having the last word," I said, twisting, knotting, and refastening Jenna's thick, amber hair in place.

"My mother's been gone this week," she said, patting the bun for good measure as she pivoted to face me. "Dad actually let me bring chocolate ice cream home last night."

"I'm coming to your place," I declared.

"Eh, party's over. She'll be home this evening."

As we strode across the sizable courtyard that separated the Wakefield Center for the Performing Arts from the Rousseau Academy of Dance, Jenna changed the subject. "Hey, I heard Zaborov will be out today."

We went through the school's side entry and paused inside the hallway. "Yeah? One could only hope."

Lena Zaborov was the toughest instructor at the Rousseau Academy of Dance. Although she'd been instrumental in my acceptance into the school, I'd not had her as an instructor during my first year as a level seven, but now, as a level eight, there was no escaping her. An accomplished dancer and teacher, the woman was a drill sergeant, and it wouldn't bother me to have a day off from her.

Jenna was about to elaborate when behind us the door opened and in stepped Evander Woodruff.

"Be still my heart. If it isn't the girl of my dreams," he crooned in his squeaky adolescent voice.

"Hey, Van," I greeted as he strutted up to us.

"Enchanté." He bowed low, his black curls glinting under

the fluorescent lights.

"So which one of us is it today?" Jenna asked.

Cocky and self-assured, the boy straightened to his full height, which only brought him to Jenna's shoulders, and he took her by the hand.

"It's you, baby. It's always been you." Then drawing her fingers close, he puckered his lips.

"Get over yourself, Woodruff," Jenna grunted and extracted her hand before his mouth could make contact.

Van merely shrugged and smiled impishly as he swept a rounded arm gracefully before his unitard-clad chest. "It's a mystery why you would deny yourself all this."

Jenna rolled her eyes. "Yeah, it's a mystery."

At thirteen, Evander Woodruff was the youngest in the level seven class. Other students his age were still level five or six, but Van danced beyond his years, and consequently, had an ego to match. He was half our size, but that didn't stop him from hitting on us every opportunity he got. And though we'd shot him down repeatedly, he seemed impervious to the rejections and insisted we'd change our minds when he hit his growth spurt.

Suddenly, Van's phone went off, halting the conversation. Jenna made a shushing sound as she glanced over her shoulder down the hall at a couple of students standing outside a classroom. "You'd better turn that off before you get busted. We're not supposed to use phones anywhere near a classroom."

Van made a whistling sound through his teeth, and ignoring her warning, withdrew the phone from the pocket of the sweat pants he wore over his unitard.

"Oooh, check it," he sputtered and tapped at the screen to reply to the text he'd received. Then a smile spread across his brown, baby face and he held up the phone for us to read the message. "It's from Liam. The theater ghost is back."

Chapter Two

*W*hen Van bolted for the door, Jenna and I rushed out after him. Sprinting across the plaza, away from the school building, we raced toward the Wakefield Center. My dance bag slapped my hip as I ran, and I laughed as I peered at Jenna behind me.

"I hope Zaborov is gone today," I yelled. "She'll crush us if we're late."

The idea of a theater ghost is utterly absurd. Still, as we approached the Wakefield, the hulking edifice that housed the opera and the ballet theaters, the excitement got the better of me and I grew breathless with anticipation.

Wheezing and giggling, we reached the Center's backdoor and found Van's friend Liam waiting inside.

"C'mon," Liam instructed and motioned for us to follow.

On each other's heels, we took the hall leading to the Griffith Theater and hurried to the backstage entry. When we'd made it through the curtains and onto the stage, we almost collided with a crowd of dance students gathered around a security guard standing in the middle of the stage. The man held a notepad, and when he wasn't looking upward, he was doodling on the pad.

Jenna adjusted the bulk of her dance bag, hiked her chin toward Liam, and asked, "So, what's the deal?"

"Look there—beyond the guard." Liam pointed to an area of the stage a couple of feet from the crowd. The floor there was peppered with shattered glass, and it was obvious the security guard was keeping the group of onlookers away from it. Naturally, the four of us lifted our eyes to the overhead lighting to see a busted stage light.

"Everybody's saying the ghost was on the catwalk last night," Liam said.

"Cooool," Van crooned. "This is awesome."

"Get out," Jenna muttered, as we moved closer.

Static energy sparked around the stage as everyone talked at the same time. The clatter of voices echoed through empty theater, making it sound like ten times more people than were actually there, as rumor and speculation filtered through the throng. I've attended many ballets, and almost every theater had its ghost story. There was always someone, or something, haunting the halls and plaguing the dancers. There was no reason why the Wakefield Center with its two theaters would be any different.

Movement overhead caught my attention. There was another security guard on the catwalk above us. I nudged Jenna to look as the man made a show of examining the damaged fixture. With an air of self-importance, he stooped forward to inspect the light's framework and the crowd around us seemed to hold its breath.

Playfully, Jenna coughed into her hand and murmured, "Rent-a-cop," breaking the silence and annoying some of the spectators.

I elbowed her and several kids around us shushed her.

"Oh, c'mon. That was funny," she whined and touched her ribs where my elbow had connected.

We continued to watch as the guard fiddled with the light a few seconds more before scooping something off the grated flooring and straightening. He studied whatever it was in his hand a moment then clenched it in his fist, grabbed the railing, and made his way carefully down the wobbly stairs. When he reached the other security guard, he opened his palm to display its contents. Collectively, we scurried over to see what he held.

"A necklace!" Jenna blurted. "The ghost wore a necklace?"

A silver chain lay draped across the guard's callused fingers. He lifted it for the other man to see and a pendant swung free and dangled in the air. I strained for a closer look, but one of the instructors noticed how many students had gathered and barked out a command, "All of you get to class. There's nothing to see here." Then she brushed aside an onslaught of complaints and shooed us off.

Deflated and disappointed, the lower level dancers grumbled as they departed. I tagged along with the stream of people, snatching a couple of backward glances. The guards had put their heads together and were speaking in low tones. I was curious about the necklace. Obviously, there was no ghost, but someone had been up there.

Leaving the same way we'd come, we stepped out of the building into the morning sun and I shielded my eyes from its blinding light. We'd made it a few steps before I realized Van and Liam weren't with us. Taking hold of Jenna's arm, I tugged her aside as the last of the students passed us by. Then I caught sight of Van and Liam. They'd paused outside the door.

"Hey, let's go—before we're late," Jenna shouted at them. But the boys ignored her and she knotted her brow.

We backtracked to join them and as we neared, it sounded like they were arguing. Well, maybe not arguing, but they were clearly worked up over something.

"I didn't do it," Liam bristled, his cheeks blooming red.

Van thumped him smartly on the chest, dismissing his declaration, and growled, "You're gonna get us cau..." but he stopped abruptly when he sensed our presence.

Liam, however, had the last word and added under his breath, "I'm telling you I didn't do it."

Jenna placed a hand on her hip and let her gaze flit from Liam to Van and back again. "What are y'all up to?" she asked suspiciously.

Van shifted his weight casually from one leg to the other, his face a mask of sugary innocence, and said, "Nothing." Then he pinned Liam with an expression that made Liam drop his eyes and look away to avoid his scowl.

When Liam finally lifted his head, tiny beads of sweat dotted the peach fuzz above his lip, and his hands twitched at his side like a nervous gunslinger. "Nothin'," he said, echoing Van's response. "We ain't up to nothin'."

The two sneaks were definitely up to something.

After an extended silence, Van spoke up. "I bet that necklace belonged to that dead dancer. Right, Liam?"

Liam's mouth pinched to one side, and what followed seemed more like reluctant capitulation than agreement. "Yeah, it probably belonged to that dead dancer."

"What dead dancer?" I asked, surprised. There'd been nothing around the school about anyone dying. I wasn't aware of anyone having passed away.

"You've heard of the Wakefield Phantom, haven't you?" Van asked and I shook my head. "There's a legend of a ballerina who died one night after a performance at the Griffith. She threw herself from the balcony because she'd been jilted by her lover."

Jenna pitched her head back and snorted. "Jilted by her lover. You're making that up."

"No, it's true," Van insisted, "It really happened. And now you've seen the evidence. It was a ghost, a phantom."

"There was no phantom," Jenna said. "The evidence was a lost piece of jewelry. There's probably someone already at the office looking for it in the Lost and Found. Stop being such a doofus."

"If I'm such a doofus, how do you explain the broken glass?"

Liam cleared his throat and mumbled softly, "Van, I told you I didn't..."

"Be quiet," Van ordered.

Jenna was right. They had a secret.

"There's something weird going on here," I said.

"I know. I know. That's what I'm trying to tell you," Van reiterated. "All kinds of weird things have been happening around this place. They found a chip bag and soda can up there last week."

"How is that weird?" Jenna asked. "A ghost wouldn't eat Doritos and drink Coke. It was probably a stage hand's trash."

"No, I'm telling you the place is haunted. Someone should call Paranormal Response Team and get Mason Riggs and his crew in here."

Jenna and I both laughed then and she said, "So that's

what this is about. You want to be on TV."

Paranormal Response Team is a reality show on the Exploration Network. It's a hugely popular ghost hunting show, and Mason Riggs, a hotty I'd ghost hunt in the dark with any day, is its host.

"You have to admit, it would be cool," Van said. "Think about it. The Wakefield Center could have its own Phantom of the Opera."

Jenna raised a halting hand. "Whoa, wait a minute there Andrew Lloyd Webber. There is no ghost. All this was the two of you, wasn't it?" She pointed an accusing finger at the boys. "Admit it."

"Nuh-huh!" Liam shook his head vehemently. "I'm telling you, I didn't do that. I didn't smash that stage light."

Jenna crossed her arms over her chest and eyed him doubtfully.

Suddenly, I remembered something Mom had mentioned some time back, and I gasped. "Please tell me you guys didn't do that break-in at the Wakefield office."

The three of them turned their surprised faces to me and after a split second of silence, they all chimed, "What break-in?"

Chapter Three

*A*ll the color drained from Liam's face, and he swerved, panic-stricken, to his friend. "Van, what is she talking about? Why would the phantom break in to anything?"

"Someone broke into the Wakefield office?" Jenna said.

"It was a while ago. I'm not sure, maybe two weeks," I replied. "Mom told me someone picked the lock and stole the cash receipts."

"Oh, man," Liam wailed, bouncing restlessly and twitching a hand frantically in the air. "We are so gonna get busted."

"You guys did that!" I exclaimed. "You took that money?"

"No, of course not," Van snapped. "We'd never do anything like that."

"Then what exactly is it that you have done?" Jenna demanded.

Van tucked a thumb into the band of his sweatpants and scratched the back of his head with the other hand. "We a... we may have planted some of the phantom evidence, but we had nothing to do with a robbery."

Liam's chest heaved so that I feared he would hyperventilate. "We didn't trash that stage light either. We didn't. I swear. You believe me, don't you?"

Jenna gripped Liam's shoulders. "Calm down. Stop wiging out. If you say you didn't do it," she looked at me dubiously, "then we believe you."

"Yeah, I'm sure there's an explanation for everything," I reassured him. Then I glanced at Van. "You said you staged some phony phantom clues?"

Van nodded. "But I don't know anything about the light or the necklace. I figured Liam did it."

"I didn't!" Liam sputtered, his face splotched purple with dread.

"It's probably like Jenna said," I told Liam. "The light fixture was faulty. Those lamps are sensitive. They can explode if not taken care of properly. And the necklace could have belonged to anyone. It's a coincidence that's all."

"You think so?" Liam said, his breathing coming under control.

"Right, right" Van said. "It was coincidence, man. That's all."

"So we're good here?" Jenna asked, and the boys bobbed their heads in agreement. "No more phantom, though," she added. "You're liable to get yourselves into a world of hurt if you keep it up. I mean if we suspected you of the break-in, the cops could have as well."

"I'm done with it," Liam said, relief relaxing his features. "Count—me—out."

We waited for Van to acquiesce. Grudgingly, he pressed his lips together and diverted his gaze. "Whatever, man." And with nothing further, he tapped Liam on the arm and motioned for Liam to follow him.

Jenna and I let the boys go and took our time falling in behind them. When they were out of earshot I commented,

"None of that explains the necklace."

"Yeah, but I'm pretty sure I know where the necklace came from," she replied.

"Yeah, where?"

"Somebody was up there hooking up."

"Eww, seriously? Hooking up—on the catwalk?"

We'd arrived at the school door, Jenna opened it, and we entered. "Sure, the staff—custodians, theater and stage hands, even the male dancers—they do it all the time. Take a girl up there, make promises to get her an audition, and then get a little action."

"That's disgusting."

"Don't knock it 'til you try it," she teased and wiggled her eyebrows.

My mouth dropped open and I stammered, "Y-you went up there with a guy? You actually, well, you know? Up there?"

Jenna grinned. "I never kiss and tell," she said. Then she left me standing there, gaping after her, as she walked to the dressing room to put away her dance bag.

Jenna was the first person to welcome me to the Rousseau Academy of Dance. Actually, she'd been the only person to welcome me to the Academy. The dance world is extremely competitive and it's difficult to spend eight hours a day with your competitor-slash-friends and have genuine relationships. Jenna, however, had been the real deal. She seemed to have an innate ability to push aside the competition aspect and simply be herself. But part of Jenna being herself was her fascination with getting a reaction from people. She loved to BS and as a result, I wasn't always certain she was being truthful.

I scurried to catch up with her in the dressing room but decided not to press her about the catwalk anymore. It was a subject I wasn't comfortable with anyway.

By the time we'd stowed our things and made it to the studio, class had begun. Scattered across the floor, our classmates were already warming up. Their violet-blue leotards, pink tights, and breezy movements made them look like delicate butterflies gracing the studio floor.

"Well, look who decided to join us." I cringed when our instructor Ms. Zaborov's voice cut across the room.

The warm-up came to a screeching halt then as the pianist on the other side of the room ground out a note that echoed the length of the studio, and all eyes locked onto us.

"You said she wasn't going to be here," I whispered.

"She wasn't supposed to be," Jenna replied.

"I hope she lets us in."

We stood inside the door unsure how to proceed. If a dancer was late to class, he or she couldn't enter unless invited. After our effrontery, I wondered whether Ms. Zaborov would allow us to participate in the first class of the day or make us sit out.

"Perhaps you would like to join the rest of us, no?" she said in her heavy Russian accent.

Embarrassed, I mumbled a thank you, ducked my head, and found my place on the cold vinyl floor.

In front of the mirror, legs extended before me, I stretched my neck and shoulders and tried not to look at my reflection. I knew my face would still be red because I could feel the remaining flush. When I finally glanced up, I caught sight of Deirdre O'Connor beside me, a frown on her face. With her next stretch, she leaned out to be closer to me and snarled,

"You'd better be glad she didn't take it out on the rest of us."

Deirdre had every reason to be annoyed with Jenna and me. Lena Zaborov was old-school. To her, everything must be traditional and done by the book. A former principal dancer with a company in Russia, it's said that if she hadn't been a dancer, she would have made a hell of a KGB operative.

I was about to apologize to Deirdre when Jenna, on the floor behind me, arched forward to grab her toes and chimed, "Piss off, Deirdre."

Unmoved, Deirdre gave us both dirty looks and continued her warm-up.

Several minutes passed, while Ms. Zaborov weaved in and out of the dancers splayed across the floor, her face impassive and giving no hint of what was going through her mind. In spite of my complaints, I'd learned a lot from her. In her day, Lena Zaborov had been one of the most sophisticated and skilled dancers to perform. I'd seen YouTube clips of her work and she appeared to float when dancing. It was like her toes never really touched the floor. She was Russia's darling and every aspiring ballerina strove to be like her. The Rousseau Academy of Dance was lucky to get her as an instructor.

It was because of her, and others like her, that we'd moved here in the first place. I hated to leave El Paso—my school and friends—but I'd gone as far as I could there. My parents knew being a student at the Rousseau Academy would increase my chances of getting into a prestigious ballet company like NYCB. I would give anything to get into the New York City Ballet. We'd visited there for my thirteenth birthday, and I'd not stopped dreaming of it since. For now, though, I had to get into a junior company like the Rousseau II for pre-professional training, and I wasn't going to do that by being late to class and making an instructor angry.

Once we'd completed floor barre exercises, we moved on to technique. It appeared Jenna and I'd gotten away with our tardy—until class was over.

"Christine!" Ms. Zaborov bellowed after dismissing everyone. "You and Jenna will remain."

"Oh, man," Jenna moaned as we hung back. "She's pissed."

One by one, dancers left the room, some giving us pitying looks before exiting. Deirdre was last to walk by. She opened her mouth to speak, but slammed it shut when she saw Jenna's cold glare. Instead, she squared her shoulders and gave us a superior grunt before sashaying out.

"I hate that girl," Jenna murmured.

We turned to Ms. Zaborov then, and she dipped her chin, slightly lowering her gaze to a point on the floor obviously meant for us. Jenna and I scuttled over to that location as she tapped the toe of her sensible, leather and suede teaching shoes.

"It would seem," she said, an invisible line holding her spine erect, "the two of you have the time on your hands, no?"

"We're really sorry, Ms. Z.," I began. "We went to the..."

"Nyet!" She cut me off with an impatient yip. "I do not wish to hear the excuses." Pursing her lips, she smoothed the front of her skirt before clasping her hands in front of her. "I think I have the solution for dancers with the time on their fingers."

Beside me, Jenna stifled a giggle as she tried not to react

to Ms. Zaborov's misuse of the slang.

Aware we were about to be sentenced, I swallowed the dread rising in my chest and remained serious.

"Solution?"

She might be no bigger than a hummingbird, but Lena Zaborov could reduce a ballerina to tears with a single look.

"Our esteemed artistic director, Mr. Darby, has asked me to help with a promise he made to the board member, Mr. Chaney. It seems Mr. Chaney has a nephew who plays—oh, what is it ..." Ms. Zaborov twirled her hand delicately in the air as if to grasp the right word. "The football! He plays the football."

I looked at Jenna and her eyes grew big. She shrugged her shoulders and made a motion with her hand to her mouth to say Ms. Z. must have been drinking.

"One of the trustees has a nephew who plays the football, and he would like us to teach the team ballet."

"Football players want to take ballet?" Jenna questioned.

"That is correct. And since you and Christine have much time, you will teach them."

Chapter Four

"I don't understand, Mrs. Zaborov. You want us to show football players how to dance?" I asked.

It wasn't unusual for upper-level dancers to teach or mentor younger students. Sometimes we did private tutoring, but that was with children.

"It is quite simple, my dear Christine. Tomorrow afternoon, the director will bring the football players, and you and Jenna will be here to greet them. Then we will set a time for classes to begin and you will assist."

Jenna's mouth moved but no sound came out. I was at a loss as well. But Ms. Zaborov, pleased she'd meted out punishment suiting the offense, gave us a dismissive snap of her head. "Now, I have a class waiting. You will excuse me." Then she proceeded, dainty and light-footed, out of the room.

In the aftermath, Jenna sputtered, "What the hell just happened?"

"It looks like we're going to teach football players to dance," I replied.

"No way. Nuh-uh. Not me. I'm not teaching a bunch of knuckle-dragging no-necks how to *plié*, much less *pas de deux*. Think what they'd do to our feet!"

"I'm not sure we have a choice." We stared at each other a few seconds before bursting into laughter.

"Oh em gee!" Jenna mocked. "We're going to have jocks in here!"

"I know. Can you imagine?" I glanced at the clock on the wall and dropped the laughter. "We'd better get moving, or we'll be late to *pointe*."

"Right," Jenna agreed. "Because if we're late to another class they're likely to make us teach the chimps at the zoo to *pirouette*."

We changed into clean, dry dance clothes and made it to our next lesson on time. It was difficult to concentrate, though. Normally I didn't have a problem dancing *en pointe*. Being on my toes made me feel like a winged fairy, but Ms. Zaborov's punishment flitted around the back of my mind. I'd never attended a football game and had no idea what to expect of football players. I wasn't even sure what Ms. Zaborov had in mind for us to do. Somehow, I found it both exciting and terrifying.

By noon, it was all over the school. Van wanted the scoop when he plopped his tray down at our lunch table. "So it's true? You're gonna teach football players to dance?"

"It's your fault," Jenna complained. "If we hadn't gone to the theater with you and Liam to check out that supposed ghost sighting, we wouldn't have been late to class."

Van grinned and said, "Bite me, Jenna. And it's a phantom not a ghost. Besides, you had fun and you know it."

Before they could get any testier with each other, several members of our class joined us and talk shifted to teaching football players the difference between ballet slippers and *pointe* shoes. By the end of the day, I still wasn't sure how I felt about it. I kept envisioning the Disney movie where hippos wearing tutus perform to Ponchielli's Dance of the Hours, only this would be helmeted, oversized teenagers sporting enormous shoulder pads above their tutus.

That afternoon, I waited outside the school for Mom to pick me up and debated as to whether I should tell her about being disciplined by Ms. Zaborov. She'd be miffed and there would be the inevitable lecture to follow. I decided to tell her the school's artistic director asked us to do it. She'd never question that. She'd likely see it as an opportunity to suck up to Mr. Darby.

When twenty minutes had passed and Mom hadn't shown up, I pulled my phone from my bag. There was a text message for me to call her when I got out of class.

"Christine," she said breathlessly, picking up after the fourth ring. "I'm in a meeting. I stepped out to take your call. I'll be late this evening so I'll have my assistant call you a cab."

"Mom, I don't need a cab. I can—"

"Just stay there. I'll bring dinner home with me. Gotta go, sweetie. See you later." Then the line went dead.

Resigned, I put my phone away and walked across the plaza to the fountain, where I heaved myself onto the concrete ledge to sit and wait. The air blowing across the cascading waterfall was cool, so I poked around in my bag for my iPod and settled back to relax.

Car after car drove by, but there was no cab and I became impatient. This was ridiculous. Leaping from the ledge, I grumbled, "Screw how it looks. I'm leaving." Then I swung my bag over my shoulder and started down the street.

With the music in my ears and the thrum of the busy streets around me, I felt energized, in spite of a full day of dance class, and it occurred to me that it was the first time since moving here that I'd done anything without Mom— even if it was only a walk home.

Maybe it was time to get my driver's license. Dad would buy me a car if I did, and I wouldn't have to rely on Mom to get back and forth to school any more. We'd talked about it before the move, but after arriving and attending class eight hours a day, school work at night, and the mental weight of it all, I had been too overwhelmed to think about learning to drive. Plus, I was terrified of learning to drive on the ant-farm streets of Houston.

A few blocks down, I slowed my pace. The traffic was lighter, the street quieter, and a rhythmic beat intruded into my own music. I stopped and plucked an earbud from my ear. The sound was ahead of me somewhere, so I stepped across the street and moved toward it. Taking out the other earpiece, I shoved the iPod into my bag.

The cadence flowed from an alley running behind a brick office building. Curious, I made my way down the building's side in that direction. Cautiously, I checked my surroundings. Within a couple of blocks of the theater, everything around me had changed. The street was dirtier and the buildings more decrepit. The aroma of ground coffee no longer poured from the Starbucks a few blocks back. Something acrid floated in the air now. It smelled like a steaming cocktail of motor oil and urine.

The music stopped and I paused. I could hear elevated voices but was unable to make out anything said. Then the music resumed, accompanied by roaring laughter. More intrigued, I took a few steps again and saw where a homeless person had set up camp. I should turn back, but the ramshackle campsite was empty so I kept going.

When I reached the back corner of the four-story, brick building, I hesitated. The sun had dipped below the adjacent structure, leaving the alley in a gray haze and giving it a creepy vibe. My heart sped up as I replayed all the horror stories Mom had drilled into me. Though we tell everyone we're from El Paso, the truth is we lived in a small suburb outside the city. So Mom filled my head with tales about the dangers of living downtown in a city the size of Houston— muggings, assaults, drug deals, she'd warned me repeatedly, and now those cautionary tales were hammering through me with every beat in the music spilling from behind the building.

Pressing my back against the bricks, I felt the heavy thump of the bass in my chest. The music issued out, echoing around me, like a rhythmic call to battle. I stood there long enough for one song to end and another to begin. Then, clutching my bag to my side, I peeked around the bend and was surprised to see a group of about a dozen people gathered in a loose circle. A mixture of ethnicities, some shuffled and shimmied, while others bounced and popped to the music's time.

When their formation shifted, I could see into the ring of figures. A young African-American man danced there, arms snaking in and out and legs nimbly swirling. After several steps, he twitched his head toward someone in the surrounding group, and a woman laughed uproariously before jumping into the center as he sauntered out. She jiggled and jolted to the music in a way that was captivating.

It was as if the music emanated from the dancer, rather than the big boom box sitting on the trunk of a car.

Their laughter was exhilarating, and I could see that taunting and bragging was a part of the performance. Completely engrossed, I became careless and before I knew it, I'd drifted from the safety of the building's shadow to stand in the open. Then someone spoke, and I knew I'd made a horrible mistake.

Chapter Five

"*H*ey, check it!" The young man who'd been in the center of the circle had spotted me. "Looks like the dancer's lost her way."

The circle opened up then, as the group turned to see me.

"What's the matter ballerina, can't find your tutu?" he jibed.

My heart raced, leaving behind the rhythm of the music to create its own, and I froze there as the guy approached me.

"So what is it, ballerina, you lost?"

How'd he know I was a ballerina? Then it dawned on me—the warm-ups, my hair bun, and the leotard beneath my shrug. And if that weren't enough, the slippers swinging from the strap of my dance bag clenched it.

He came closer then, dressed in an oversized red-and-black-striped polo and a pair of well-worn Nikes. His braids swished like a living creature as he cocked his head to study me, and suddenly, I was embarrassed by my pink, zebra-striped dance bag. It looked juvenile—it made me look juvenile.

"C'mon, Dionte, you're scarin' the girl." I looked past the man to the woman who'd been in the center of the dance-off.

She'd come up behind him. Breathing hard, she wiped sweat from her brow and said, "Don't mind Dionte, he's all bark."

When I looked at him again, he did just that—barked. He and the others who'd gathered around me laughed when I jumped.

"Hey, it's cool," he teased. "I was only messin' with you. You can dance—if you think you can hang." Then he took a step back and snapped his shoulders a few times, making them appear liquid as they undulated beneath his shirt. Before I could blink, he executed a back flip that sent the others into a round of cheers.

"I'm Magdalena," the woman said, ignoring Dionte's display and offering me her hand.

Timidly, I took it and gave it a gentle shake. "I was—I heard your music." I pointed stupidly to the boom box on the car.

"We were having a little fun. Wanna join us?" Smiling genuinely, she flicked a thumb over her shoulder, pointing to her friends. She was pretty, with creamy tan skin and chocolate curly-Qs that framed her face. Wearing skinny jeans, a multi-colored tunic, and gold bracelets that jangled at her wrist, she exuded confidence.

There was no moisture in my mouth, but I managed to say, "No, I can't. I have to go."

Retreating a few feet, my back connected with something solid. I spun around and came face to face with a grinning old man. He was toothless and when he spoke, he reeked of alcohol.

"I'll dance with you, darlin'," he slurred.

I shrieked and stumbled a few feet. When the group of dancers laughed at me again, I bolted down the alley and didn't slow my pace until I'd reached the thoroughfare. I stopped long enough to snatch a glance backward. The old man was hobbling toward the makeshift camp, hesitating long enough to do a little jig to the music, and the dancers were returning to their concrete dance studio. My heart pounded and I was breathless. I couldn't imagine what kind of an I-told-you-so Mom would have given me had I been mugged. It hadn't been all bad, though. Something about the encounter excited me. This trumped Van's ghost hunting by a mile.

My pulse had slowed to its normal rate by the time I reached our apartment building. Inside the elevator, I smiled at my own childish behavior. They must have thought me an idiot, running down the alley like I had.

To avoid the elevator music, I pulled my iPod from my bag again and thumbed through the playlist. The doors started to slide into place when suddenly an arm jabbed through the narrow opening and forced them apart once more. A man in a business suit stepped inside, followed by a blond-haired guy I recognized from a few months back when I'd seen him by the rooftop pool. We made eye contact as he reached for the button panel, and I averted my gaze, at once aware how small the elevator was.

When he'd pushed the button for his floor, he waved a hand in the air to get my attention. Then he pointed to the panel. I'd forgotten to choose my floor. Embarrassed, heat crept up my neck and I raised my hand, all five fingers spread apart. He smiled and pushed the fifth-floor button, and my stomach fluttered as I bit my lip to keep from smiling back at him.

In a few swaggering strides, the guy was across the

elevator and leaning lazily against the handrail, stacking his suede chukkas one atop the other. After arranging his plaid over-shirt so that it hung loosely away from his tee, he clipped his thumbs casually into his jeans pockets.

For the second time in less than thirty minutes, I felt uncomfortable in my own skin. I seriously wished I'd changed into street clothes before leaving the studio. Fighting the desire to adjust the waistband of my sweats, I pretended to have great interest in my iPod. If only I'd taken my hair down, rather than leave it in the somber bun I wore for school every day.

The doors closed and the elevator lifted, gently gliding skyward, and I glanced at the boy. He was cute, really cute, and my stomach fluttered again when he caught me looking at him.

When we stopped at the third floor, the door opened and the man exited. Slowly, the younger one dragged himself from the handrail, taking a wide step that brought him close to me. A full head taller than me, he paused long enough to nod slightly as if telling me goodbye. I sucked in a ragged breath, pulling in the smell of cologne that no doubt had the word noir in its name. He was so close I could have touched the cleft in his chin, and my fingers itched to. I'd never seen such an impressive dimple. And his silver-blue eyes were out of this world. Images of a lone werewolf popped into my mind. I'd definitely read too many of the paranormal romances passed around the Academy.

At last, he stepped off the elevator, but I didn't breathe again until the doors closed and the elevator resumed its upward trek. I had no idea who he was. I'd only seen him the one time last summer by the pool.

We hadn't been in Houston long and Dad had left for Norway only two weeks earlier, leaving Mom and me alone in a still unfamiliar city. The only people I'd met were my fellow dance-mates, so I was lonely and missing my friends back home. Lounging on the rooftop that day, I felt truly dismal. Then he showed up. I desperately wanted to go over and introduce myself. I spent probably an hour staring at a tattoo on his back, a snake with its mouth open and fangs bared. But I never worked up the courage. Plus, I doubted he even noticed me because he was with a couple of guys and a tall, leggy brunette whose two-piece would have kept him from noticing an elephant on the rooftop.

It was just as well. My demanding schedule didn't allow much time for a personal life, and Mom would have frowned on me getting involved with anyone at this stage in my training. I was on the verge of making ballet my career. It was what we'd always wanted, and I knew she'd stop at nothing to get me there.

Chapter Six

I had homework to do, so after grabbing a banana and a bottle of water I sat down at my desk and booted up my laptop. Like most of my classmates, I took online high school correspondence courses. Full days at the studio left no time for regular school attendance. It sucked the life out of social life, but it was what I'd chosen.

Opening the English composition I'd been working on, I struggled to focus. The dancers in the alley kept popping into my head. Part of me wanted to go back there. I wanted to watch them dance, to pick apart their technique and learn how to turn my bones to quicksilver like that fellow Dionte had. His intense, fast-paced animation was so very different from the controlled, disciplined moves to which I was accustomed.

Again, I tried to wrap my mind around the comp paper, but the cute guy in the elevator replaced the dancers in my thoughts, and I really had no interest in school work then. Did he live in the building? If he did, surely I would have seen more of him by now. And short of going to the concierge downstairs and asking if they knew the tall, golden-haired hotty making an occasional appearance around the place, I didn't know how to find out who he was.

Eventually, after staring at the blank document on my laptop screen forever, I managed to wrangle my thoughts together and worked on the composition until I was interrupted by a text from Jenna.

Bring your helmet and shoulder pads tomorrow!

I'd completely forgotten about Ms. Zaborov's arrangement. I was about to respond to the text when the video chat rang. It was Marisol, so I answered it instead.

"Hola, chica, what's happening in the great city of El Pa..." I sputtered to a halt when I got a good look at her face. I pulled the laptop's screen closer. "Whoa, what happened to you?"

The girl on the monitor smiled and I could see it pained her when she flinched and her hand flew to her swollen jaw and busted lip.

"You should see the other girl," she said, obviously trying to make light.

"Marisol, please tell me you didn't get into it with Guadalupe."

She avoided the monitor for a moment. When she looked back, her face was wreathed in remorse. "I only meant to warn her."

"Oh, Mar, you didn't."

"She's the one who threw the first punch. She said I called her a skank."

"Did you?"

"I didn't call her a skank. I told her to keep her skanky hands off Carlos. It's not my fault if she read more into it."

Marisol Mendoza, for all her wisecracking, tough-girl exterior, was the sweetest person I knew, and the one I most regretted leaving behind when we'd moved. She does have a short fuse when it comes to Carlos Vega, though. Unlike Jenna and her fascination with ambiguity, Marisol was an open book.

"What'd your parents say?" I asked.

Marisol grimaced and shrugged. "I haven't told them yet. Mom was asleep when I got home, and Dad hasn't come in from work." Trying to appear nonplused, she put on a good front and added, "I got three days suspension."

But I knew Marisol was worried. Her mother tended to sleep a lot —which was code for she was loaded again—and it made her dad overly protective of Marisol and her sister Inez.

"He's gonna go nuts, you know that, right? You'll be grounded so long you'll forget what it's like to see anything outside the four walls of your bedroom."

"Yeah, but Carlos is his fishing buddy. I doubt he'd stop him from coming over. So that's something." She picked up an ice pack and gingerly pressed it to her cheek. "But I called you to get my mind off this crap, so what's going on in H-town?"

In order to tell her about the football players, I had to start from the beginning with the ghost hunt in the theater and Ms. Z.'s retribution. I was about to share my encounter with the group of dancers in the alley when I heard Marisol's father calling her name from somewhere in her house.

"Uh-oh, Dad's home." She sat up straight and slapped the ice pack down on the desktop. "Time to face the music."

"Keep your head low," I advised. "Do your chores without being told, bake his favorite chocolate cake, and you'll be back in his good graces in no time." She nodded, but I could see I'd lost her as she girded herself for the conversation with her father. "Message me later," I added. "And try to stay out of trouble."

Setting my status to Offline after we'd hung up, I finished the comp paper. It was late by the time I typed the last sentence, and Mom still wasn't home with dinner, so I strolled down the hall toward the studio, passing Dad's theater room on the way there.

The home theater had been a deal he'd struck with Mom to get what we wanted in the new apartment. He'd agreed to let her decorate the entire place how she liked if we could turn the third bedroom into a dance studio for me and let him have the den for his big-screen TV. It hadn't been that great a sacrifice on Mom's part. She was on board with me having the practice studio, and she was more than happy to have the television out of the living room.

We'd been so excited then, eager to move to Houston and the new place. Having never lived in anything like it before, a high-rise apartment building, it was a new adventure. Back in El Paso, we'd lived in a simple wood, gable-front house where there was a yard to be mowed, trash to put on the curb, barking dogs in the neighborhood. Apartment living was novel and we'd been enthusiastic about the change. But something had gone wrong. We'd grown so far apart. I resisted blaming myself, but the truth was if we'd never moved—if I'd stayed in dance classes there—maybe Dad would still be with us.

At my studio door, I paused, kissed my fingertips, and pressed them to the laminated surface of a vintage New York City Ballet poster. It was a sort of good luck ritual. One wall of the studio had floor-to-ceiling mirrors, while the others were lined with various sized posters of Manhattan, Time Square, and panoramics of Lincoln Center. My oasis. And I never entered without a kiss for luck.

Moving to the heart of the room, I locked eyes on the Time Square poster, did a *relevé* onto the balls of my feet, and performed a series of *chaînés*, quick turns along an imaginary line on the floor. With sweat pants on it was impossible to see my form, so I gave it up and went to rifle through CDs for something to listen to. But rather than choose one of them, I turned on the satellite radio and scanned the channels until I found one playing hip-hop.

Every beat brought back the dancers' high energy and free-style movements. How does a person teach that, let alone learn it. The baggy clothes obscured a dancer's frame. How would you know if you screwed up wearing clothes like that? In ballet, you always knew. The instructor might never say so, but you knew. It was in the narrow slant of their eyes, lips pressed together dismally, or the impatient bellowing of *again*! You always knew.

Losing myself in the music, I faced the great mirror and began snapping my fingers to the throbbing bass. Then I added some shoulder rolling, attempting to mimic Magdalena's gestures. I had to override the voice in my head that chided, "You look like a poser-white-girl," to lean forward and pop my upper body the way she had. It felt awkward and gawky, so I cranked up the music hoping the vibration would help. Technique was usually my strong suit. I simply needed to find the right approach. I jerked and moved but my undulating looked more like a worm squirming on hot pavement than hip-hop dancing.

"What are you doing?" someone yelled.

Startled, I lost my balance, but righted myself and spun around to see Mom in the doorway, her arms folded tightly across her chest.

"What is going on here?" she shouted.

Chapter Seven

Winded, I placed my hand on my stomach and wheezed, "I was messing around."

She mouthed something I couldn't make out, which annoyed her, so she stomped into the room and switched off the sound system.

"What are you doing?"

"I was street dancing."

"Street dancing? Why?"

"I don't know. I thought it would be fun."

"You should be concentrating on your piece for the second company audition, rather than that foolishness. You don't want to blow it again."

She'd thrown a barb I elected to ignore, and said, "It's not foolishness, Mother. It's art."

"Art?" she scoffed and turned to leave the room, obviously expecting me to follow. "Really, Christine, you can't compare night club dancing to art. Ballet is art, dear."

"Don't be such a snob," I replied as we entered the kitchen to unload bags of Chinese carry-out onto the counter.

"I'm not a snob. I believe there's a place for that kind of dancing. It is called street dancing."

"But don't you think it takes as much ability and coordination as ballet?" I took paper plates from the cabinet and placed them before her. "Not to mention skill."

"I suppose so. But it's, well, it's crass, honey. Uncouth. And I don't like you doing it."

With a tired sigh, she settled onto a stool at the breakfast bar, opened a Styrofoam container, and began spooning lo mein onto the plates. We'd been taking our meals this way since Dad left, no longer eating as a family in the dining room. It was the two of us now—paper plates and plastic cups.

"Speaking of crass and uncouth," I said, sitting across from her and claiming a wonton. "We're going to teach football players to dance."

"Come again?" Her chopsticks wavered.

"Mr. Darby asked Ms. Zaborov to choose a few dancers to teach a group of football players to dance. It's a favor for a board trustee, and Jenna and I were chosen to assist Ms. Zaborov."

At the mention of Mr. Darby's name, Mom's eyebrows rose and her suck-up meter kicked in. I couldn't really fault her for that, though. All the ballet mothers thought that Mr. Darby was a genius.

"Really?" she said and took a sip of water. "I've heard of that before—professional players taking ballet. It's supposed to be good for them. Mr. Darby asked you to do it?"

"Ms. Zaborov recruited Jenna and me to help."

"That's interesting. It must be a public relations thing. I suppose it's all right, as long as it doesn't interfere with your own studies. It might be good for you. It may get you noticed, put you in front of Mr. Darby more often."

This was another change since Dad left—her over-ingratiating. She claimed it was for me, to help my career, but in truth, her behavior started when we moved here. She had been a big fish in a little pond at her firm back in El Paso. But here, she was a little fish in a big pond, and she struggled for status.

"You're probably right," I agreed, and neglected to tell her that getting noticed is what landed me in the predicament in the first place.

"I'm not sure how it will affect my schedule. I might be later than usual some days." I don't know why I'd said that, but I thought of the dancers in the alley, and using this for more time alone.

"We'll have to make sure you keep enough money on you for a cab in case I can't be there to pick you up."

"Okay."

She continued to talk, stuff about school, her job, but I lost track, rolling ideas around in my head. This football-ballet thing might not be bad after all. It might even lead to something cool.

The next morning, Mom was pleased with herself and all but said so as we stepped into the elevator to leave.

"I'm glad to see you took my advice. Your makeup looks nice this morning."

I let her believe what she wanted. The truth was, I had taken extra care, but not because of her reproach the day before. I'd hoped to run into the hotty in the elevator again. So I'd straightened my hair and left it down, wore street clothes, and added a pair of teardrop earrings. I'd have to undo it all when I got to the school, but at least there'd be no repeat of yesterday.

Riding the elevator down, I held my breath as it approached the third floor. But it kept going, and it wasn't until I heard Mom's voice rise that I realized she'd been speaking.

"Did you hear me?"

"No, I'm sorry. I zoned out."

"I asked you if I should be there at five this evening to pick you up."

"Oh. Well, I don't know yet. Ms. Z. scheduled us to meet the team this afternoon after class. I don't know what time it'll be over."

Fumbling through her purse, she took out her wallet and gave me a twenty-dollar bill. "In case you need a cab."

Absent mindedly, I crammed the twenty into my bag, my thoughts still on the possibility of an encounter with elevator dude in the lobby. No such luck, though. The lobby was empty except for the concierge.

After Mom dropped me off, I went in and found Van outside studio D. Surrounded by a crew of lower level girls, most of them around twelve or thirteen, he appeared to be impressing them with his posturing and posing. As I neared, I overheard him say, "Yeah, I'm gonna be the one to expose him. I've already emailed the producers at Paranormal Response Team. I haven't heard back from them yet, but I know they're gonna love it when they learn there's a phantom at the Wakefield Center."

"Van," I interrupted, "what are you doing?"

He whipped about, surprised to see me there. His eyes registered that he'd been caught doing the very thing he'd promised Jenna and me he wouldn't do, but he never skipped a beat in front of the girls.

"Oh, hey, Princess. I was telling them about my plan to expose the theater phantom."

"Van," I said, turning his name into a protracted two-syllable word. "I thought we decided there was no ghost and you would drop the Paranormal Response Team thing."

A couple of the girls giggled, and Van stiffened. "You and Jenna decided there was no ghost. I say there is, and there's been evidence of one."

I gaped at him, but before I could dispute, he pressed on.

"I'll find a way to get the show's crew out here, and when I do I'll be famous for being the dancer who caught the catwalk phantom."

The bevy of girls snickered and Van smiled, basking in their adoration.

"It might be a good idea for you to stay off the catwalk," a male voice interrupted.

We looked around to see Mr. Sims the custodian in the hall with us. He stood before the wall thermostat, a screwdriver in one hand, and the thermostat cover in the other.

"A theater in the dark, especially backstage and the catwalk area, can be a dangerous place," Mr. Sims said, brandishing the screwdriver toward Van.

The boy squared his shoulders and looked ready to pop off something snarky. I was prepared to pinch him if he did. Mr. Sims was one of my favorite people at the school. He was kind and gentle, and always went the extra mile. I wasn't going to let Van disrespect him. I didn't have to worry about it, though. Van took the you-know-you-wanna-let-me-have-my-way approach and flashed the man a cheeky grin.

"Come on, Mr. Sims. Don't you think it would be cool for

them to tape what goes on around here at night? They could set up their night-vision cameras on the catwalk and catch it all on video."

I couldn't believe my ears. The little stinker had had no intention of letting this go when Jenna and I talked to him the day before. It was evident he'd been working on the hoax for some time.

"I know what goes on around here at night," Mr. Sims said, "and that's why I'm telling you to keep out of it."

Jenna's account of people sneaking in afterhours must have been on mark. Mr. Sims didn't want Van privy to it.

"So, we have the class in the hall today?" Ms. Zaborov had materialized out of nowhere, and her arrival put the skids on the conversation, frightening the girls who squeaked and scurried back into their studio.

But the ever-confident Van simply bowed low to Ms. Zaborov and said, "Lovely to see you this morning, Ms. Z." Then he moseyed down the hall.

With the others gone, Ms. Zaborov looked to me. "I would not think it advisable to be late to class again today, Christine."

"No, ma'am," I responded. Then she walked away, leaving me alone with Mr. Sims.

"I've been here a long time," he said as he watched Ms. Zaborov enter a classroom down the hall, "and nobody scares me like that woman does."

I laughed. "Look, I'll talk to Van. In fact, I already have, but apparently I'm going to have to be more convincing."

"That's a good idea," Mr. Sims said. "Somebody needs to stop him. That catwalk is unsafe, and there's no telling what would happen if he ran face to face with that phantom."

Chapter Eight

*M*r. Sims resumed his work, but I remained, surprised and staring after him. What had he meant—run face to face with the phantom? Had he bought into Van and Liam's ruse? Surely not. He must have known about the rendezvous occurring there, and the idea of discussing it with me embarrassed him, or worse, maybe he thought I was one of the late-night visitors. I blew it off and went on to the dressing room to change for my warm-up before technique.

Jenna was already at the barre, stretching, when I joined her. I noticed she, too, had taken more time with her makeup that morning.

"So how do you feel about dating a football player?" she asked as she did *pliés*.

I bent my knees in unison with hers. "Wouldn't that be a little like the Incredible Hulk meets Odette?"

"It might be a pleasant change," she said. "I'm tired of dating nothing but ballet dancers." Then she swept her foot forward and stretched her pointed toes to add *tendus* to her *pliés*.

Copying her moves, I searched for a way to change the subject. In this, I suppose I was a bit like Mr. Sims. Talking about sex made me uncomfortable, and any time Jenna discussed boys there was a chance sex would enter into the conversation. And I knew she'd done more than just talk about it when, after a pregnancy scare last summer, her mother put her on birth control.

Truthfully, I'd never actually dated. Most of my crushes had been on dance-mates. Once, when I was fourteen, I had a horribly naïve crush on Mr. Agretto, an instructor at my last school. In his day, he'd been a premier dancer with the New York City Ballet, which when I looked back, I could see was a large part of the attraction. I had imagined him the greatest dancer in the world and spent hours dreaming that one day we would be married. A ridiculous childhood crush.

Since enrolling in the academy, I'd been too busy to become involved with anyone. It was something I tried not to dwell on because it left me feeling inadequate, as if I lacked something other girls my age had. So any time Jenna brought it up, I did what I could to avoid admitting my inexperience. I didn't have the courage to tell her I'd hardly been on a first date, much less to first base.

Marisol was the only one who knew about my nonexistent love life. She'd been there since its beginning. Our freshman year, she'd set me up with Dennis Umber. He and I had attended a movie once, but he'd talked incessantly about video games so it went nowhere. After that, I'd wanted to date, but I simply didn't know how. It seemed to come natural to everyone else, pairing up and going out. And now, well, I felt like a nonparticipant, like there was a schedule to be followed and I was so far behind I'd never get caught up.

"Don't you think we should wait to see what they look like before lining up dates?" I asked. "I mean, they could be ugly."

She rolled her shoulders in a catlike stretch. "I figure there must be, what, at least a dozen of them? Odds are one of them has to be good looking. And I have dibs on him."

"Sinking to a new low aren't you, Newsom?" Deirdre O'Connor said, having sidled up behind us. "No, wait," she amended, and paused as she couldn't resist looking at herself in the mirror. When she'd corrected her posture and run a thumb under the leg of her leotard to snap it in place, she continued, "You do have the feet of a linebacker so maybe they are more your style."

Jenna smirked like she didn't really give a crap what Deidre had to say and responded, "At least I can get a date." Then she flipped her off.

Ms. Zaborov entered the room then and strode over to us. "Ladies, I trust you have not forgotten our little arrangement for this afternoon."

We all bowed to our instructor then Deirdre slunk away, probably afraid she, too, would be dragged into lessons with the football team.

"No, ma'am, we haven't forgotten," I replied.

"Good," she said then clapped her hands and called the class to order.

The day passed quickly. At lunch, Van sat with the girls he'd been entertaining earlier that morning, and I learned he was going to perform in a recital with them later in the month. It was probably better that he hang around them as much as possible, since they were closer to his age. It had to be hard for him, being so much younger than the dancers with which he trained. He was stuck in the middle with the boys his age jealous of his skills, while the older male dancers resented him rising through the ranks so quickly. If he'd been any other boy, one without Van's brazen self-confidence, he might not have been able to do it.

In repertory that afternoon, we rehearsed Swan Lake. It was grueling. Our instructor Mrs. Hahn, also known as Atilla the Hahn, was merciless and made everyone miserable. She seemed to have little patience with me especially. From the moment class began, she was on my case, declaring some of my executions utter failures.

"You must feel it, Christine," she bellowed, pounding her pearl-handled cane on the floor. "You must emote believably. If you do not feel it, the audience will not feel it either. Your technique might be good, but your swan has the heart of a sloth." She swiveled about and her black wide-legged palazzo pants rippled around her calves. "Deirdre, would you please show Christine how it's done?" She snapped her fingers, and her long silk sleeve slipped above her wrist, revealing an ugly scar.

I'd heard rumors about that scar and the walking cane. Most of it was ridiculous, but she'd obviously suffered an injury or been in accident. And, though she was still a strong, toned woman, whatever had occurred had put an end to her dancing.

Deirdre moved forward to do Mrs. Hahn's bidding, making a point of looking down her nose at me as she came between my dance partner and me.

"Okay, Peter, let's show her how real ballerinas dance."

But before the pianist could hit the first note, Ms. Zaborov entered the room and spared me further embarrassment.

"Please pardon the intrusion." She dipped her head toward Mrs. Hahn. "I would need Christine and Jenna now."

Then she motioned for us to join her.

We cut a quick curtsy to Mrs. Hahn and rushed to Ms. Zaborov's side. I, for one, was glad to leave.

"Lena," Mrs. Hahn called after Ms. Zaborov, and the three of us paused at the door. When she'd closed the distance between us, Mrs. Hahn said, "You know how I feel about this football business." Ms. Zaborov acknowledged her with a slow blink and slight nod. "And we both know nothing can be done about it, but I don't think Christine should be working with you in this."

Ms. Zaborov hesitated, looked at me serenely, and responded, "Director Darby gave me liberty in my choices. I am happy with the ones I have made."

The tension between the women crackled.

"But Christine has much work to do if she is to audition again this fall," Mrs. Hahn pointed out.

"I do not believe it a problem for Christine to miss a few moments of repertory twice a week," Ms. Zaborov said.

"If you recall, Lena, I followed your lead concerning Christine's dancing last year, and look how that turned out. You do remember her behavior at the second company audition?"

Ms. Zaborov's face was impassive, but I silently prayed that they would just shut up. I didn't want to think about that audition, and I definitely didn't want it rehashed and discussed in front of the other students doing their best to get close enough to eavesdrop.

Taking a deliberate step, the petite yet formidable Russian woman moved closer to Mrs. Hahn and stared up into her eyes.

"I stand by my decision then, and I stand by it now. But of

course, if you would like to take it up with Director Darby, then I would be happy to—"

"No, no, no," Mrs. Hahn sputtered. "That won't be necessary. I merely wished to state my opinion."

With a husky inflection, Ms. Zaborov replied, "Duly noted. Now, girls, we shall go," and we left the room without looking back.

Chapter Nine

*I*didn't breathe easily again, until we'd made it down the hall and rounded a corner to stop in front of Ms. Zaborov's office. "Wait here. I shall return," she instructed and disappeared behind the door.

"That was intense," Jenna said the minute Ms. Z. was out of sight. "What was that about anyway? You auditioned for the second company last year. I didn't know that. How'd you manage that your first year here?"

Hesitant, I averted my gaze. I really didn't want to talk about it. Jenna was the closest thing I had to a best friend in Houston, but after almost two years at the Rousseau Academy, I'd learned not to let other dancers see my weaknesses, and I wasn't sure how she'd react.

She saw me distancing myself and said, "Listen, you don't have to tell me if you don't want to. I know how Mrs. Hahn can be. I was just curious."

I shook my head and rolled my lips in and out to moisten them. "It's okay. I don't mind." I pulled her a couple of steps from the office door and spoke softly, "Ms. Zaborov invited me to audition. She told my parents that she thought I was a good candidate for the second company."

"Seriously? As a first year, you were asked to audition for Rousseau II? Wow, that's amazing. So what happened? Why aren't you in the second company?"

My breathing sped up and the walls of the hall felt confining. I tugged at the collar of my leotard and stretched it away from my throat to blow cool air down the front.

Again, Jenna noted my resistance. "You choked, didn't you? Oh, man, Christine, I'm sorry. But don't be so hard on yourself. It happens to all of us. "

I shook my head. "Not like that it doesn't."

Her brow furrowed. "What do you mean?"

"I have performance anxiety," I told her.

"Well—yeah—who doesn't? Shoot, I always feel like I'm going to pee my pants before going out on stage."

Self-loathing settled in the pit of my stomach and I sighed. "It was more than anticipation. I had a panic attack right there in front of everyone, dizziness, nausea, heart pounding. I ran off the stage blubbering like a baby."

"Ohhhh," Jenna lamented. "That is bad."

"Sometimes when I'm super stressed I get this pain in my stomach, and when I do I sort of freak out."

Jenna tilted her head to the side. "What do you mean you get a pain in your stomach?"

I clasped my hands together, lacing my fingers into tight knots reluctant to talk about it. At the same time, it had been bottled up for so long talking about it might be a relief.

"It's kind of a medical condition," I said. "The doctor told my parents it's like post-traumatic stress disorder."

"Huh? Post-traumatic stress? Isn't that what soldier's get?"

"It can happen to anyone. It's an anxiety disorder brought

on by something traumatic. I almost died, or at least I feared I would, when I was six years old and that's what caused it."

"Get out!" Jenna exclaimed. "How? I mean what happened?"

"There was a recital coming up and my grandmother was supposed to attend—I was six so it was important to me, you know?" Jenna nodded. "Then about a week before, I became ill. It started with sharp pains behind my navel"—automatically, my hand went to my stomach where I pressed the heel of my palm into my bellybutton—"Mom took me to the ER and they told her I had a bladder infection. The doctor sent me home with antibiotic and said I would improve. But instead of getting well, the pain worsened and moved into my side.

"By then, it was only a few days before the recital, and I really wanted to perform, so I didn't tell my parents. It wasn't until my temperature went higher and I could hardly walk that I finally told them. Mom and Dad took me back to the emergency room. For some reason they argued, my parents and the doctor. He insisted it was a urinary infection and they should take me home. I was so sick, though—horrible pain and I was terrified. My parents were on the verge of losing it because they didn't know what was wrong with me. I just knew I had cancer or something."

"Did your parents take you home again?" Jenna asked.

I shook my head. "My fever was so high, I'd grown delirious. I remember looking at the nurse behind the counter and her face seemed to melt because it felt so hot in the room. The next thing I knew I'd thrown-up all over the Admitting desk. After that, they got their crap together, did some tests, and found it was my appendix. My appendix had burst and I had to have emergency surgery. They said I could have died."

"Wow!" Jenna murmured.

"From that point on, I don't remember much. But they took out my appendix and I stayed in the hospital for several days."

"So you missed the recital."

"Yeah, but that's not all. About a week after I came home, I fell ill again, running fever, nausea. We made another trip to the surgeon and they discovered tissue left behind during the surgery. It had turned septic, and the infection was in my blood stream. So I had surgery again and stayed in the hospital for another week before they got the infection under control."

"Holy cow, that's awful," Jenna said, shocked. "But what does that have to do with your performance anxiety?"

"It came back."

"Your appendix?"

"No. The pain. A month after my recovery, I was at dance class and started to have stomach pain and vomiting again."

"No way," she sputtered.

"Once more, we were back at the doctor's office with more tests. I kept imagining all kinds of horrible things, like they'd missed something else, a tumor, or a disease. The tests results were fine, but the doctor told my parents that I was having phantom pains. He said that I'd suffered such trauma that it had affected me emotionally, and I might have to deal with it for the rest of my life."

"You're kidding."

"When I get stressed, it flares up. Mom thinks I should be able to control it by now, and I know it's in my head—it's not real and I'm not sick—but I feel it just the same—the nausea and stabbing pains."

"And as a first year dancer at Rousseau, auditioning to get into the second company triggered it," Jenna concluded.

"Yeah, I totally freaked, left the room in tears."

"I'm really sorry, Chris. What a bitch Mrs. Hahn is bringing it up like that. But look, I got your back, all right? If we're chosen for the auditions, we can practice together. Maybe I can help you get through it."

A soft breath filtered from my throat and the tension dissipated and it felt like a load had been lifted off me. Jenna truly meant what she said, and in a setting where your friend pool is also your competition, I was glad to have Jenna Newsom as a genuine friend.

Ms. Zaborov opened her office door then and stepped out to lead us to an empty studio where Jenna and I went to the barre to pass the time while we waited. She never brought up the subject of the failed audition again, and I knew that was because she got it.

A few moments had passed with Jenna and me at the barre, when Ms. Zaborov commanded, "Attention, ladies. We have guests."

We whirled around to face the door and pulled up—hips level, shoulders and spine straight, and head up.

Director Darby entered the room first. Smiling, he stepped aside to let two men follow. I presumed one to be the trustee, while the other had to be the football coach, because he wore a Polo shirt with Davis High School Diamondbacks embroidered on the chest. Advancing into the room, they let a procession of very tall, very burly, and very scary boys amble in. Although, I wasn't sure boys was the right word, as most of them were larger than the men who preceded them.

From the corner of my eye, I saw Jenna's face take on an especially satisfied appearance. She practically grinned, obviously finding the choices to her liking. Then the last player entered the room and I gasped. Instantly, my palms began to sweat and my heart did a nosedive as I stared across the room at my elevator guy.

At the sound of my sharp breath, Jenna's head snapped my way.

"What's the matter?"

"I know that one. I've seen him in my building."

Chapter Ten

*I*could hardly believe my eyes. The hotty from the Templeton Tower's elevator was standing in the level eight dance studio. And though it wouldn't seem possible, in a navy blue crew neck sweater, crisp khakis, and gray boat shoes he looked even hotter than the day before.

"Who is he?" Jenna whispered.

"I don't know his name, but I've seen him around my building a few times."

"He's cute," she observed, "but I think I like the one with the red hair and freckles—looks a little like Ron Weasley on steroids."

At that moment, Ms. Zaborov ever so slightly swiveled her head, her neck elegantly elongated. Though the group around her wouldn't have discerned it, Jenna and I knew she was annoyed with us for murmuring behind her back. Her eyes conveyed the message, If you embarrass yourselves, and thereby the Rousseau Academy, I will have your heads on a platter!

We shut up.

Director Darby motioned elevator guy forward, and he stepped out of the line-up of behemoths and moved to where the board member stood by Ms. Zaborov. I guessed my elevator guy was the trustee's nephew Ms. Z. had mentioned, because the man was proudly patting him on the shoulder.

I strained to listen as they made their introductions, but I couldn't hear when Mr. Darby said the guy's name. He wasn't as big as the others were, maybe five-ten. I noticed his hair wasn't actually blond either. It was more a light, sandy brown with blond highlights that seemed natural, like he'd been in the sun the entire summer.

Ms. Zaborov signaled for us to join her. "Girls."

Striding up next to my instructor, I couldn't bring myself to look at elevator guy as Ms. Zaborov extolled our accomplishments.

"These are two of the Academy's finest dancers, Jenna and Christine. They have graciously volunteered to assist us in this endeavor."

Any other time, I would have been thrilled to hear her speak of us in such a manner, but not now. Now it was disconcerting.

When she looked at us again, to let us know she'd finished, we bowed and curtseyed, paying *révérence* to both her and Director Darby. That was when elevator guy recognized me. I saw it in his wolf-blue eyes, and the corner of his mouth curled into a smile that made my heart squeeze.

"Girls, this is Mr. Howell, the football coach," Director Darby said. "And this is Mr. Chaney. I'm sure you will recognize him as a member of the Rousseau Ballet Company's board of trustees."

The man stepped forward to shake our hands. "Thank you girls for helping us with this."

Ms. Z. responded for us. "They are more than happy to

assist."

"Perhaps you'd like to take a tour of the facilities," Mr. Darby suggested to the group. "Maybe we could even step over to the Wakefield Center and see the two theaters there, the Griffith and the Werner."

"That sounds like an excellent idea," Mr. Chaney said.

"Wonderful," Ms. Zaborov concluded. Then she stepped to the door to lead the procession out of the studio and into the hall to explore the rest of the school. This left Jenna and me to bring up the rear.

We walked along slowly, making the occasional stop for Ms. Z. or Mr. Darby to comment on a particular aspect of the school's construction. Since elevator guy was pulled from the line-up in the studio, he was now near the end of the parade, only a few feet in front of me. I was relieved to have him there rather than behind me. I couldn't have taken it knowing he was there, possibly checking me out. This was, of course, hypocritical, as I was totally checking out his killer derriere.

Jenna was doing her share of ogling his bottom, too. She elbowed me, cast her eyes that direction, and fanned her hand in front of her face. "WOW," she silently mouthed.

After Mr. Darby decided we'd seen enough of the school, we traipsed across the plaza to the Wakefield Center where we took a cursory look at the Werner Theater, used primarily for the opera, and then we went to the other side of the building to tour the Griffith Theater.

We were treading our way down the theater aisle, when Jenna saw her chance to get closer to the redhead. Fully aware of her figure in her dance clothes, she zigzagged through a few boys, who tried to catch her attention, until she was beside her target. The movement caused a shift in the line of young men, and elevator guy took a couple of steps to fall back closer to me. When Mr. Darby and Ms. Z. paused at the orchestra pit and fell into a deep discussion, he spoke to me.

"So, you live in Templeton Towers?"

Answer him. Answer him. I tried to pull up words. Answer him. But all I could do was smile and nod.

Chapter Eleven

"My name's Raoul. Raoul Chaney. I've seen you at Templeton Towers." He paused and it was obvious he waited for my response.

I glanced at Ms. Zaborov, who was still conversing with Mr. Darby, and swallowed my anxiety to whisper, "Yeah."

"You know, usually when a person tells you his name, you give yours."

My face heated up and I was sure it was red. "Christine Dadey."

"Nice to meet you, Christine."

"Nice to meet you," I murmured, hoping Ms. Z. wouldn't hear me talking and consider it impertinent.

"I notice you keep looking at your teacher. You afraid of her?"

I glanced at him to see if he was mocking me, but his smile only made my insides feel warm.

"Don't let her size fool you," I said. "That woman eats football coaches for breakfast."

He laughed, a sound that was smooth and velvety.

"Do you live in the Towers?" I asked.

"My father does. I live with my mother in River Oaks."

"Oh," I mumbled and we fell quiet for an awkward moment.

"So you're going to teach me to dance like Hilarion?" he asked

I lifted my brows in surprise.

"What?" he chuckled. "My uncle is on the board of trustees. Don't you think I've seen a few ballets?"

I was embarrassed that I'd been so obviously close-minded and presumptuous. Nonetheless, I was astounded to learn he was familiar with Giselle.

"I know about Hilarion's unrequited love for the fair maiden, Giselle. How she falls for Duke Albrecht who deceives her by posing as a peasant to get close to her, and the lovesick gamekeeper Hilarion who tries to break them apart."

When I couldn't summon a reply, he grinned at my discomfiture.

"Although, I suppose," he added, "dancing like the jealous Hilarion would be a dumb choice, since he dies in the end."

"I'm sorry. I didn't mean to imply you were—"

"Culturally or intellectually warped because I play football?" He finished my sentence.

I bit my lip to keep from laughing. "Yeah, that."

From the front of the line, I heard Jenna clear her throat.

She gave me a warning glance, so we quieted and the group moved forward to circle up the aisle and out of the theater.

As we trailed across the plaza, returning to the school, Raoul walked beside me. I sensed him watching me. When he glanced away, it was my chance to get a closer look at him. He had an athlete's body, and his steps were lithe and energetic. He would have made a powerful dancer.

Back in the studio, there was a lot of discussion between Ms. Zaborov and the coach about what to expect from the classes. She even asked Jenna and me to demonstrate a few poses while she narrated. "Ballet will help players learn to find their center of gravity and gain balance while in complex positions," she said.

"I admit," Coach Howell said, "I'm not sure about this, but I know professional players who've taken lessons and they say it improved their game. Some claim it cut down on injury."

"I cannot say about the football injuries," Ms. Zaborov responded, "but I know a well-trained dancer is a strong, healthy dancer."

Once schedules were discussed, it was decided the boys would forgo two days a week of strength training in the gym to come to the studio to practice with us. After a lot of hand shaking, and the promise of returning on Thursday dressed in workout clothes ready to train, the group departed. The last thing I noticed as they filed out the door was Raoul turning to wink at me, and without thinking, I raised my hand and waved a small goodbye.

When the room had emptied, and she was certain they were out of earshot, Ms. Zaborov turned to us and said, "Thank you, ladies. You conducted yourselves admirably. And now, on Thursday, we will see if we can whip these oafs into dancers." Then she gracefully left the room, and Jenna and I burst into laughter.

On our way to the dressing room, Jenna poked me in the arm and asked, "So did you get his number?"

"Seriously? We barely had time to say three words to each

other and you want to know if I got his number."

"Maybe they weren't the right words." She grinned and raised her open hand to my face.

"Are you kidding me?" I grasped her wrist and ogled the ink phone number written on her palm. "You got his phone number? Already! Did you even get his name?"

"Yeah, it's Troy,—uuuh—something or another. I forget the last name."

"You don't waste any time."

"You snooze, you lose," she said.

I may not have moved as quickly as Jenna had, but I was pleased with myself nonetheless. I'd been nervous the whole time, and if he hadn't initiated the conversation, I'm not sure I could have, but we talked—that was something.

After we changed clothes, I noticed it was almost five, and since I hadn't told Mom otherwise, she would be picking me up shortly. Jenna and I walked outside together where we saw her mother already parked on the street, waiting for her.

"I'll catch you later," Jenna said as she went to the car and slid in.

Behind me, I heard the school door open and saw Van and Liam exit together. Not long after, Mr. Sims came out, a toolbox in one hand and an overstuffed trash bag in the other. When he spotted Van, a worried shadow passed over his face, and I remembered I was supposed to talk to Van again. But Mom pulled up then, so it had to wait. But as I climbed into the car, I promised myself I'd do it tomorrow.

As she maneuvered through traffic, she told me about her day. I caught bits and pieces about her wonderful assistant, Cooper, before I zoned out, thinking about my own day. I was surprised I hadn't gotten nervous when Ms. Zaborov had asked us to demonstrate some of the basics for our all male audience, and I wondered if I would when we actually started the lessons.

After we'd parked in the garage, we took the stairs to the main lobby, and as we stepped out, I thought I heard my name called. I glanced about and heard it again.

"Christine!"

Following the direction of the voice, I was surprised what I saw. Raoul Chaney was striding purposefully across the marble floor toward us, smiling and motioning for me to join him.

Chapter Twelve

Surprised to see him there, it took me a couple of beats to speak. "Raoul? Are you visiting your father?"

He shook his head. "I came to see you."

Stunned, I blinked in rapid-fire and felt Mom staring at me. I opened my mouth a couple of times before words finally came out.

"Mom, this is Raoul Chaney. His uncle is a trustee on the Rousseau's board. You remember I told you about the football team. He's a player."

"Yes, of course. It's nice to meet you, Raoul." She extended her hand.

After he shook it, we stood there for a couple of stiff seconds before he asked me, "Is it okay—umm—can we talk?"

"Oh, yeah, sure. Mom?"

"Right," she said and smiled. "I'll see you upstairs." Then she headed for the elevator, her heals clicking on the marble floor as she went. I watched her press the button a couple of times, unsuccessfully trying to hide her grin.

Once she'd stepped out of sight, I faced Raoul again. Neither of us spoke, only stared at each other. The longer the

67

silence spread between us the more my breathing sped up.

"So, you wanted to talk to me? Did something happen at the studio? Because if you left anything behind, I have a key card; I can get you in."

He chuckled, again with the dulcet tenor sound that made my spine shiver. "No. I wanted to ask you out."

I stopped breathing altogether then, convinced I'd heard him wrong. "C-come again?"

"I'm asking you out, Christine. Unless, of course, you're seeing somebody."

"No! No, I'm not seeing anyone. I'd love to go out with you."

"Great. How about Saturday? I have a game in Katy Friday night, but I could—"

"Saturday sounds wonderful." I'd cut him off and I feared coming across desperate.

Reaching into his pocket, he pulled out his phone and extended it to me. "Put your number in."

I took it and keyed in my name and number, trying not to let him see my fingers tremble.

When I passed it to him, he looked at the screen. "Thanks, Christine Dadey. I'll text you later."

"Okay." I backed toward the elevator. "I a—my mom," I stammered and pointed toward the doors.

"I'll see you at practice Thursday," he said, as I stepped into the elevator. Then I jabbed the fifth floor button several times and watched him walk toward the exit, my heart still hammering in my chest.

After the elevator doors closed, I squealed and did a series of *pirouettes* until my dance bag threw me off balance. I stopped and looked up at the security cameras. I didn't care if they saw me. I was too excited. In fact, it was too bad Mrs. Hahn couldn't see me, emoting the hell out of my moves.

When I stepped through the apartment door, Mom appeared out of nowhere. "What was that about?"

"He asked me out," I replied, and I knew I had a cheesy grin on my face.

"He asked you out?"

"Don't sound so shocked." I slipped my dance bag off my shoulder and headed toward my room.

"I didn't mean it like that, honey." She tagged close behind me. "It's, well, we haven't talked much about—"

"Dating?" I finished her sentence as she sat on the edge of my bed. "We don't talk about much of anything—other than ballet."

"Christine," she chided, "I'm trying to talk to you now. Would you sit down?"

I dropped my bag on the floor, exhaled audibly, and settled into my desk chair.

"My point is we don't really know this boy. Who is he?"

"Oh, that. Well, like I said, his uncle is a trustee, he plays football, and his father lives here in Templeton Towers."

"His father lives in the Towers?" she said and paused. "I don't know, Chris, maybe we should talk to your father about this."

Now she wanted to talk to Dad!

"Mom, I've already told him I'd go." She hesitated, and I pressed on. "I promise I'll tell you where we're going, and I'll even check in—if you want me to."

She was about to speak when the doorbell rang. "We're not done here," she remarked and left the room to answer it.

I heard the door swing open, and her voice carried down

the hall. "Hey, Cooper. I'm glad you were still at the office. Come on in?" It was her office assistant. She'd evidently left something at work. Maybe he would keep her occupied while I shot an email to Dad. It was a preemptive strike. And if the email didn't work, I'd call him and beg.

Chapter Thirteen

I took my time with the email. I needed Dad to understand how important this was to me. Norway was seven hours ahead of us. It was the middle of the night for him, so it would be tomorrow morning before I'd get a response. When it came down to it, I couldn't see either one of them telling me no. I was almost eighteen and they should be happy I was going out with a guy that practically lived in the same building, not to mention his family was connected to the Rousseau Ballet.

After I'd hit SEND I logged into the school website to do some homework and noticed Jenna was online, so I shot her an IM.

You there?

Yeppers

You'll never guess what happened!

???

Raoul asked me out

Who?

Football guy. he was in the lobby when i got home

No way!

Yeah! can you believe it

So you going?
Of course i'm going
But your mom?

My text alert went off then, interrupting my IM response, so I plucked my phone from my dance bag. I didn't recognize the number, but the message made it clear who it was and my heart skipped a beat.

I forgot to give you my number. Save it to your phone.

Quickly, I saved Raoul's phone number to my contacts and replied.

Got it!

My response seemed lame, but I didn't know what else to say. Then my IM alert sounded.

You still there??
Yeah, but he's texting me right now
Cool. Call me later

Then Jenna logged off.

My text alert chimed again.

Hi

He wants to talk. He wants to talk to me! I responded,

Hey
How long have you lived in the Towers? He asked.
Two years.
Why haven't I seen you?
Don't know. I saw you.
Yeah? When?
Last summer by the pool.
Why didn't you say hi?

I didn't want to answer that question, so I shifted to something else.

What position do you play?

Quarterback

Though I knew little about football, I did know the quarterback was the star of the show.

So you're football's principal dancer.

Are you calling me a prima donna?

A smiley face followed the question, but I didn't bother explaining that prima donnas were in opera not in ballet because I knew what he meant.

You didn't answer my question.

What question?

Why didn't you say hi at the pool last year? We could've gone out already.

My heart did a flip-flop. We could have gone out already? I gave myself a mental head-butt for not mustering the courage to talk to him back then.

You were with a girl and some other guys. I thought she might be your girlfriend. I didn't want to be the chick who broke up your relationship.

I couldn't believe how bold and confident I sounded, as though it were a given that he would choose me. I supposed it was easier to be sexy in a text because he couldn't see how I paced the floor and sweated abundantly.

That was my sister. She's in college now.

Inwardly, I breathed a sigh of relief. I so did not want him to say she was his girlfriend. Then something dawned on me.

Now I get it.

Get what?

Your snake tattoo. It's a diamondback—for the football team.

The second I'd hit Send, that moment when the text couldn't be stopped, I realized what I'd done, what I'd just admitted.

So, you really were checking me out.

I hammered my fist into my forehead. Stupid, stupid, stupid. This was why I didn't date. I can't seem to do it right. Now he was going to think me a lecher.

That's not fair. You've seen me in my swimsuit but I've never seen you in yours.

His comment made me tingle all over. I was disappointed when he said,

I have to go. Dinner with my mother.

K. See you later.

Falling onto my back, I lay staring at the ceiling, feeling warm and fuzzy. I was going out with a football player. Who would have ever thought it?

Eventually, I gave up my daydreaming and dragged myself to my desk to do homework. But it was impossible to concentrate. I had to tell Marisol, so I pulled up my contacts and called her. She smiled when her face appeared on my laptop screen. Her lip wasn't as swollen and a scab had formed over the cut.

"What's up, *chica*?" she asked.

"You're not going to believe this. You know the football thing I told you about?"

She nodded.

"One of the players asked me out."

"Shut up!"

"Yeah, and get this—his dad lives in my building." I blabbered on for a solid fifteen minutes, giving her every detail, some twice. I even read her some of the texts and told her how I'd inadvertently confessed to staring at the tattoo on his back.

"Wow, I've never seen you this excited over a boy."

A giggle turned snort erupted from me. "I know, right. But he's different. He's really nice."

"Your mom's letting you go out with him?"

"She hasn't exactly said yes, but she hasn't said no either. If she does say no, I'm going to call Dad."

I reached up and loosened my hair from its confines, shook it out, and wrapped the strays behind my ears, and said, "Mar, what if he wants to you know—I don't—I've never—"

"Put out?" she supplied.

"Jeez, Marisol, some people think of it a tad more romantically than that."

"I'm sorry. I guess I've been hanging around Carlos's friends too much. But we've talked about this. You don't have to do anything you don't want to. But if you wanted to—" her voice trailed off teasingly.

"Marisol! I haven't even gone on a first date with him."

"Don't worry about it so much. If you do you'll be so tense the guy will think you're weird."

"Thanks for the encouragement."

"You should just have fun. Don't worry about anything else right now."

I nodded. "Yeah, you're right."

"Marisol, have you seen my soccer shorts?" Marisol's younger sister, Inez, had entered the room, and I could see her behind Marisol, searching through her sister's things.

"I gotta go," Marisol said. "I ripped Inez's shorts and she's not gonna be happy."

"Wish me luck."

"You don't need luck, momma. You got this. And get some

pics. I want to see what this guy looks like." Then the screen went black.

I closed my laptop and my stomach growled, so I headed for the kitchen to see what Mom was preparing for dinner. When I opened my bedroom door, I heard voices filter down the hallway. Not just voices—laughter. Was Mom's assistant still here?

I padded down the hall through the living room to the kitchen but stopped short. Mom was at the sink washing vegetables, and a man, I presumed her assistant, was standing beside her, chopping peppers on a cutting board. Mom tossed her head and laughed as he reached around her waist to take a cucumber from the counter where she'd laid it.

"Mom?"

The two of them spun around. "Chris," she said, and fumbled to turn off the water. "I was making dinner, and Cooper dropped by to leave some paperwork." Her words flooded out like a waterfall, and her cheeks blushed dramatically. "Since he was here, I thought I'd ask him to stay for dinner."

My gaze went from her to the man standing next to her as she grabbed a towel and wiped her hands. "Cooper, this is my daughter, Christine. Chris, this is my office assistant, Cooper Nance."

The man smiled at me and held up the cucumber and knife. "I'd shake your hand, Chris, but—"

"Christine," I corrected.

"Christine," he amended.

I stood there staring at them, and the three of us formed a silent triangle.

"Well," Mom said, her voice jittery, "I think that's about it. The salad is tossed and the bread is ready to come out of the oven. Chris, you may want to wash up while we set the table."

While we set the table?

"We're sitting in the dining room?" I asked.

"Of course, honey. Now go clean up."

I lingered a moment, reluctant to walk away. But they continued with their tasks, still laughing and talking but not quite as intimately.

When I returned from the bathroom, I walked into the dining room and saw Mom had pulled out her best tablecloth, and she and Cooper were placing the food atop it. I sat down and watched Cooper pull Mom's chair out for her before he settled himself in at the head of the table.

What the hell?

Mom cleared her throat as she scooped pasta onto her plate. "Would you like salad?" she asked me, and offered the bowl. I took it and realized the tension in the room was as tangible as the bowl in my hand.

Unapologetically, I observed Cooper Nance as he passed Mom the garlic bread. He was nice-looking with dark eyes and even darker hair. He was clearly younger than she was, probably late twenties or early thirties. A handsome man.

"Your mother says you're a ballerina," Cooper commented.

"Yes," I responded sharply.

"Do you like it?"

"I've been doing it all my life; what do you think?"

"Christine!" Mom censured.

I lowered my gaze, surprised by my own insolence. But this guy was hitting on my mother, right in front of me. Not to mention sitting in my father's chair. Did they expect me to pretend it wasn't happening?

Neither of them tried to include me in their conversation after that. It was extremely uncomfortable, and after a few minutes of pushing food around on my plate, I asked to be excused. Before walking away, I narrowed my eyes and glared at Mom, but she ignored me and continued talking to Cooper.

In my room, I left the door open and sat on the edge of my bed to listen to them down the hall. It didn't sound like they were doing anything inappropriate. Maybe I was overreacting. Maybe Cooper had merely been delivering Mom's work, and she was being courteous like she said. After all, he had no way of knowing he was sitting in Dad's chair. And it would have been rude for Mom to make him move.

The situation had really dampened my mood, so I picked up my phone and reread Raoul's texts.

Mood improved

Chapter Fourteen

*D*ear Tina Ballerina,

I can't believe my baby girl is growing up! I hope you know this email is turning your old man prematurely gray. Honestly, I saw one in the mirror this morning! Joking aside, sweetie, this Raoul doesn't sound like a bad guy. And I suppose you have to go on a first date some time. I'm sorry I'm not there for it. I'll talk to your mother today, but I can't see any reason why you shouldn't go.

Xoxo

Dad

I read the email before I'd even brushed my teeth. If Dad was okay with it, I couldn't see Mom having grounds to stop me. But my excitement didn't last. When I went to the kitchen for breakfast, Mom was there at the breakfast bar waiting for me.

"You went behind my back," she said accusingly.

"What are you talking about?"

"Don't take that stance with me. You know what I'm talking about. Emailing your father."

"I email Dad all the time."

"Christine, we're not going to dance around this. I had an email from him this morning."

"Oh."

"You didn't even give us time to work it out." She sounded wounded, which made me feel a little guilty.

"Mom, this isn't a competition between you and Dad."

"I know." She drummed her fingers on the countertop before sighing and swiping at a stray hair.

"Everyone I know is or has been dating for a while," I said. "Most of them have their driver's license and I'm older than they are."

"Whose fault is that?" she countered. "You could have had your license a year ago when your dad offered to teach you. But you didn't want to."

She had me there.

"This is different," I said. "Marisol has been dating Carlos for years. And every girl I know has been dating for a while. I just want to feel normal, like everyone else."

She let out a long, slow breath and slapped her hands on top of the counter.

"Short of doing a background check on this boy, I guess I'll have to trust your instincts on this."

I yipped and ran to throw my arms around her neck.

"I can go?"

"You can go," she relented. "Your dad will call me later this morning, but I know how he feels, and I can't keep you locked up in Templeton Towers like Rapunzel forever."

When I released her and bounced up and down, she raised a finger. "But! You have to check in with me at least once. Okay?"

"Absolutely!"

She kissed me on the cheek. "Now eat before we're late." Then she left the room.

We talked about the date on the drive to school. I mean really talked, even laughed about it. We agreed she'd take me shopping for something new to wear after class on Friday. It was a nice little mother-daughter, commercial-worthy moment. Until her cell phone rang.

"Cooper," she nearly gushed. "I'm on my way right now. I just have to drop off Christine."

I watched her as she chattered. She was coquettish and effervescent. This wasn't right. She shouldn't be flirting with him. He might get the wrong idea, like she was available or something.

When she hung up and dropped the phone on the seat, she was beaming and it annoyed me.

"Mom, what's going on?"

"What do you mean?"

"Uh—let's not dance around this," I said, throwing the same words she'd used on me right back at her. "What's going on with you and Cooper Nance?"

She took her eyes off the road long enough to glance at me. There was confusion in her gaze, but I wasn't sure if it was genuine or feigned. "He's my assistant."

"Yeah? Well, from where I sit, it's looking like a lot more."

"Don't be silly." She rolled her lips together—a nervous habit. "He's my assistant. I don't know what else you think might be going on." She rolled her lips again.

Easing the car to the curb in front of the school, she said, "So, we have a date Friday to get you ready for your date!"

It really chafed that she would treat me like I was twelve, dismiss the topic, and think I wouldn't notice. I figured two could play this game of half-truths, so I said, "Don't bother picking me up this afternoon. I'll be late."

"Oh, okay," she replied without pressing me.

I stepped out of the car and slammed the door on her friendly wave and enthusiastic goodbye. I didn't feel like making nice with her. I didn't even feel bad for lying to her about being late tonight. It was Wednesday; there were no football players coming to the studio today. But I didn't want her picking me up. I wanted to be alone.

Chapter Fifteen

I sought out Jenna as soon as I'd dropped my bag in the dressing room. "I think my mother might be cheating on my father," I said as we loosened up. "At least she wants to."

"Seriously?"

"Yeah, she and her new assistant are getting awfully chummy."

"You had to know it might happen, Chris, with your parents separated like they are. I mean, do you honestly think your dad isn't getting a little action over in Norway?"

I lowered my leg from the barre. "Separated? My parents aren't separated. Dad's out of the country because of his job."

Jenna gave me a sympathetic look that made me feel uncomfortable. Stepping closer, she said, "Tell me you see what's going on here."

"Going on where?" I was confused, and Jenna's knowing gaze made me uncomfortable.

"Your parents concocted this working out of the country scenario to get away from each other—and to protect you while they did it."

I shook my head, while something cold permeated my

stomach and I felt nauseated. My parents weren't separated. But the longer I stood there, quietly hanging on to my denial, the more I knew it was true. They were apart and not simply because they were on different continents.

"I'm sorry, Chris, but it's time you faced it. Your parents are probably going to divorce."

Divorce? No, that couldn't be right. My breath caught in my throat and I felt weak-kneed. Jenna continued to stare at me compassionately and I wanted to cry. I rolled my lips in and out, and when I realized I'd mimicked Mom's nervous little tick, I did burst into tears.

"Oh, don't cry." Jenna took me in her arms. "People divorce all the time. It'll be okay. You'll see."

A few dancers entered the room and she released me, and I twisted away to hide my face from the others.

"Go to the bathroom," she suggested. "I'll tell Ms. Zaborov you started your period."

Without hesitation, I obeyed.

I spent some time in the restroom, splashing water on my face, trying to wrap my head around the truth that had been right in front of me. I was relieved Jenna was the only one aware of how clueless I'd been. Then I wondered if Marisol had guessed it. She knew my parents better than Jenna did. Had she seen it, too?

When I could no longer hide in the bathroom, I joined the class, but my bout of crying left me tired and distracted, and it was evident in my work the remainder of the day.

"Christine!" Mrs. Hahn bellowed and slapped her hand on top of the piano to halt the music during repertory. Then she walked toward me, the thud of her cane audibly marking every step she took. "There is no feeling. Where is the anguish, the agony? Has your heart never been broken?"

I stared at the dance floor and felt the eyes of my classmates on me.

"In spite of Duke Albrecht's betrayal," she continued, "Giselle loves this man. Yet you dance like you are going to the local Wal-Mart. Where is the drama? Where is the grief and shame? You must act, not merely flit about! This—" she waved a hand in the air around me—"this is mediocre, and if you can't improve, we may have to rethink your audition for the second company."

From across the studio, Deirdre snickered as a few soft gasps issued from the other dancers. Mrs. Hahn let the word mediocre float around the room like an ominous specter settling eventually on me. "Perhaps you should take some time and reexamine your goals here, Christine—if you are to get beyond this plateau."

Mediocre and plateau—words that have the ability to flay a dancer alive. If only Mrs. Hahn knew, my heart really was broken. I kept seeing Dad, thousands of miles away, forlorn and alone. That should qualify as grief and anguish. Yet I couldn't translate it into my dancing.

"I'll get it, Mrs. Hahn. I promise."

"I hope so, Christine. I really hope so."

Since I'd already auditioned and failed, I wasn't sure what might happen if denied another opportunity. Would they keep me on as a level eight? If so, I would be the oldest in the class. I was already older than most of them now.

She dismissed the class and everyone left the room, except Jenna. She waited until Mrs. Hahn had departed and said, "Don't let her get to you. She's an old hag past her prime who gets her kicks dogging dancers."

"Jenna!" someone exclaimed, and we whirled about to see Ms. Zaborov standing inside the door. It was obvious she'd overheard Jenna's acerbic insult.

Beside me, Jenna swallowed loudly and I wondered if this could get her kicked out of school.

For a long moment, Ms. Zaborov stared at us. Finally, she said, "You may go, Jenna. I would speak to Christine."

Jenna glanced at me, unsure, and then curtsied to Ms. Zaborov before hurrying out the door.

I readied myself for whatever Ms. Zaborov was about to dish out. No doubt, it would be a reiteration of Mrs. Hahn's harsh critique.

Then she did something strange. Casually, she walked a circle around me, her eyes roving up and down. At last, she spoke, "I believe I should work with you for the audition."

"What? I mean, ma'am?" This wasn't what I'd expected, and I thought I'd misunderstood.

"You need my assistance," she said pointedly.

"Yes, ma'am. But Mrs. Hahn—" I indicated the door the woman had exited.

"Eh, I shall speak to Elaina, but first, I must know if you wish to work with me."

"Yes," I replied without hesitation. "Of course. I would be honored to work with you."

Ms. Zaborov is the best—the best. In addition, this would get Mrs. Hahn off my case, and that was my main concern right then.

"I will talk to Elaina. But consider it done."

"Yes, ma'am," I replied, and like that, she was gone.

Both stunned and elated, I ran to catch Jenna in the dressing room. When I threw myself into a chair next to her dressing table, she asked, "Did she say anything about what I said? Shit, I thought she was going to kick me out right then and there. Is she kicking me out?"

"No, no. She didn't say anything about that. She wants to tutor me."

"What? Like private lessons?"

"Yeah, can you believe it?"

"I told you so," Jenna said, a satisfied glint in her eyes.

"What do you mean?"

"You're a lot better than you give yourself credit for. Ms. Z. wouldn't give you the time of day much less offer to personally mentor you if she didn't think you were good. This should help you get past the panic attacks."

I hoped Jenna was right. I didn't know what Mrs. Hahn wanted, so I didn't know how to please her. I felt with Ms. Z. I had a better chance. At least maybe I wouldn't be excluded from the audition.

Chapter Sixteen

*I*t wasn't until we'd left for the day and Jenna climbed into her mother's car, that I remembered I didn't have a ride home. I decided not to call Mom or a taxi and walked instead.

The warm, late summer air was soothing and made me slightly lethargic. I'd been on an emotional roller coaster all day, and I didn't care much for roller coasters. They threw off my equilibrium.

As I strolled down the sidewalk, my mind was all over the place, jumping form one issue to another. With Ms. Zaborov in my corner, I'd have a buffer between Mrs. Hahn and me. Then there was my conversation with Jenna. I couldn't believe how blind I'd been about my parents. The image of Cooper Nance and Mom cozied up to the sink together still nagged me. Had she been cheating on Dad all along? Was that why he went to Norway in the first place? Thinking about it caused my stomach to hurt, and I ground my fist into my midriff.

"Oh, no, please don't let me have a panic attack here on the street."

Weaving through pedestrians, I concentrated on my

breathing, trying not to let my inside take over my outside.

"I will not have a panic attack. I will not have a panic attack."

The familiar cold sweat oozed from my pores, and I paused there, willing it to go away. I needed a diversion to get my mind off the anxiety rising in my chest. Glancing around, I worked to get my bearings and realized I was at the alley where I'd seen the street dancers. Hesitating for a brief moment, I found myself walking down the passageway alongside the office building. When I rounded its corner, I saw the alley was empty. Disappointed, I circled about to leave.

"Hey," someone yelled. "Hey, girlie!" I'd been so distracted I hadn't noticed the snaggletooth, homeless man seated at his camp. For a moment, I considered running, especially when he said, "Hey, come 'ere. I got somethin' for ya." He must have seen the hesitation on my face because he explained, "Magdalena left ya somethin'."

At the mention of Magdalena's name, I gave in and walked to where he perched on a milk crate. "What are you talking about?

"I got it here somewhere." He pilfered through tattered coat pockets, patting down his chest until he found what he looked for. "Here it is!" He pulled a folded piece of paper free from his jacket and held it out to me. "Magdalena said if you came back to give this to ya."

Cautiously, I took the paper from him and unfolded it. It was an advertising flyer for an event at Discovery Green, a park downtown only a few blocks from our apartment. It read,

Dance-Off

Saturday, August 27th 6 p.m.

Hosted by Urban Honesty from Street Feet Studios

A photo inset at the bottom showed a group of dancers performing at a similar venue. It was the crew I'd seen in the alley.

"Magdalena wanted you to give me this?"

"Yep," the man replied, flicking a mosquito away from his face.

Magdalena was inviting me to the event. I glanced at the day and time again. Saturday, the day of my date with Raoul. He hadn't mentioned where we were going, and I wondered if it would be inappropriate to ask if we could attend.

Refolding the paper, I unzipped my dance bag to put it away. Shoving the flyer inside, I saw the twenty-dollar bill Mom had given me for a taxi the day before. I pulled it out and handed it to the man.

"Thanks," I said, and then I headed home.

Chapter Seventeen

*W*hen I arrived at the apartment, I went straight to my room and my laptop to do a search on the dance troupe. Turned out they have a studio in the Montrose area. I was impressed with their repertoire of multicultural, modern, and even traditional offerings and I was embarrassed to admit I thought they were a street gang. I'd never stopped to consider they might be professional dancers. And I'd accused Mom of being a snob.

After viewing the Street Feet Studios website, I thought of calling Marisol to talk to her about Mom and Dad but changed my mind. I'd had enough of the roller coaster for one day. So I logged on to the correspondence school site to complete a math assignment.

Not long after, Mom arrived home. I could hear her in the foyer. Then she appeared at my door. "I'm home. How was your day?"

I looked at her. "Fine."

"That's it? Just fine?"

She sagged against the doorframe and yawned. I thought of confronting her about Cooper again, but I wasn't sure if I wanted to know. It was one thing to think my parents were having trouble in their marriage, but the idea that Mom may have cheated, which consequently led to Dad's move to Norway, was more than I was ready to face.

"Yeah, just fine," I said.

"Well, dinner will be ready in about an hour." She shoved off the doorframe and rolled her head, massaging the back of her neck with her fingertips. "That is if I don't fall asleep making it."

I finished the math by the time she called me to eat. This meal was no less awkward than the one with Cooper Nance the night before. We both picked at our food, and for the most part, sat silently pretending to have a meal together. After a few failed attempts to engage me, she finally gave up, and I went to my room, where I stayed the remainder of the evening.

It was much the same the next day, as she was on her cell the whole morning, even on the drive to the school. When I stepped out of the car, I told her the same thing I had the day before. "I'll be late."

Her only response was a hurried wave as she continued her phone conversation and drove away.

Several times throughout the day, Jenna asked me if I was okay. "I shouldn't have said anything about your parents," she lamented at the lunch table.

"Forget it. It's not your fault my family is screwed up."

"I know what will make you feel better." She wiggled her eyebrows and took a draw off a bottle of water then plopped it onto the table. "Raoul Chaney."

Immediately, I smiled.

"Thought so."

"Are you nervous about this afternoon?" I asked.

She shook her head and nibbled a carrot. "Nah, I figure it has to be better than dancing with the stuck-up boys around here."

As the time approached four, Ms. Zaborov came for us during repertory again. She and Mrs. Hahn barely acknowledged each other, and I wondered if the competition between ballerinas ever went away. It obviously hadn't weakened between these two.

We waited a few minutes and gradually, two and three at a time, the football team trickled into the room. As they'd promised, they were in workout clothes not too different from what male dancers wear, sans the tights. The logo on their T-shirts was like Coach Howell's, only on closer inspection I noticed the D in Davis High School was fashioned from a snake, its head forming the top of the letter, mouth open and fangs bared. These people were serious about their football.

I'd never been one to chew my nails. In ballet, hands were as instrumental as feet and were to be kept clean and manicured, but now, watching the super-sized, testosterone machines enter the studio, I had to resist the urge to gnaw off a couple of fingernails.

"Don't look so scared," Jenna teased. "They won't bite."

Oddly, when Raoul walked in, I realized I was no longer nervous. Quite the opposite. I wanted to impress him with my art, to show him who I was and of what I was capable.

Unfortunately, an awkward, invisible line appeared in the room, separating Jenna and me from the boys. We stood on our side, and they on theirs. Eventually, Ms. Zaborov entered and broke some of the tension.

"Ah, and here we are, ready to work, no?" A couple of the

boys murmured a response, but Jenna and I remained silent.

Without pause, Ms. Zaborov stationed herself before the group and proceeded to lecture them on the importance of proper training for any physical sport or activity. She was a pixie among giants, but I knew she could snap one like a twig if need be.

Her discourse complete, Ms. Z. moved across the floor to the barre and commanded, "Christine, if you would please," and I joined her.

"First, we will start with turnout. Christine will demonstrate."

Placing a hand on the barre, I stood tall in sixth position. I felt exposed—in my leotard and tights, since Ms. Z. wouldn't allow us to wear a dance skirt because it concealed hip alignment.

"You see,"—she waved a hand for me to move—"notice how the hip is turned out." I opened my knees, and keeping my heels close, I gradually adjusted my toes outward. "This allows for greater extension of the leg. Christine has excellent turnout."

From somewhere in the crowd, a boy said, "Give me a few minutes with her and I bet I can make her hips turn out."

Sniggering and high fives bounced around the room, as heat shot up my neck and traveled all the way to my hairline. I tried not to look at them, and in averting my gaze, caught sight of Raoul in the mirror. He elbowed the guy beside him and gave him a dirty look. Then he mouthed something I couldn't make out, but the guy grimaced and threw his hands in the air in mock offense. I couldn't be sure, but it looked like Raoul Chaney had defended me.

Chapter Eighteen

*M*s. Zaborov didn't acknowledge the outburst. I was the only one who saw the tick at the corner of her eye that revealed her irritation. She remained professional and in control.

"We will try these on the floor first."

Then she had Jenna and I execute the moves, lying on our backs, soles of the feet together to allow gravity to pull our knees toward the floor. Though this was the more provocative pose, no one made a lewd remark this time. Satisfied the boys were at last serious, Ms. Zaborov dispersed the team across the floor and put them to work.

It was slightly comical to watch the boys follow Ms. Zaborov's commands. Their massive bulk didn't respond so well to the unfamiliar movements. There was an occasional grunt, and someone complained, "Whose idea was this?" By the time class was over, the Davis High Diamondbacks realized they had greatly underestimated Lena Zaborov's ability to inflict pain, and I felt sure they'd gained a new respect for ballet in general.

As the team left, Jenna and I toweled off and Raoul sauntered over to us.

"We still on for Saturday?"

A cool shiver trickled down my back, and it was hard to tell if it was the droplet of sweat that ran the length of my spine, or the sound of his satin-smooth voice that caused it.

"Yeah," I said, "we're still on for Saturday."

Jenna wrapped her towel around her waist and tied it. "What does it take to get that guy Troy to make a move?"

Raoul glanced across the room where Troy was down on one knee, tying his shoe. "Troy's kind of shy."

"Good thing I'm not," Jenna stated and left us to walk purposely toward him.

"So, you need a ride home?" Raoul asked when we were alone.

"Yeah—no. I mean, yes, but I can't leave now. I have to stay for some one-on-one with Ms. Zaborov."

"Let me get this straight." He shifted his weight from one leg to the other. "You've been here for eight hours and now you're staying for more torture?"

"I know—masochistic, isn't it? But Ms. Zaborov is helping with my weaknesses because I'm planning to audition for the Rousseau Ballet's junior company.'

"Weaknesses! If you have weaknesses, I sure don't see them."

His compliment was flattering, but I didn't know how to respond. So I raked a slippered toe across the floor to have something to focus on, while I tried not to do or say the wrong thing.

"I have a few minutes before we start, though—if you want to get some water and talk," I said.

"I could use some water."

Guiding Raoul from the studio to the kitchenette, we

passed several dancers along the way, including Deirdre. Unable to conceal her curiosity, she ogled us. And with an unexpected burst of confidence, I looked down my nose at her in the same manner she had me the day before.

Inside the kitchen, I removed two bottles of water from the refrigerator and we sat at one of the tables. Raoul chugged down half of his before taking a breath to ask, "So what do you want to do this weekend? We can grab something to eat, maybe at the Aquarium."

"I've never been to the Aquarium."

He looked at me quizzically. "You've never been to the Aquarium? But it's only two blocks from here."

"I guess we never took the time. Mom works a lot, and between my online classes and my dancing, I stay busy."

He probably thought me a loser with no more personal life than I had.

"Your parents are divorced, too? How long?"

The mention of my parents sent a pinching sensation through my stomach.

"Mine have been divorced since I was ten. My father remarried, and now I have two stepsisters."

"My parents aren't divorced." I shook my head. "My dad is out of the country on business. He'll be home soon."

"Oh, I thought it was just you and your mother."

Not wanting to discuss my fractured family, I scrambled for a different topic and remembered Magdalena's invitation.

"There's a festival at Discovery Green Saturday. Could we go there?"

"Yeah, sure."

"We don't have to stay long. There's a dance group performing and I'd like to watch them."

"Ballet? Don't you get enough of that here?"

"No, it's not like that. It's hip-hop."

He cocked an eyebrow. "Hip-hop, huh? Is this some sort of ballerinas-gone-wild thing?"

"No," I snickered. "They're from a studio over on Montrose, and I've never seen them perform. It's free, open to the public."

"I'm cool with it. We can eat at the Mexican Cantina around the corner from the Towers then walk to Discovery Green."

"Great."

Movement at the door caught my eye. Mrs. Hahn had entered the room.

"Christine. What are you still doing here?" Supporting herself with the cane, she hobbled into the room.

"I'm staying late to rehearse with Ms. Z."

"Is that right?" She moved to the refrigerator to get a sport drink. "So Lena is tutoring you?"

"Yes, ma'am."

"Well, I suppose she knows what she's doing." She directed her attention to Raoul then. "And you are?"

"This is Raoul Chaney. He's one of the football players taking classes. His uncle is a Rousseau board member."

"Douglas Chaney's nephew?"

I glanced at Raoul and he nodded. "Yes, ma'am."

"I suppose that's the cost of doing business," she said. Then she exited the room, leaving her insult to do its job.

"Who was that?" Raoul asked.

"Mrs. Hahn. She's not keen on football players taking lessons at the Academy."

"No kidding."

I looked at my watch. "I better go before Ms. Z. comes looking for me."

We stood at the same time, and I took one last drink of water, tossed the bottle in a nearby trashcan, and started to walk away. Raoul caught my hand and gently tugged me to a halt.

"Saturday," he said. Then he leaned in and brushed his lips across my temple. My heart dropped to my knees, as he released my hand and strolled out of the room. Barely breathing, I raised a shaky hand to the warm place his lips had touched. Then my knees buckled and I flopped into the chair I'd just vacated. How I was supposed to dance after that?

Chapter Nineteen

*F*or the next hour, Ms. Zaborov drove me beyond reason. I danced until my legs cramped and I couldn't go on anymore.

"This was good," she contemplated aloud.

I took a towel from my bag, collapsed to the floor in an exhausted heap, and thought good for whom?

"You do not have to rise," she said, meaning I didn't have to get to my feet to curtsy and thank her. "Class is over. You have done well today. Now, go home and get some rest. We will work again tomorrow."

When I'd cooled down and caught my breath, I hauled myself to my feet and slipped into my sweats and shrug. It was getting late, and since the homeless man in the alley now had my taxi money, I would be walking home.

Outside the school, I'd paused on the stoop to fish my iPod from my bag when I noticed Van walking briskly across the plaza toward the Wakefield Center, lashing his head about conspicuously as though making sure no one followed.

"That little stinker," I mumbled and charged after him.

At the building's back entry, I swiped my key card and swung the door open. Once inside, my eyes had to adjust to the partially lit hallway before I could go on, so I stood and listened for Van. It was quiet. Eerily quiet.

"Van!" I whispered into the barren hallway. "Evander!" But there was no response.

Ambling through the dim corridor, passing dressing room doors and walls lined with theater posters, Van's dead dancer story popped into my mind. I had to admit, the theater was a good setting for it. The place made a person feel like a spook could be lurking around every turn. A shiver ran down my spine, and I laughed at myself for being so silly. There was no ghost. It was a cleverly concocted scheme for Van to get attention, but the enormous, empty building was creepy nonetheless.

I took the path leading to the Griffith Theater's backstage entrance, making my way to the wings. If he intended to plant more evidence, he might already be on the catwalk.

"You are so busted," I shouted and leaped from behind the heavy velvet curtains. But there was no one there. Stepping farther out, I craned my neck upward to the single truss light that illuminated a small spot on the stage. "Van? You up there?" I made a few turns around, peering into the inky recesses of the theater. "Van?" My phone rang then and startled me. "Crap!"

I dropped my bag onto the floor and fumbled the ringing phone out of it.

"Hello?"

"Where are you? I called your house and there was no answer," Jenna said.

"I'm at the Wakefield."

"What? Why? Are you still with Ms. Zaborov?"

"No. I thought I saw Van sneaking in. I'd intended to bust

him, but he's not here. What's up?"

"I wanted to know how it went with Raoul. I saw you leave together."

"We went to the kitchen to take a break. And it went great. He kissed me."

"Shut up!"

"Just on the brow. But still, I think he really likes me.'

"Aww, my little duckling is turning into a swan."

"I don't think a baby swan is called a duckling."

"Don't ruin my moment here with a science lesson, Christine. You know I suck at science."

"There's something different about him," I said, crossing my legs and folding them beneath me to sit down on the stage floor. "I don't get as nervous around him as I do most guys. I mean—I get nervous, but in a good way."

"Ooooh! This sounds serious."

"C'mon, you know what I mean."

"Yeah, I do." She turned sober then. "And I think it's cool."

I reclined and lay flat on the floor, too exhausted to care how dirty it was. Sprawled there like an octopus, I rested, even after Jenna had hung up. The gloomy quiet wasn't so unnerving anymore. It was strangely peaceful, tranquil. Outside was a city of millions trying to get home to their evening meal, yet there was solitude here in the theater that was comforting.

Closing my eyes, I pictured the hundreds of dancers who'd graced this floor. I imagined what it would be like to perform here in a real troupe, not merely as a student or in a junior company, but as one of the main company.

Suddenly, I found my second wind and I scrambled to my feet. "Okay, Mrs. Hahn. Let's see if we can feel it in here."

Without any music, I started to dance. I wanted the music to be inside me, or at least for it to appear that way. I imagined myself the lead with an audience here to see me perform in a famous ballet. In my fantasy, there was no panic attack. I was free to dance. Free to be me.

I *pirouetted* around the stage, leaping and twirling, Ms. Zaborov's directions echoing in my mind. Then I saw movement behind the curtain and froze mid-rotation when I heard, "You really shouldn't check your formation in your shadow like you do. It reveals your lack of confidence."

Startled, I stumbled back a couple of steps and a bird-like shriek slipped from my lips. I was not alone.

Chapter Twenty

*M*y shrill chirp bounced off the walls of the empty theater, and the building went stone cold silent once more. Gasping for air, my breathing roared in my ears and my heart beat heavily.

"Who's there?" I demanded and squinted into the darkness.

On the verge of calling out again, the words jammed in my throat as Jenna's statement came flooding back to me; 'They take girls up there to get a little action', and I realized I may have stumbled upon someone's make-out session.

Glued to the floor, I didn't know what to do. I would die of humiliation if a couple were on the catwalk hooking up. Tentatively, I lifted my gaze to peer overhead ready to bolt if I saw any bare skin. To my relief, the catwalk was empty.

Then I heard, "If you continually check your form in your shadow, you'll never be free to move."

I cast about. Was he behind me?

"Van, are you messing with me?"

"Your technique is flawless, but you stifle your gift with it."

To my left. He was behind the curtain to my left.

"Who's there?" The voice had a gravelly edge to it. There was no way it was Van's high-pitched, juvenile speech.

Rather than answer me, the guy continued his critique. "You worry too much about your form. You should trust your body to do what it's trained to do."

I trod over and yanked back a curtain. "Who's there? Are you one of the Diamondbacks?" That of course was ludicrous, because the only formation they knew was on a football field.

Then it dawned on me. "Oh, you're a security guard. Well, I was about to leave," I explained to him. "I was looking for Evander Woodruff, and I—"

"I'm a dancer."

"Pardon?"

"I'm a dancer."

"Oh. A member of the company?"

"Not this company."

"What company are you with?"

"I'm not."

"You're not making sense. And where are you?" I twisted my head like an owl.

"Behind the curtains."

"Yeah, I got that." It sounded like he'd moved so I did a one-eighty to follow his path. "But why?"

He hesitated. "It's what works for me."

"What?"

"Let's just say I have my reasons." His tone was superior and sounded strangely familiar. "But I saw your dancing," he said. "And your technique really is outstanding, but you're uptight and it shows."

"Excuse me." I sputtered.

"Don't be offended." He chuckled. "I just think some of your steps were stiff and it needed to be pointed out."

"And you think you're the one to do that."

"Well, yeah. It doesn't seem anyone at this ridiculous school knows how to help you."

"Wow," I scoffed. "What are you eighteen? Nineteen? And you think you can instruct me better than the professionals at the Rousseau Academy can. Arrogant much?"

He laughed again and I picked up my bag.

"I get enough critiquing, thank you. I don't need it from a poser hiding behind a curtain."

When I'd reached the rear of the stage, he said, "It's your loss." And I paused.

"If you're so brilliant," I replied, my pride having been vexed, "then step out and show me." He didn't respond, so I went on. "Let me tell you what I think. I think you came here to meet up with a girl, a student probably, and she stood you up. Or maybe you're a perv who gets his kicks ogling ballerinas?"

"A perv? You mean because of the way I'm lunging out to grab you and drag you away."

I ignored him and continued, "But I don't see any reason why I should let a groupie evaluate my performance?"

"I told you I'm a dancer. I could give you a rundown of my training, list my instructors both in the states and in Paris, but it would be easier for me to show you?"

"You've danced in Paris?" I didn't bother masking my skepticism.

"You don't believe me."

"No. I don't."

"Then let me show you."

I waited for him to come out then, but he didn't. Instead, he commanded, "*Développé*."

Surely, he didn't mean for me to follow his command. Seconds ticked by and it became clear that that was exactly what he meant.

"But there's no barre, no—"

"Just do it," he said. "*Développé*."

Rolling my eyes doubtfully, I pulled up straight and moved into fifth position. Slowly bringing my right foot up to *passé*, I unfolded it out behind me to angle my body at ninety-degrees.

"Hold," he commanded.

I did, which wasn't easy on my already fatigued legs.

"Shift your weight and lean to the left. There. It's modern. To make it contemporary, curve your neck, tilt your head, and wrap your arm around close to your neck.

"Now see yourself in a peasant girl's dress, performing Giselle to contemporary choreography."

"I can't." I dropped out of position to rest my leg. "Mrs. Hahn would never allow me to perform anything with a contemporary expression."

"Mrs. Hahn? Are you going to let that has-been dictate your future?"

"I don't have much choice. She and Ms. Zaborov hold all the cards."

He was quiet so long I wondered if he'd left. Then he spoke again and his tone was more solemn. "I could help you."

I wiped the sweat from my neck. "You?—could help me?"

"Of course you'd have to stop trying so hard to be a ballerina and learn to concentrate on character. You could probably benefit from sense memory exercises, too."

"Wait. What? Are you saying you want to tutor me? No thanks. I have a tutor proficient in torture. I don't need another."

"You're right. You don't need tutoring. You need transforming." He said this as if it were the most obvious thing in the world.

Shaking my head, I took up my bag again and backed toward the exit. "You know what I think? I think you're a wannabe dancer—maybe a stagehand hoping to get lucky—but I have enough instructors to keep me busy. I don't need one whose method includes hiding behind a curtain."

Chapter Twenty One

I walked home in the dark, but hardly noticed. Replaying the conversation with the guy behind the curtain, I'd completely forgotten about Van. The man had said he was a dancer, but he never said with what company. And he never said how he knew Mrs. Hahn or Ms. Zaborov.

His comments gnawed at me, mostly because they hit home. For as long as I could remember, all I'd wanted was to become a principal dancer. It had never occurred to me that I was trying too hard. Was that what Mrs. Hahn had been getting at?

Arriving at Templeton Towers, I upbraided myself for letting what was most likely a stagehand's flippant comments bother me so. Although, I didn't totally dismiss the notion that I needed to concentrate on characterization more, I pushed the incident aside.

It was close to eight o'clock. Mom would surely be mad, possibly furious, that I hadn't called or texted, but to my surprise, she wasn't home either. When I checked my phone, I saw I had text messages, one from her and several from Jenna.

Mom's text said she was working late and that there were

leftovers in the refrigerator. Jenna's were all small talk. I was exhausted, too tired to care, so I ignored her texts. All I wanted was to soak in a hot tub and go to bed. I didn't even care about food. It wasn't until I was falling asleep that the truth penetrated my foggy brain. If Mom was working late, so was Cooper Nance.

The next morning, Mom buzzed around, humming and smiling, as she prepared for work.

"You're awfully chipper this morning," I said, placing my cereal bowl on the island.

She smiled. "Am I? I don't know that I feel chipper. I had trouble falling asleep last night."

A knot of anxiety tightened in my chest.

"Why couldn't you sleep?" I asked

She shrugged a shoulder and opened the refrigerator to remove a bagel. "Work, I suppose."

"Mom, how long has Mr. Nance been your assistant?"

Her brow furrowed as she popped the bagel into the toaster.

"Hmm, I don't know. Several months now. Originally, he was a temp, filling in for Britta while she went on maternity leave. Then when Britta decided to stay home with the baby, we hired him full time. Why?"

"No reason," I replied, trying to do the math in my head. But I couldn't recall how long it had been since she'd told us about Britta quitting, whether or not it was before Dad left for Norway?

When she dropped me off at school, I saw Van approach the entry, and I called out to him. He stopped and waited for me to catch up to him.

"Princess," he said as I approached.

"What were you doing at the Wakefield last night?" I demanded.

His lips curled into a smug, satisfied grin. "That's for me to know and you to find out."

"Van, you need to stay out of the Wakefield after hours. It's wiggin' out Mr. Sims."

"Sims is an old woman. He worries too much."

"Evander," I enunciated. "You need to let this go. He's right. It can be dangerous in there when it's dark."

"That's exactly what I'm going for—mystery and danger in a haunted theater. Did you see this week's episode of Paranormal Response Team?"

I shook my head.

"They were at an old drive-in theater looking for the ghost of a kid who'd been run over there. Car backed over him and crushed him."

"Eww, Van, that's horrible."

"I know, right. So can you imagine how cool it would be for them to come here?"

He opened the door and hesitated there. "Don't worry so much. I know what I'm doing." Then he walked into the building, letting the door slam behind him.

Chapter Twenty Two

*M*y concerns about Mom and Mr. Nance filled my thoughts all day, and I forgot to tell Jenna about my encounter with the guy in the theater. It wasn't until the end of the day that I thought about him again. I wondered who he was and almost mentioned it to her, but if it turned out he was a security guard analyzing my performance I'd be embarrassed. I mean how crummy a dancer would I be if a rent-a-cop could see my flaws. Or worse, what if he had been there to meet a girl and I'd interrupted.

Mom picked me up that afternoon and we went to the Galleria to shop. We were there for several hours when I finally chose a shimmery, champagne-colored dress with spaghetti straps and a ruffle trimmed V-neck. I accessorized with aqua-colored earrings, a pearl cuff bracelet, and a pair of stacked wedge sandals. I thought Mom was going to cry when I stepped out of the dressing room.

"Oh, Chris, baby, you look beautiful."

I spun around in front of the tri-fold mirror and the dress swirled about my legs. "You think so?"

"I wish your dad were here to see you."

Happy to hear her expressing kind thoughts toward Dad, I tried to perpetuate it. "Here." I pulled my phone from my bag. "Get a picture and we'll send it to him."

Swiping at her nose, she smiled and took the phone from me. "Say first date," and she snapped the photo.

After we'd made our purchases, we went for dinner at a nearby restaurant and the remainder of the evening was more like the way things used to be between us—before Dad left. I knew we could return to normal if he would only come home.

At the apartment later that night, I pulled up some homework and tried to catch up on lessons I'd let slide during the week. But I kept daydreaming of Raoul, his defending me before his coarse teammate, his reaction to my unusual life-style, and his kiss. I tried to keep a straight head, to not be naïve and over romanticize everything, but still, he seemed perfect.

In the middle of my musings, Mom knocked on the door and entered the room. She circled around a few times, straightening and tidying up. Then eventually, she perched on the edge of my bed to address the real reason she was there.

"We need to talk." Her spine was rigid and her features tense. "I'm still concerned about this boy. I would feel much better if we knew Raoul's parents."

"Mom, please don't get parental."

She smirked and knit her brow. "Asking a parent not to be a parent is like asking the sun not to be hot or snow not to be cold."

I rolled my eyes.

"I'm being serious," she said.

"Okay, okay."

"You're—well—"

"Mom, we've had this talk, and I've had sex-ed."

"Yes, but you weren't actually dating then. Now that you are, I need to know you understand the consequences of the choices you make."

Then she pulled something from her pocket and tossed it on my desk next to the laptop. It was a condom.

"Crap, Mom, I just met this guy. I don't think—"

"Nobody ever thinks, Christine. That's my point. Don't stick your head in the sand and ignore this, only to end up like Jenna last year."

I sucked in a breath. She knew about Jenna's pregnancy scare.

"And with the strain ballet already puts on your body," she continued, "I don't want you on birth control. I don't think the hormones would be good for you."

"Mom—" I stood, hoping to put an end to the sticky conversation, "—I'm not going to do anything stupid. As far as Jenna is concerned, well, I don't know why Jenna does what she does; sometimes I think it's for the shock value. But I'm not Jenna, and I don't plan on ending up in that situation."

Taking the hint, she rose to her feet. "Promise me you will keep this in mind."

"I promise."

Moving closer to me, she pulled several strands of my hair through her fingers and sighed. "I love you, Tina Ballerina. Don't ever forget it." Then she hugged me to her and kissed the top of my head.

Chapter Twenty Three

Seated before my laptop at nine the next morning, I was ready for my weekly video chat with Dad.

"Morning, sweetheart," he said when he appeared on screen.

"Afternoon, Dad," I replied, since it was four p.m. where he was.

"So tell me about this boy. I want every detail."

I made a puny attempt not to sound too girly, but before I knew it, I'd completely gone off the deep end and gushed over how fabulous Raoul Chaney is. Dad let me prattle, and when I finally allowed him a turn to talk, he told me about his week and a trip to a restaurant where he'd sampled reindeer.

"Eww, reindeer. That's disgusting." This brought us to a lull in the conversation, and I thought it a good place to bring up the subject of his return. "Dad, when are you coming home? We miss you."

Exhaling audibly, he dragged a hand across his stylish, close-cut beard—something he'd added after his move to Norway—and said, "Baby girl, it's complicated."

"Complicated? You pack, get on a plane, and come home.

How complicated is that?"

"It's not that simple, sweetheart. Your mother and I—" he averted his gaze, tussling a hand through his wavy, brown hair. "We haven't exactly—" his cell phone rang then and he raised a finger, extracted it from his coat pocket to look at the screen, and said, "I need to take this. It's work."

"How convenient," I muttered.

"Christine, please don't be like that. I can't help the way things are right now. Please smile. Don't let this ruin your big day." His phone continued to ring. "Now I really do need to take this. I love you. We'll talk later." Then the screen went blank.

"I love you, too, Dad," I mumbled to the unresponsive monitor.

In spite of my father's well wishes, a shadow had been cast over my day. I lay around the rest of the morning, watching television and fretting about the two of them. What had driven them apart? Dad's job? Mom's job? The move to Houston?

Around three, Jenna called which finally got my mind off it.

"So, I have some fabulous ideas for your hair tonight."

"Oh, yeah?"

"I'll come over and help you with it."

"Your mom will let you drive over?"

Jenna had only had her license for a couple of weeks.

"She went shopping with a friend. I plan to harass Dad until he gives in."

"Sounds like a plan," I replied.

A short time later, Jenna arrived and I showed her my outfit, of which she thoroughly approved.

"We need to do something to accentuate the earrings and your long neck. What have you got over here?"

She walked to my desk to pick through my hair accessories. After sifting through various clips and bows, she paused. "Hey, what's this?" Turning to face me, she held up the condom Mom had left behind. "You plan on gettin' busy tonight?"

My face warmed, and I stood to snatch it away from her. "No. That's my mother's version of the talk."

"Well, trust me," she said as she maneuvered me into the chair and began brushing my hair, "it's not all it's cracked up to be."

"What? But you do it all the time."

"Not all the time," she said defensively.

"Sorry. That came out wrong."

Silence.

"Look, sometimes it's just what you have to do. You know, to get a guy."

"Jenna—" I wanted to say something, but I didn't know what because in truth, I feared she might be right. I caught her reflection in the mirror. She was chewing her bottom lip, and for the first time since I'd known her, Jenna Newsom had a crack in her armor.

"If it's how you get one, then how do you keep one?" I regretted the question instantly because everyone at school knew Jenna kept a pair of *pointe* shoes longer than she kept a boyfriend.

Unable to make eye contact with me, she said, "Boyfriends are highly overrated. Besides, we have to get you one before we worry about how you keep him."

She stayed for about an hour after she'd done my hair, and

when she'd gone, I watched the clock and paced the floor because I didn't want to sit down and wrinkle my dress. Certain the anticipation was going to kill me, I almost jumped out of my skin when the doorbell finally rang. But when I opened it and saw Raoul's face, my apprehension dissolved. Dressed in a pair of straight-leg trousers, he wore a black leather jacket over a button-down shirt that was open at the collar. Very hot.

A smile spread across his face as he removed his sunshades and stuffed them into a pocket. "Wow you look—"

Mom entered the foyer then and interrupted his compliment.

I motioned for him to come in. "Mom, this is Raoul Chaney."

"We've already met," Raoul said and stepped forward to shake her hand. "Nice to see you again, Mrs. Dadey."

I held my breath as they exchanged a few words. When she asked about his parents, what his father did, where his mother lived, I worried she might scare him away. But if he was uncomfortable he never let on.

When it came time to leave, Mom smiled at me and admitted in my ear. "Okay, so he's a nice guy."

Chapter Twenty Four

Raoul was right about the Mexican Cantina. It was charming. The atmosphere made me feel as if I'd stepped into an impromptu party, with festive colors, rustic hardwood furniture, and live mariachi music playing in the background.

Throughout the meal, we compared battle wounds. I told him about my blisters and sprained ankles, while he shared the after-effects of a quarterback sack. We ate tons of chips and salsa, followed by fajitas with beans and rice—heavy foods I normally avoided, but I felt so light I almost needed the weighty dishes to keep my feet on the ground.

"You don't eat like a girl, much less a ballerina," Raoul observed.

"Umm, thanks?"

"No offense," he stammered.

"None taken." I shrugged. "I'm fortunate in that I can eat whatever I want and not have a weight issue. A lot of dancers struggle with it, though."

"Tell me about your dancing. Is it what you plan to do? I mean, will you go to college?"

There was a time when dancing was the only career option

I even considered. But after what had happened at the audition my first year here, and Mrs. Hahn pressuring me, doubts had crept in. On the one hand I didn't know if I was cut out for it, while on the other I didn't know what else I would do.

"It's all I've ever known," I said. "I got my first pair of ballet slippers when I started beginners' classes, and I haven't stoped dancing since. So, yeah, it's what I plan to do. If I can, that is."

"What do you mean?"

"It's not that easy. Ballerinas reach a certain phase where they advance only if the instructor or choreographer wants them to. If you're not good enough, well, you don't advance. A person could spend years training and still not make it into a recognized company. And it's highly competitive. Often, there are more dancers than there are positions.

"What about you? Do you plan on pursuing professional football?"

"Nah, I started playing when I was in elementary, and it sort of stuck. But I don't care to keep it up after high school."

"But you must be good if you're a quarterback."

"Not to brag," he said with a cocky grin, "but it comes naturally to me. Coach is after me to pursue it, and I've had a few colleges approach me, but it's not what I want to do. My old man is a lawyer, so he wants me to get into law, but I don't know if it's for me. To be honest, I think I might like architecture. I enjoy building things."

I knew right then I liked Raoul Chaney, really liked him. He wasn't shallow and it made me respect him.

We had walked to the restaurant, so after dinner we strolled down the block toward the park. A breeze ruffled strands of my hair free from its clip, and when I'd tucked them behind my ear and let my hand fall to my side again, Raoul took it in his. I smiled so big I had to look away for fear of appearing downright goofy.

Cars lined the streets and people carrying folding chairs and portable coolers filled the sidewalks. The closer we got the more the music beckoned. A small crowd had gathered on the green in front of the raised platform, and the group of dancers I'd seen in the alley was on the stage performing. The speakers blared, their hair and limbs flailed, and energy, tons of energy radiated from the dais.

"So how do you know these people?" Raoul shouted. "They don't exactly look like the ballet type."

"I met them at a street practice," I yelled over the clamor of the music.

"They're good," he observed.

I was glad he appreciated their style of dance and I hoped he wouldn't regret our coming here.

Up on stage, I spotted Magdalena among the group at the same time she glanced out and saw me. She smiled and waved, made her way to the edge of the stage, and motioned for me to come near. I couldn't have imagined what she was about to do.

Chapter Twenty Five

*T*aking Raoul by the hand, I made my way to the front. When we were a few feet from the platform, Magdalena leaped down and said, "You made it!"

"Yeah, I got your invite from that guy—umm—"

"Barney," she supplied.

"Right, Barney."

"Well, I'm glad you came. Who's this?"

Raoul stood quietly beside me.

"This is Raoul. Raoul, this is Magdalena."

"What's up?" he responded.

Magdalena acknowledged his greeting and directed her attention to me again. "I don't even know your name," she said, leaning in for me to hear her.

"Oh, right. I'm Christine."

"Well, Christine, you ready to dance?"

"What?"

"We're about to crank this thing up." She turned to the stage and motioned to the others, who then responded to her mimed commands and several left the stage to scatter throughout the crowd.

Suddenly, the music transitioned and the dancers from

the troupe selected partners from the crowd and began to dance. In some cases, it was a bit awkward, as the onlookers were hesitant. But by degrees, movement spread through the crowd as spectators became participators.

Before he could protest, Magdalena grabbed Raoul, intent on dancing with him. I half expected him to balk, but was surprised as I watched him slip into the moves as if he did it all the time. Tapping his foot and nodding with the music, he let Magdalena whip around him. Gradually, he added motion, sliding side to side and popping his shoulders. It was incredibly hot, and when he came up behind her, placed his hands on her hips, and began to grind, I actually whooped aloud.

"So, ballerina, you come to dance, or you jus' gonna stand there?"

I pivoted to see Dionte behind me. He was grinning with his hands outstretched in an open dare. Instantly, I regretted coming here. I thought the crew would be performing and we'd merely watch. The idea of attempting the type of moves they were executing in front of strangers terrified me, made me feel vulnerable, exposed. To discourage him, I wrinkled my nose and shook my head.

Dionte threw his head back and laughed. "C'mon, momma, I'll show you how it's done." Not giving me a chance to decline, he drew me to a spot near Magdalena and Raoul.

Following his lead, I warmed up and the more I moved, well, the more I moved. Observing others around me, I relaxed and pushed my inhibitions aside. A couple of times, I saw Raoul watching me. Once, he playfully arched his brows and pursed his lips to say oooh.

When Dionte tried to teach me how to grind, though, I

was embarrassed and became clumsy and ungainly again. In ballet, every move is specific, even has its own name. It's ordered and complex and you know the next move you're going to make before you make it. Hip-hop's free-style is the opposite, and I didn't know how to transition.

"I'll take it from here," someone said, and I spun to see Raoul behind me.

"You got it, man," Dionte said and bowed out.

Suddenly, every nerve in my body tingled and a peculiar fear seized me. What if I stepped on his toes or elbowed him in the face? Back in El Paso, I'd busted a male dancer's nose as we'd practiced for a recital. He'd taken it well, it did come with the territory, but this was different. I wanted Raoul to like me. In that split second, I tried to come up with a way to decline, change the subject, run like crazy, anything to get out of dancing so closely with him. Then he took me by the hand and I knew there was no backing out.

Spinning me about to stand behind me as he had Magdalena, he nestled his hands into the folds of my skirt to rest low on my hips. Snuggling up close, he whispered into my ear, "Excellent turnout." And his simple parody of Ms. Zaborov made me relax. We moved together naturally then, and I realized the guy really had skills. I was having so much fun I never wanted it to end. Unfortunately, the group had the stage for an allotted time, and when it was up, the dancing was over.

While the troupe prepared to leave, bundling wires and packing their gear, Magdalena sauntered over to me.

"I'm glad you came, Christine."

"Yeah, me, too. Thanks for inviting me."

"We have some other events around the city; they're

posted on our website, if you'd like to attend."

"Ballerina!" someone hollered and I glanced up on stage to see Dionte hovering close to the edge not far from Magdalena and me. "If you ever wanna dance on the wild side, we can always find a place for you."

I chuckled. "I'll keep that in mind." Then Raoul and I watched them load their things onto wheeled carts and leave.

Still breathing hard, Raoul swiped a wayward lock of hair from his eyes. "You want something to drink?"

"That would be great."

"Stay here. I'll be right back."

The crowd lingered, still energized and unwilling to leave. Frenetic energy filled the air, and Raoul had to press his way through the tightly woven horde toward the food court.

With him gone, I remembered I was supposed to call Mom, so I took my phone from the pocket of my dress and dialed home. The phone on the other end rang a few times, and Mom picked up. I was about to say hello when someone bumped into me, throwing me off balance and knocking the phone from my hand.

"Hey!" I cried and went to my knees to retrieve the phone before someone stepped on it.

A male voice said, "Pardon me," as I scrambled to snatch the phone from the ground.

I struggled to my feet to accept the apology only to realize I didn't know who'd said it. A woman stood before me, a baby in a knapsack on her chest. It obviously wasn't her. Next to me, a couple of middle school boys pushed and shoved one another, as an old woman attempted to break them apart. But there was no man standing there and it had definitely been a male voice. Surveying the crowd an odd sensation passed over me, like something familiar, something I couldn't put my finger on. There were tons of people around, so I shook it off. Whoever it was had moved on.

"Hello? Christine?" I heard Mom's voice tiny and distant, so I placed the phone to my ear again.

"We have a bad connection. I can't hear you," she said.

"No, it's all right. I dropped my phone."

"Oh, okay. That's better. I can hear you now."

"I'm calling to check in like I promised."

"Are you having fun? You sound out of breath. Why are you out of breath?" Her voice raised slightly in alarm.

"Loosen up, Mom. We've been dancing."

"Oh. Where did you go that there's dancing?"

"We're down the street at Discovery Green. There was a hip-hop festival."

"Hip-hop? What is it with you and hip-hop lately?"

I opened my mouth to reply but was interrupted by the sound of a man's voice in the phone's background.

"Mom? Is someone there?" The phone went chillingly quiet. "Mom?"

"Of course not," she said at last. "It's the television."

I glanced up to see Raoul striding toward me. "I have to go."

"Don't forget curfew," she warned.

"I won't."

I hit the End button at the same time I envisioned Cooper Nance at our apartment, ensconced comfortably in front of Dad's big screen TV.

Chapter Twenty Six

"This was all they had," Raoul said, offering me a canned soda.

"It's fine." I reached for the Coke and noticed my pearl bracelet was gone. "Oh, no!" I cried and went to the ground again.

"What's the matter?" Raoul stooped in front of me.

"I lost my bracelet." The crowd had opened up some. I could now see the area around us, but there was no sign of the bracelet.

"Someone bumped into me. It must have come off then."

"What does it look like?" Raoul asked.

"Two strands of white pearls."

"I don't see it anywhere. Was it expensive?"

Shaking my head, I stood up. "No, not really." I gripped my wrist where the bracelet had been. "It was fake. It's no big deal."

Then I noticed Raoul had a red, white, and green Mexican serape draped over his arm.

"Where'd you get that?"

"Found it on a chair under the portico where the picnic tables are. I thought we'd spread it on the grass and chill for a while."

"You found it?"

"I'll return it," he said. Then he took my hand and we started walking. "C'mon, let's go over there." He pointed to a slope of grass not far from the pond. When he'd spread the blanket on the lawn in front of the water, we sat down and relaxed.

"You didn't tell me you could dance," I said.

"You never asked." He raised his soda can to his smirking lips. Then he placed the can on the ground, lay back on the blanket, and folded his arms leisurely under his head. "It's hard to see stars in the city, but sometimes here in this open area, you can spot a few."

"You come here often?"

"More when I was a kid than I do now."

He stared up at the sky, and lazily pointed upward. "Hard to believe they're several hundred thousand miles away, huh?"

I craned my neck to look up even though right then, a star could have plummeted to earth for all I cared.

"You can't see them like that," he said. Then he sat up, shed his jacket, and molded it into a pillow. Before lying back down, he draped an arm around me and tugged me close, pulling me down beside him to share the improvised pillow. "You can see better from here."

Deep in my stomach, a pleasant tickle developed, and I held my breath for fear I'd do something to ruin the moment. We lounged there for some time, him talking about the constellations and me pretending to care about pollution blocking the view. Then he lifted himself up on an elbow to gaze down at me. His eyes were like the blue moon overhead, and his cologne was delightfully dizzying. I wanted to take a deep breath and hold it, so I could somehow keep that scent with me always. Then I did something I'd wanted to do since the day I first saw him in the elevator. I pressed my fingertip into the cleft of his chin.

With a light touch, he took my hand in his and kissed the finger. Then he leaned down and pressed his lips to mine, and something warm and satisfying swept over me. The only kisses I'd ever had were pecks stolen by young dance partners in a studio. None of them was ever so utterly mesmerizing as this.

Raising his head a fraction, he allowed his lips to linger ever so slightly above mine, teasing and tempting. I felt a smattering of whiskers and tasted a trace of soda on his lips.

I'd wrapped my arms around his neck to pull him back, when we heard, "Eh-hum. No PDA."

Raoul groaned and lifted his head. Over his shoulder, I saw a park security guard.

"It's cool, man," Raoul said without taking his gaze off of me. "We're leaving anyway."

Getting to his feet and boosting me up with him, Raoul slipped back into the jacket and snatched the blanket from the ground. "I don't want you to be late on our first date. Something tells me your mother wouldn't allow another if you were."

Another? Another! He wanted to go on another date with me!

On our way out of the park, we walked by the picnic area for Raoul to return the blanket. There were few people around now, so I watched the ground for my bracelet on the outside chance it might still be there. More than likely, someone had probably found it and kept it.

Hand in hand, we retraced our steps to Templeton Towers. Raoul did most of the talking on the way home, while I contemplated how hours could pass like minutes.

Back at the Towers, inside the elevator, Raoul moved close to me. A confident grin curling his lips, he backed me against the wall, and I grabbed the handrail behind me to keep steady. When he ran a hand through my hair, I quivered and was glad for the railing.

"Damn—" he sighed, "—you are hot."

His words reduced my insides to mush, and my lungs refused to take in air. Finally, I stammered, "So, are you staying at your dad's tonight?"

"Mm-hmm," he groaned, planting a kiss on my eyelid.

"Will you be around in the morning?"

"No, Dad's making me go fishing with him." He trailed kisses down my cheek. "We're leaving for Galveston before the sun comes up," he whispered into my ear.

"Wow, you won't get much sleep, will you?"

Mental head-butt. Could I have sounded more lame?

"Christine," he said.

"Yeah?"

"I'm gonna kiss you again." And he did—a long, slow kiss that coaxed my lips apart with his. Then the elevator stopped at my floor and the doors squeaked open. Raoul moaned and let his head fall into my neck, sending shivers up my spine.

Inhaling deeply, he lifted his head and stepped back, allowing me to exit the elevator. In the hall, I stopped to look at him. "I had a great time."

"Yeah, me, too." He raised a hand and mussed his hair.

"So, I'll see you later," I told him.

"Later," he said, and the elevator doors closed.

The apartment was dark, but I doubted Mom was truly asleep. She would have waited up to know what time I came in.

As I readied for bed, I replayed the night's events over and over again. Between the dancing and kissing Raoul, I couldn't remember ever feeling so exhilarated.

I looked at the clock for the last time around three a.m. My final thoughts should have been about Raoul. But they weren't. The last thing that went through my mind before falling asleep was the dancer behind the curtain and his declaration, "Your technique is flawless, but you stifle your gift with it."

Chapter Twenty Seven

*A*round ten-thirty the next morning, I awoke to find Mom standing by my bed. "Get up, sleepyhead." She shoved my feet aside and sat on the bed next to me. "Here." Offering me a glass of juice, she sipped from the cup of coffee she'd brought for herself. "I let you sleep as long as I could stand it, but I'm dying to know how it went."

I'd never kept anything from my mother, and I was aware that that wasn't necessarily normal. I'd seen Jenna's relationship with her mother, disagreements, contention, strife, but it had only been since Dad had left that Mom and I'd begun butting heads. Before that, we were close. Yet now, I wanted to keep last night to myself. I didn't want her intruding into it.

I sipped the juice and pushed my hair out of my face. "It was nice."

"Did he behave appropriately?"

"Yes, Mother. We had a great time. We went to the Mexican Cantina down the street, and then we went to the festival, where we hung out the rest of the night."

"So, are you two an item now?"

I nodded and smiled. "Yeah, I think we'll go out again."

Sweeping a hand forward, she cupped my cheek and smiled.

My cell phone vibrated on the nightstand next to my bed. I picked it up to see a text from Jenna that was simply a series of question marks. "It's Jenna. She wants to know about last night."

"I get it." Mom rose to her feet, looking a little disappointed. "Let me know when you're ready for breakfast, or maybe I should say brunch, and I'll make you waffles." Then she leaned in and kissed the top of my head.

After she left, I looked at my phone again and saw Raoul had texted around six-thirty this morning.

Ugh! really don't wanna be here. rather be with you. mandatory Sunday dinner with mom tonight, school and football tomorrow, so I won't see you till Tuesday.

A spark of heat shot through me as I realized he'd been thinking about me when he left early that morning. Not only thinking about me but also anticipating our next encounter.

Downing the remainder of my juice, I dialed Jenna. Unlike Mom, I told Jenna everything, the dancing, the kissing, and the possibility of more.

"Damn, girl, sounds like you hit the jackpot," she said.

"I know, right. He's really cool."

"So you seeing him again tonight?"

"No, he has a family thing." Then I had an idea. "Hey, can you get the car tonight? Maybe we could attend Romeo and Juliet?"

"Yeah, I guess so. If it's to go to the ballet, Mom would probably let me."

One of the benefits of being a level eight student was free admission to ballets. It was especially encouraged for understudies and dancers wanting to absorb all they could from professional performances.

"I can be there around six."

"I'll be ready," I replied and we hung up.

After showering and getting dressed, I found Mom in the kitchen stirring up waffle batter.

"Jenna and I are going to see Romeo and Juliet tonight," I said, realizing I'd told her rather than asked.

"Oh? Well, did you want me to drive you?"

"No, Jenna's going to pick me up."

"Jenna's picking you up? I don't know if I like that. She hasn't been driving long."

"Mom, the theater is five blocks from here. Barring hurricanes, earthquakes, and other natural disasters, I think we can get there safely."

"All right, then. But be careful."

"Always."

Chapter Twenty Eight

*A*fter gorging on waffles, I tried to video chat with Marisol but couldn't get her online. Since it was Sunday afternoon, I figured she was at some of her family's for dinner; they had big family meals every weekend. So I spent the day cleaning my room, hand-washing a couple of leotards and repairing a pair of slippers.

That evening, while finishing my make-up and dressing for the ballet, Jenna called. "I am so pissed," she spat into the phone. "Mom won't let me go tonight."

"What? Why not?"

"They got my grades. I'm flunking math and science. I'm grounded until I show some improvement." She mimicked her mother's decree. "Can you believe it? Show some improvement! She sounds like Zaborov! I'm sorry. If you still want to go, maybe your mom can take you."

"It's fine. Do you want some help with your math? I could come over."

"Thanks, but I'll do it. Why should you have to suffer too?"

After our goodbyes, I paced my bedroom floor. Dressed and ready to go, in a pink backless dress and strappy silver heels that added four inches to my five-foot-five frame, I looked fierce. I didn't want to stay in the apartment, so I picked up my handbag and headed for the living room.

Mom was on the sofa, reading a book. I was about to ask if she'd drop me at the Wakefield when I realized she was wearing her frumpy around-the-house-clothes and her hair was piled atop her head, a clip barely keeping it in place. There was no way she would go in public like that. She glimpsed up at me right then.

"You look beautiful," she said, and in that moment, I made up my mind.

"Thanks. I'm meeting Jenna downstairs." I started for the door before she had time to respond.

"Don't stay out too late. You have school tomorrow," she called after me.

"I won't."

Then I closed the door on her last words. "Be careful."

I didn't relax until I was out of the building and trudging down the street. There was no reason for her to doubt me and catch the lie, yet I was antsy. But as the balmy, evening breeze wrapped my skirt around my knees, and the theater came into view, I shrugged off the uneasiness. It was worth it, even if I were caught.

At the box office, I got a mezzanine seat ticket, which would allow me to see the dancers at every vantage point. I found my place in the gallery, two from the front row, and sat down as the lights flickered, signaling the ballet's start.

Once the show was underway, I studied Claudette Sunderland, the principal dancer playing Juliet. As she flowed gracefully across the stage, I struggled to discern what it was that truly made a prima ballerina. What did she have that the Mrs. Hahns of the ballet world looked for? What did she have that I didn't?

Immersing myself in the music and the performance, I pushed aside self-absorption and allowed the ballet to carry me away. Several movements passed and they were deep into Scene 2 of Act 1 when I experienced a strange sensation and a chill passed over me. Straightening in my chair, I wondered what had caused it. The air conditioner maybe?

The ballet went on, and when the Dance of the Knights commenced, the sense that something wasn't right nagged me. The heavy one-two, one-two rhythm of the music accelerated my unease. The horns and the bass resonated, while the strings played a dark, forbidding march, and I had the overwhelming feeling I was being watched.

As inconspicuously as possible, I surveyed those around me. The seat to my right was empty, so I casually lay my handbag in it as a way to look down the row of seats. Nothing seemed out of order there. Furtively, I twisted my neck to peer over my shoulder. Everyone behind me was lost in the ballet.

It was ridiculous and probably only my conscience, the guilt I felt for having lied to Mom. I focused on the stage again then, determined to enjoy the rest of the performance.

Like always, Claudette Sunderland inspired the crowd. At the end, everyone went to their feet and remained there until the last curtain call. All around, men and women alike oohed and aahed over her performance. Envy, jealousy, and rivalry were emotions every dancer was familiar with, but in this setting, even the best of people longed for that kind of adoration and appreciation. There wasn't a person in the theater who didn't dream of being Claudette Sunderland, including myself.

Slowly, theatergoers began leaving but I remained in my seat, in no hurry to go home.

The auditorium was almost empty, and I knew at some point security would do a walk-through to ensure the building was clear, but I still didn't want to leave, and I had no intention of doing so.

Shoving to my feet, I hurried downstairs to the powder room, where I hid until everyone had gone. Holing up in a stall on the back row, I finally heard the familiar voice of one of the ushers. "Anyone here? Closing time. Lights out." Then after a pause, every light but one went off. As my eyes adjusted, I counted to twenty before leaving the stall to walk across the room.

Cautiously, I opened the powder room door and peeked through the gap. The hall was empty and dark but for a couple of low lights. The door grated on its hinges as I opened it. I worried the usher might have heard it, so I counted again before stepping out to tiptoe quickly down the corridor, thankful for the plush carpet muffling the sound of my heels.

Wending my way through the theater to get backstage, I started to question what I was doing. It wouldn't hurt to go in Claudette's dressing room for a few minutes, would it? No one would ever know.

Hers was easy to find. Her name was scrolled across it in sparkling, metallic letters. But was she still inside? Doubtful. She would have gone out to meet with her devotees at the building's back exit. Nonetheless, I raised a hand, knocked, and waited. With only the occasional wall sconce glowing, the hall was shrouded in gray and gave off a creepy vibe, but rather than frightening me, it only added to the strange sense of adventure propelling me forward.

When there was no answer, I knocked again. The silence swelled around me, and I made my next move, grasping the doorknob and giving it a slow, deliberate twist. The frame responded with a severe groan as the door coasted open.

"Ms. Sunderland? Are you there?" My voice echoed dully back to me.

What I was about to do was wrong, but I wanted to do it anyway. Glimpsing around the dim foyer once more, I slunk in to the room.

It was like entering my dreams. This was every ballerina's fantasy brought to life. Pausing in the middle of the chamber, I took it in—a principal dancer's dressing room. Flowers covered every available space, on the dressing table, a sideboard, the floor, everywhere. Pink, white, and yellow, in vases and wrapped in tissue paper, their sweet aromas competed with one another, leaving the air with an indistinguishable odor.

To my right stood a garment rack laden with flamboyant costumes made of chiffon and lace, sparkling crystals and rhinestones, and I thought them more beautiful than the flowers. Easing closer, I ran my hands across a couple of them, letting shimmering fabric glide luxuriously through my fingers. My conscience began to bother me again, intruding like this was wrong, but I overrode it and stepped closer to Claudette's dressing table.

The room was in shadow with only the gloomy light from the hallway filtering in. Still, I could see Claudette's personal effects scattered across the tabletop. My hands tingled with the desire to reach out and touch her things, but I came to my senses and decided to go.

As I turned to depart, there was a swooshing sound, followed by a sudden clatter behind me. My heart shot to my throat and I whirled about, expecting someone to have emerged from behind the dressing screen. But the only thing there was an open duffle bag, which had slid from a chair to the floor spilling its contents everywhere. Laughing at my jitteriness, I scooped up the hair accessories, an Ace bandage, and a bottle of Tylenol, crammed them back into the bag, and returned it to the chair.

My pulse still raced as I backed toward the door surveying the room, hoping it looked the same as it had when I'd entered. Before fleeing, I pinched a pink flower from a nearby vase. One missing flower wouldn't be noticed. Gingerly, I wove it through my hair to tuck it behind my ear.

In the hallway, I leaned against the closed dressing room door and listened to the empty building. Overhead, an air vent rattled and a light down the hall buzzed frenetically. Unlike the night I looked for Van, this was a Sunday and everyone had gone. There'd be no stagehands or cleaning crew until Monday morning and it was as if the place waited for something.

To my right, the hall led to the rear exit and the faint hum of the street outside. To my left was the route back to the stage—go home one way, stay a little longer the other. There would be a single guard on duty at the Wakefield's main entrance on the other side of the building, so I had the Griffith Theater entirely to myself. Tittering slightly, I slipped off my shoes, grasped them in one hand and my bag in the other, and took off running that direction.

Pushing through the curtains, I hopped onto the dance floor and placed my shoes and handbag in the corner. Then I tiptoed to center stage to spring onto the balls of my feet and do a series of *pirouette*s. The chirp of my bare feet on the floor and the swish of my dress fueled my fervor. I imagined Claudette's dressing room mine, with my things adorning the dressing table. Exhilaration coursed through my limbs, and I threw my head back and laughed aloud. When I could leap and prance no more, I drifted to a halt to catch my breath.

Then out of the darkened, deserted theater, I heard, "So there is a dancer inside struggling to get out."

Chapter Twenty Nine

*A*lmost immediately, I knew who it was.

"You scared the crap out of me—again!" I bellowed, and a low chuckle rumbled from behind the heavy, velvet drapes.

My hand pressed to my overexerted lungs, I breathed deeply. "I see you're still behind the curtain. But I suppose that's where a stagehand would be, wouldn't he? Behind the curtain."

"Ouch. And here I thought you were a nice girl—not like the Academy snobs looking down their noses at the hired help."

"Ah-ha! So you are a stagehand."

"I never said that. What I said was you're a snob."

"I am not!"

He half laughed half snorted.

"What are you doing here?" I asked him.

"I came to see the ballet. Isn't that why you're here?"

"Of course, but that's not what I meant. The ballet has been over for an hour. Why are you still here?"

"I might ask you the same thing."

The pink flower chose that moment to fall from my hair

and float to the stage floor.

"You were playing the ballerina, weren't you?" He teased.

His voice had moved from where it started at my right to the curtains behind me.

"Don't worry," he said. "I'll keep your secret."

My face heated and I bent to recover the flower then stood to face his voice.

"You won't tell Mr. Darby or the theater manager?"

"I said I wouldn't tell."

Spinning the flower between my fingers, I asked, "Why do you stay behind the curtain?"

"I don't like the stage."

"But you said you're a dancer. What kind of dancer doesn't like to be on the stage?"

"This kind."

He'd been yanking my chain long enough. Two could play this game.

"So, are you handicapped or what?"

An unpleasant silence stretched between us and I realized I'd stumbled onto something.

"Oh, God, you are."

Backtrack-backtrack-backtrack.

"I'm so sorry. I don't know why I said that. I didn't mean to..."

"It's okay. You could say I have a handicap, and I prefer to keep to myself. That's all."

"So are you a dancer or not?"

"I am."

"But you're disabled?"

"No."

"But you said—"

"That I prefer to keep to myself."

I took a step closer to the curtain. "I'm confused. You said you could help me, but you won't come on stage?"

The velvet rippled as he ran his hand across it on the other side and he moved back to where he'd started. "You should go," he said. "It was absurd of me to offer to help you—considering I can't even bring myself to step onto the stage." His voice cracked with emotion, something in it akin to my panic attacks.

"Sometimes the stage terrifies me," I confessed. "But being here alone like this, it's freeing."

"Solitude can be freeing," he said.

We were quiet a moment. Then I said, "There are impaired people who dance, you know—even some in wheelchairs. Why don't you come out and show me what you can do? If you want to dance, you should."

"It's not my dancing that would repulse you—but my face."

"Ohhh."

"That's right. Cinderella's prince isn't so charming anymore," he murmured.

"What happened?" When he didn't answer, I felt compelled to press him. "Will you tell me? I promise I won't say anything catty. I didn't know before—I didn't mean to insult you. I would never have said such a thing had I known."

"It was a fire." The response was short and clipped, and when he continued, his voice was so low and fractured I had to inch nearer to hear him.

"One night a couple of years ago, I came home to flames shooting out of my mother's upper floor window. Sirens blasted from a distance, so I knew the fire department was coming, but it was difficult to tell how far away they were, no way of knowing how long it would take them to arrive." He paused for a beat then said painfully, "I couldn't leave her there."

"You went into the fire?"

"I found her unconscious in her bed and managed to get her onto my shoulder to haul her downstairs. About halfway down, an overhead beam gave way and struck me in the head and knocked me out."

"Oh, my God. That's horrible. How did you escape?"

"The fire department arrived. I woke up in the hospital the next day with my face and head bandaged."

"And your mother?" I asked.

Silence was his answer and a shudder ran through me.

"Oh, no," I whispered. "I'm sorry."

"Thank you," he said. "It took me a long time to even think about dancing again. I just didn't care. I didn't want to live much less dance."

Totally absorbed, I slipped closer to the curtain, a longing to express comfort rising up in me.

"That's why I watch the ballet from the shadows. There's no place for the scarred—the ugly—in ballet. So I come here and cower behind the curtains and remember what it was like to have once been the dancer the audience adored.

"I watch the company and wallow in self-pity," he said. "It's macabre, but I can't seem to stop myself. Then when I saw you dancing, I thought I could help you. I know that sounds ridiculous. But I really miss it—you know—the music, the audience, and the stage. I miss it a lot."

Fixing my eyes on the flower still in my hand, I tried to

process everything he'd said. For months, I'd worried that my entire life was wasted on an elusive dream. Now, to meet someone who'd attained and lost it was more than I could wrap my mind around.

"I'm starting to think it's impossible," I confided. "Maybe I should stop torturing myself and bow out before the second company auditions rather than suffer the humiliation of having Mrs. Hahn or Ms. Zaborov reject me."

"Don't talk like that," he commanded. "You have to stop making allowance for failure. Don't expect to fail."

I didn't have the courage to tell him I'd already tried and failed. In light of what had happened to him, my panic attacks and botched audition seemed trivial.

"You are a gifted dancer, better than any of the girls you're up against. But I do think I could help you. If you would let me."

His voice had taken on a hopeful intonation, and I felt sorry for him. He sounded so lonely.

"I have tutoring with Ms. Zaborov," I said. "And then there's the football team. I'm not sure when I could squeeze it in—maybe at night."

"Come when you can." There was anticipation in his tone now. "I'll give you my cell number, and you can text me when you're coming."

Squeezing the flower's stem, I lodged the bud behind my ear again.

"I don't even know your name," I said.

"Erik."

"And you don't know mine."

"I will when you tell me."

"Christine," I replied and smiled.

Then I padded across the stage, slipped my feet back into my shoes, and retrieved my handbag. "Give me your number," I said, pulling out my phone. "I'll have to think this over, though."

Every reason why this was a bad idea sounded in my mind. I didn't even know the guy. But he seemed so sad, so lost.

"I understand," he said then recited the phone number. "I'll wait to hear from you when you're ready."

Chapter Thirty

"You're late," Mom said from her post on the sofa.

"We stayed behind to talk with some of the company." The lie rolled off my tongue effortlessly. "Plus, you know how the theater district is at night. The traffic's crazy."

She stood, stretched, and appeared to accept my excuse for being late. "Well, I'm going to bed." She kissed me on the cheek as she walked by. "G'night, sweetie."

"Good night. See you in the morning."

In my room, I changed into pajamas, and readied for bed. As I brushed my teeth, images of a house fire and burned flesh plagued me. Staring at my reflection in the bathroom mirror, I touched my nose, eyebrows, and even my ear. Looks were important, if not everything, to a dancer.

"Cinderella's prince isn't so charming anymore," he'd said. So he must have been handsome before the fire. In my mind, I envisioned the possibilities, dark hair, warm, olive skin, green eyes that twinkled when he lifted a dancer over his head. But now, what kind of damage had the fire caused?

The whole matter drove home how precarious my own situation was, and it set that familiar roiling in my stomach in motion. Marisol. I needed to speak to Marisol. If anyone could talk me down, she could.

It took several rings before Marisol answered the call and her face appeared on my laptop. Her hair aimlessly disheveled, she yawned widely. "What time is it? I was asleep."

"Mmm, I don't know, eleven, eleven-thirty maybe."

"Oh, c'mon, Chris, I have school tomorrow."

"Me, too, and I'm sorry, but I really need to talk. I met this guy—"

"I know, you told me." She scratched her cheek. "So how'd it go with R—what's his name?"

"Raoul, and it went great, but that's not what I'm talking about."

"Hmm?"

"I met a guy at the ballet. He wants to tutor me."

"What are you talking about?"

Slowing down, I took the time to unpack everything and told her about meeting Erik the first time when searching for Van, running into him again tonight, and even his experience in the fire.

"Man, Chris, that's bad." She was wide-awake now. "So this guy can't dance anymore?"

"It's not that he can't—he doesn't. Think about it, he went through some major trauma—lost his mother, his looks. The damage to the outside is probably nothing to what it did to the inside, to his heart and emotions."

She nodded. "Did you see him? Is he creepy looking?"

"No, he wouldn't come out from behind the curtain."

"Then how is he going to coach you?"

Shifting a shoulder, I said, "I'm not sure he's thought it

through. More than anything, I think he misses the dancing world—he wants someone to share it with. I know that's how I would feel," I added.

The clock at the bottom of my screen rolled over to midnight, and I knew I needed to let Marisol get back to bed. "What do you think, Mar? Should I do it?"

"I don't know, Chris. The whole thing is kinda weird."

"A lesson or two couldn't hurt anything," I said. "It might make him feel better. After all, what ballet teacher isn't a former dancer? If he can't dance, teaching might fill the void."

Marisol yawned again. "Cool. Now can I go back to bed?"

"Yeah, I'll let you know how it goes. Love you, *chica*," I said and clicked the End Call button.

After closing my laptop, I crawled into bed and stared at the ceiling for a long time. My fate as a dancer was in the hands of Ms. Zaborov and Mrs. Hahn. They were playing tug of war with it, and my career hinged on the winner of that game. Depending on the outcome, I could be burned as easily as Erik had been.

The next morning, I'd planned to tell Jenna about Erik as soon as I got to school, but I had a dentist appointment and didn't arrive until the end of *pointe* class. When I walked into the studio, I discovered Mrs. Hahn and Jenna in a heated conversation.

"Haven't I been doing what's asked of me?" Jenna demanded angrily.

"Remember your place," Mrs. Hahn warned, and I saw Jenna's jaw tighten as she battled to keep her temper and her tongue under control.

"This had to be addressed," Mrs. Hahn told her. "Now, it's

up to you." Then leaning on her cane, she walked away, saying, "Good morning, Christine," as she passed me on her way out.

"Good morning, Mrs. Hahn." I dipped my head and gave her a slight curtsey.

Aware I was there now, Jenna turned her face away. With her head bowed, she swiped at her eyes and I heard a sniffle.

"Jenna?" I moved toward her. "Are you okay?"

"She's such a bitch!"

"What happened?"

She pivoted to face me. "Apparently, I'm getting fat!" She pinched a hunk of leotard and skin around her midriff. "Must have been the stupid ice cream," she mumbled under her breath.

"She can't be serious," I marveled.

"Have you ever known Attila the Hahn to be anything but serious? I suppose I'll have to start skipping a meal, at least until I drop a few pounds."

"Jenna, that's not—,"

"Save it, Christine," she interrupted. "It is what it is." Then she stalked to the door. "I'm going to the bathroom." As she stormed out, she all but ran into Ms. Zaborov.

"Jenna?" Ms. Z. called after her, but Jenna barreled on.

"She and Mrs. Hahn had a disagreement," I said when Ms. Zaborov looked at me quizzically.

"Perhaps I should speak with her."

"Actually, I think she needs some time alone."

"Ah," Ms. Zaborov sighed. "I see. It is just as well because I would speak with you, Christine."

My stomach recoiled. What now?

"I wish to talk about this new man in your life."

Chapter Thirty One

*N*ew man in my life? She knew about Erik. How could she?

"Your mother called to enquire about the young football player," Ms. Zaborov said.

"Oh." I almost laughed at my misunderstanding. "My mother called you about Raoul?"

"Naturally, your mother is concerned for you and your career."

"Naturally." I sneered.

"Christine, you cannot fault her for being concerned. Frankly, her concerns give me pause as well."

"What do you mean?"

"I do not know if it is a good idea for you to be thinking of boys at this time, especially a boy from the football players. You are in a tenuous position, my dear." Though she tried to sound sympathetic, there was wary caution in her voice. "You should be focusing on your art right now."

Anger bubbled up, and I found myself echoing Jenna's sentiment from earlier. "Haven't I been doing what's asked of me? I'm teaching the class you gave us. I'm working with you after hours. Do I have to give up my personal life, too?"

"Control yourself, my dear. I am merely saying there comes the time in every dancer's life when she must make the choice. And sometimes that choice does not allow for boys and the dates."

"A choice," I mumbled.

"I am confident you will do the right thing, Christine." Then in an uncharacteristic move, she stepped close to me and wrapped a strand of hair behind my ear. "Your mother and I only want what is best for you, *lapochka*."

Though I didn't know the term she'd used, I figured it an endearment—something Lena Zaborov doled out sparingly.

"Now, I must go make some calls. I will see you this afternoon."

Choices, the word reverberated through my head as Ms. Zaborov left the room. It comes down to choices, yet Jenna couldn't eat what she chose, and now I couldn't choose to date whom I wanted. I resented the hell out of Mom for going behind my back to, of all people, Lena Zaborov.

If it all came down to choices then maybe I would make one that would blow their socks off and choose to give up ballet.

Chapter Thirty Two

*T*hat evening, I pretty much ignored Mom, though it took little effort on my part because she had her face buried in work she'd brought home from the office. After my conversation with Ms. Zaborov, I'd planned on coming home and telling Mom to keep her nose out of my business, but by the time she'd picked me up I'd run out of steam. Instead, while she dug into work I entombed myself in my bedroom.

Everything had gone to hell. Jenna was fighting with her weight, and consequently Mrs. Hahn, Ms. Z wanted me to give up possibly the greatest guy I'd ever met, Mom and Dad were knocking on divorce's door, and a wounded young dancer had lost his dreams to a cruel fate. Could life suck anymore?

It was time to take control—at least where I could.

I picked up my phone from the nightstand next to my bed and sent a text message to Erik.

Meet you at 11 at the theater?????????

The number of question marks might have been overkill, but that was a late hour. It might not work for him, or he could have even reconsidered his offer from the night before.

A few seconds passed when my message alert sounded. It

was a simple *see ya then.*

With the exception of the ballet on Sunday, I'd never sneaked out of the house before, and here I was, barely twenty-four hours later, doing it again.

When Mom went to bed around ten, I waited half an hour before changing into my dance clothes then another fifteen minutes before skulking into the hallway. Motionless, I listened for any sign of activity from her room. When it seemed safe, I hooked my dance bag over my shoulder and crept down the hallway, stealing out the door and into the night.

On the way down in the elevator, in the lobby, and on the trek up the sidewalk, I kept a watchful eye on my surroundings, walking a little faster when I passed the alley where Barney the homeless man camped.

Arriving at the Wakefield Center, I went around back, swiped my card to get in, and moved quickly down the hall. Through the curtains and onto the stage, I dropped my bag to the floor and waited. It was so quiet. Was he here? Had I risked Mom's wrath for nothing?

Then I heard him from behind the big, heavy drape. "I didn't really think you'd come."

"I'm the one who texted you remember?"

"I know, but I wouldn't have blamed you if you hadn't. No doubt I sounded strange—hiding behind a curtain asking you to dance for me."

I pressed my lips together and considered my answer. "Everything in my life right now is strange. Nothing is the way it was supposed to be. Why should dancing be any different?"

"Sucks," he commiserated. "But I made a promise to

myself last night," he said. "I decided if you came back, I would put the last two years behind me and make the best of what I have left. So no more Debbie-downer for either of us. Got it?"

"Got it." I agreed then asked, "Now, what do you want to do first?"

Striding to the center of the stage, I warmed up and followed a few commands he issued. He wanted to see more of the technique I'd been taught. After a short while, though, I gravitated closer to the curtain and we ended up sitting near each other—the red, velvet material the only thing between us—and talked about ballet.

He'd trained under several of the world's best teachers, and preferred a blend of the Vaganova and American, or Balanchine, method because he said it prepared a dancer for a company with a more diverse repertoire.

"A ballerina should learn to dance more than one way."

He truly was what he claimed to be, or had been—a world-class dancer.

Sometime later, I went home, but I was awake into the wee morning hours, thinking. Choosing to visit Erik had turned out to be the right thing. If only for a while, I had helped him enjoy the realm of ballet again. And his enthusiasm for my abilities boosted my ego, which of late had been flat-lining. It was the start to a friendship that would be beneficial for us both.

Chapter Thirty Three

*I*was sluggish the next morning, and Mom was surprised to see me have coffee with my breakfast. But the caffeine didn't help near as much as the text I received from Raoul.

Can't wait til this afternoon. wanna see if I can out *plié* you.

What the coffee hadn't done, anticipating seeing Raoul did, and I found the energy to get through my morning classes.

Jenna and I never talked about Mrs. Hahn's scolding, but at lunch, she barely nibbled a few carrots, and when Van came up behind her and snatched a stalk of celery from her plate, I feared she might bite his hand.

Unaware he might be poking a sleeping bear; he took a seat beside her. "So, either of you lovelies going to attend my performance next weekend?" he asked.

"What performance?" Jenna snapped.

"I have the lead in the level five's recital next Sunday. Of course, it's only for the recital. I'll still train with level sevens."

At her best, Jenna doesn't have a lot of patience with

Van's boasting, but I dreaded to think how a hungry Jenna would react.

"I'm grounded," she snapped. Getting to her feet she picked up her tray. "I can't go anywhere for a while." Then she stomped away.

"What's up with her? Somebody put bitching powder in her tights?"

"Cut it out, Van. She and Mrs. Hahn have been going at it, and trust me, you don't want in the middle of it."

"Whatever." He shrugged and shook it off. "How 'bout you, my soon-to-be first wife? You coming?"

"I don't know, Van. I have a lot on my plate right now."

"Yeah, I heard you have another man in your life, and I'm deeply wounded.

"What? Who told you?"

"The whole school knows, and you've ripped out my heart." He clutched both hands to his chest. "I thought it was you and me all the way. And now I find out you're hooking up with a football player."

"First, you'd have to have a heart for it to be ripped out." I flicked a slice of cucumber and he dodged it. "Second, we are not hooking up! We've only been on one date, so how does everyone already know?"

"Nothing is secret around here, not even the phantom. It's a matter of time for him, too."

"You still trying to convince everyone there's a ghost in the Wakefield?"

"Shhh," he hissed and leaned in closer, conspiratorially. "Stupid Paranormal Response Team shot me down," he grumbled. "But I've emailed Supernatural Sector. They may not be on a major network, but it's TV and that's all that matters."

Just then, several girls took up seats at a table adjacent to ours and Van said, "Ah, there's a pot of honey that needs stirring," and the heart-breaker-in-training left me to go join them.

Later that afternoon, I was relieved to see Jenna perk up some when Troy arrived for class. It made me wonder if she really liked him, or if it was simply the chase she enjoyed.

When Raoul sauntered in, I sucked in a breath, somehow having forgotten how gorgeous he was in only a few short days.

He walked straight to me and leaned down to plant a kiss on my lips. I was both thrilled and mortified. Immediately, I took a step back,

"What's wrong?"

"Nothing, it's ummm, well, we can't do that here." I flagged my hand outward.

"Oh, right," he grinned. "Here you are the teacher and I, the lowly student." He bowed humbly. Then he stepped closer, dipped his head, and leaned forward very near my cheek. "So you think later maybe you can give this naughty pupil a few private lessons?"

I didn't have to look in the great mirror to know my face was red. And right then I was certain of one thing; there was no way Mom or anyone at this school would to stop me from seeing Raoul Chaney.

Chapter Thirty Four

Tuesday night, Jenna took both a math and science test and passed, improving her mood immensely. "I talked Mom and Dad into letting me have the car Friday night," she said as we waited for our rides outside the school Wednesday afternoon.

"How'd you do that? It was only a couple of tests."

"Troy asked me to come to his game, and I promised if they'd let me go, I'd stay in and study the rest of the weekend. How do you feel about watching the Diamondbacks play?"

"Seriously? That would be awesome."

"Good. I didn't want to go alone."

"So you and Troy are hitting it off?" I asked.

"Yeah. It's slow, but I think I like that."

"Aw," I teased and gave her a playful shove, "my little Jenna is growing up."

"Bite me," she snarled.

Mom pulled up then. "So text me the details," I said, opening the door and climbing in.

"Details?" Mom said as she entered the flow of traffic. "What details?"

"Just guy stuff," I replied.

"Guy stuff?"

"Jenna and I are going to a Diamondback's' game Friday night."

"Is that right?" Her voice held a challenging pitch.

"Well, that is if you let me."

"Jenna is seeing one of those football players, too?"

"You don't have to say it like that."

"Like what? I was simply asking."

"There's nothing wrong with Troy or Raoul. They're both nice guys, and I would think you'd be glad I'm seeing someone whose family is connected with the Rousseau."

"I would prefer you not see anyone right now, Christine."

"So I've been told."

Mom's head jerked sideways. "What's that supposed to mean?"

"I know you talked to Ms. Zaborov. She doesn't approve either."

"Well, that should tell you something, honey. Lena Zaborov knows what it takes to be a principal dancer. She dedicated her life to it."

"Yeah, and look at her now—a woman alone, with no life outside the ballet school where she teaches."

I understood Lena Zaborov's decision to dedicate her life to ballet, but other dancers date—even marry and have children. This really came down to my mother wanting to maintain control of my life.

She never told me whether I could go to the game or not, so I took it as a yes and planned accordingly.

Later that night, I sent a text and met Erik at the theater. He'd managed to get a remote control to operate the stage speakers, and surprised me by playing some contemporary pieces of music for me to practice to. It wasn't until he asked me to perform a scene from Giselle that he switched to classical. That's also when he commented on my lack of concentration.

Pausing the tune coming through the onstage speakers, he said, "Okay, Ballerina, something's on your mind. What's bothering you?"

Catching my breath, I tugged my hair out of its ponytail, flattened and smoothed it in place, and wrapped it back in the band again. I pulled a bottle of water from my bag and had a few swallows.

"My mother is on my case about what she views as my lack of dedication."

"Yeah, mothers can be a pain in the ass sometimes, but fortunately you still have one."

Mental. Freaking. Head. Slap.

"Oh, my gosh! I'm so sorry. I can't seem to stop saying the wrong things around you."

"Look, Christine, you don't have to keep apologizing. What happened to me wasn't your fault. I should have said that differently. What I meant was, well, a ballerina's life is like a vortex. The amount of dedication and passion it generates forms a great whirlwind that can't help but suck in the people around her. Of course, your mother would be picked up and carried away by it."

This knocked off kilter. Consumed by my frustration with my parents, I hadn't thought about all they'd had at stake in my succeeding, or failing, at the Rousseau.

"How'd you get so wise?" I asked, smiling.

"The hard way," he replied.

Chapter Thirty Five

*T*hursday, in the school kitchenette after the Diamondback's practice, I told Raoul about Jenna and me making plans to attend their upcoming game.

"So it will be my turn to show off," he teased.

"Show off?" I replied. "You think I show off?"

He stepped closer to me, wrapped his arms around my waist, and smiled. "Did I say show off? I meant to say shine. It's my turn to shine."

"Mmmm," I groaned and pulled away. "I have to go. Ms. Zaborov is waiting."

"You still doing the one-on-one with her?"

"Afraid so. The second company tryouts are in the spring of next year; until then it's work, work, work."

"All right," he grazed his lips across mine, "I'll see you tomorrow night." Then he walked out the kitchen door.

"Yeah," I called after him. "I'll be the one in the tutu."

Later that day, Ms. Z. and I practiced for close to an hour before she decided to stop for the evening. "This was good," she observed. And though she'd said this before, this time was different. She really meant it and her smile proved it. "Excellent work, Christine," she said, and I curtseyed and thanked her.

On my walk to the apartment, I made a mental note to tell Erik about Ms. Z.'s compliment when I went to the theater that night. But upon arriving home, I found a note from Mom saying she would be late again. There would be no trip to the theater, since I had no idea when she'd be in. Instead, I made myself a sandwich, did some homework, and crashed with my literature book sprawled across my bed a short while later.

"Christine. Christine!" Mom shook me awake the next morning. "Did you sleep like that, sweetheart?"

I glanced down at the slouchy shorts and tee I'd slipped into the night before, and the literature book that lay crumpled under my hip.

"Yeah," I yawned and stretched. "I guess so. What time did you get home? Where were you?"

"I was at work. You better get moving if you're going to shower and have time to grab breakfast."

She left my room and I doubted her at work story. It was turning into her go-to excuse. More than ever, I needed to find a way to convince Dad to come home. If he were here, Mom wouldn't be working late so much of the time.

The extra sleep did me some good. I wasn't at all tired at the end of school that day. Of course, anticipating attending Raoul's game might have had something to do with that.

Jenna showed up at the apartment at six. The stadium was on the south side of town. Traffic would be heavy, rush hour on a Friday, so we had no time to waste.

"Be careful," Mom said as we started out the door. "Be home by eleven-thirty. No texting and driving. And certainly no drinking and..."

"Mom. Don't be ridiculous. Give me a little credit."

She laughed. "I'm your mother. I don't do credit."

With that, I kissed her goodbye and we left.

Traveling across town, Jenna cut into the I-59 traffic. We listened to music and talked for a while when it occurred to me that I'd never told her about Erik. Between my practices with Ms. Zaborov, and her putting in overtime on her homework, we hadn't had a decent girl talk in days.

"If I tell you something," I said, "can you keep it a secret?"

"I'd take it to the grave."

"I'm being serious. You have to keep it to yourself."

Drawing her gaze off the rode a second, her brow furrowed. Then she put her eyes back on the freeway and smiled wickedly.

"You're telling me Christine Dadey has a secret? Now that's a shocker."

Chapter Thirty Six

"I'm not a total goody two-shoes," I said.

"Yes, you are, but that's a subject for another time. Right now, I want to know this juicy secret."

"I met this dancer; his name is Erik, and he's promised to teach me some things, help me get Mrs. Hahn off my back."

"Okay," Jenna prompted, "and this is a secret because…"

"Well, other than Marisol, no one else knows."

"Isn't that generally how a secret is defined—no one knows? The question is why you've kept it a secret."

"I've been meaning to tell you, but haven't had the chance. I met him after the ballet the other night—the night we were supposed to attend Romeo and Juliet—I went by myself. Well, actually, I met him before that."

Traffic had stalled, so while we crept along at a snail's pace, I relayed everything to Jenna. I told her he'd caught me sneaking into Claudette's dressing room, but I omitted the fire and the fact that he'd stayed behind the curtain for our practices. She'd probably think me nuts if she knew."

"You're shittin' me," she jibed.

"No, no. It's true. I've practiced with him a couple of times now. His method and strategy is different from anything I've experienced. He's all about varied styles, and muscle and mental energy."

She nodded. "Cool. So where's his studio?"

"That's the thing. He doesn't have one. I've been sneaking out at night to meet him at the theater to practice, and Mom doesn't know."

"Dayum, girl. When you decide to have a secret, you go all out. Maybe there's a bad girl underneath that leotard, after all."

"Stop it," I said. "He truly is helping me."

"If you say so. But you can trust me. Your secret is safe. Whoa, there's our exit," she said, pointing at a green road sign, and we dropped the topic altogether.

Jenna soon located the stadium parking lot, and before long, we were seated in the stands with the other excited fans.

I know nothing about football and the whole occasion was a bit extraordinary. The stadium was gigantic, filled with people wearing the Diamondback's team colors, drinking from cups with the team logo, and blowing air horns at unexpected times. Fortunately, Jenna was no novice. She has a younger brother who plays peewee and her dad is an aficionado. So while we waited for the players to take the field, she gave me a quick tutorial on running, passing, punting, and tackling. I learned the most important thing was to get the ball into the opponent's end zone.

My anticipation built as we waited with the noisy crowd, the smell of freshly made popcorn and something sweet I couldn't identify, floated on the air. Then without warning, a band commenced playing and the people around us went wild, some screaming louder than the deafening air horns.

"Here they come," Jenna yelled, and we rose to our feet along with the others and started clapping to the music.

From where we were in the stands, we had a clear view, but I was ill prepared for the way the boys we'd been teaching to *plié* and *jeté* would look in football uniforms. They were enormous! With the pads, their shoulders had doubled in size. This made me a little concerned because Raoul was not as big as they were. They would trounce him. I hoped his helmet would keep his brain intact. Then Jenna informed me it wasn't the size of Raoul's teammates that mattered, but of the other team. To my horror, the Springer High Razorbacks were no less humongous. They were going to kill Raoul.

It turned out there was no need for me to worry. Raoul was good. He was fast, light on his feet, and when he threw the ball, it went where he intended. No wonder colleges were pursuing him.

During a break, Raoul ran to the sideline, pulled off his helmet and picked up a Gatorade bottle to squeeze a stream of pale, green liquid into his mouth. I have no idea how he did it, but he spotted me. Our gazes connected and he smiled. Then he placed the bottle on the bench, kissed two fingers, tapped them to his heart, and then pointed to me. My own heart went buttery and warm. If I wasn't careful, I was going to lose it entirely to this boy.

Chapter Thirty Seven

I slept in the next morning and when I woke, I lay in bed with my phone, going through pictures, reliving the night before. Jenna and I had met Troy and Raoul at the Frozen Tundra Ice Cream Shop after the game. I'd snapped a bunch of random photos, but one of Raoul wiping a smear of ice cream off his nose made me laugh aloud. Thinking about how the creamy confection came to be there caused me to tingle all over.

Raoul had scrunched his nose in disgust when he saw me eating mango-flavored ice cream. I tried to get him to taste it, but he refused, and when I called him a sissy he'd said, "I'll try it. On one condition.'"

"What?" I'd asked.

"If you feed it to me."

I had seriously backed myself into a corner. It was my fault. I'd offered for him to taste it. But the look he gave me said he'd like to taste more than ice cream.

Jenna egged me on. "Go ahead, I dare you," she'd said.

So I'd taken my pink, plastic spoon, scooped up a sizable amount of the yellow-orange treat, and placed it into his mouth. Slowly, excruciatingly slowly, he'd closed his lips around the spoon, letting them linger as he made eye contact with me. Then he dragged his mouth off the spoon and licked his lips sensually before saying, "Mmmm. More."

A flush had shot up my neck then, and thinking about it now caused a repeat sensation. I'd tried to play it cool—pretend I knew how to act sexy—and tunneled out another scoop. On my way to his mouth with it, Jenna jibed, "Sheesh, you two keep that up and you're gonna melt all the ice cream in the place." Then she bumped my elbow and I lost control of the spoon, causing the ice cream to jostle up Raoul's nose rather than into his mouth.

Grinning now, I set the photo as my phone's background, and after flipping through more of the pictures, I chose a couple of Raoul and me to send to Marisol. Then there was a knock at my door. I sat up in bed. It would be Mom. I shoved my phone under the bed covers a second before she opened the door and poked her head in.

"If you don't get up soon," she said, you're going to miss your chat with your dad."

"I'm up," I said. "Be dressed in a minute."

She was closing the door and I stopped her.

"Have you seen my purple shrug?"

"No. Did you check your closet?"

"Yeah, and the dirty clothes hamper, too, but there's no sign of it. Maybe I left it at school."

"Probably," she agreed and left me to get dressed.

Throwing on a sloppy tee and a pair of running shorts, I had my laptop booted up and ready for the call when it came.

"So you've already been out with him again?" Dad asked when I told him about the football game and ice cream afterwards.

"It wasn't exactly a date," I replied.

"You haven't wasted any time," he ribbed. "A week ago, you hadn't even been out, and now you're his personal cheerleader. You tell him I said he'd better treat you right. He doesn't want me to come over there."

"That's a great idea," I said, jumping on his suggestion. "If you came home you could meet him."

He opened his mouth then closed it again, and after fiddling pointlessly with his keyboard, he asked, "Is your mother there?"

I shook my head. "She went grocery shopping, but I can have her call you when she gets home."

"That's okay. Maybe another time."

"This is wrong," I complained. "It's just wrong. You two don't talk to each other; you're not even in the same country for heaven's sake. What gives? When are you coming home?"

"Don't worry about it. It will fi…"

"Don't worry about it?" I interrupted. "How can you say don't worry about it? I think Mom's cheating on you, Dad."

Oops, hadn't meant for that last part to slip out.

He stared vacantly at me a few seconds, let out a long sigh, and leaned back in his chair, stretching so all I saw was his upper chest and shoulders. When he reappeared, he looked sad.

"I didn't want you to find out this way. I had hoped we'd get it worked out."

"Find out what? Get what worked out?"

Tugging at an earlobe, he groaned then drew his hand across his face. "Christine—baby—I'm the one who cheated. I cheated on your mother. And then I ran away."

My mouth flew open and I gasped like I'd been sucker-punched, gurgling noises rising from my throat.

"I didn't want you to find out like this. But you've been so persistent. And if your mother..." he waited a moment, "...well, if you mother wants to see someone else, I suppose I don't blame her."

Perched on the edge of my seat, I scooted my laptop closer. "This can't be happening," I muttered more to myself than to him.

"It wasn't supposed to come out like this. It wasn't supposed to come out at all. But I don't want you blaming your mother for our separation."

Separation. There, he'd said it. Their separation.

He continued to talk. I could hear and see him but none of it made sense.

"You cheated? But...but..."

"I'm so sorry," he placated. "I'd really hoped you'd never have to learn of it. I came over here for a while to give things time to cool down, and now your mom and I seem to be stuck in limbo."

My stomach burned and I felt sick. "You cheated?"

"Christine," he touched his monitor as if he could console me through cyberspace, "I'm so sorry."

"Sorry!"

The overwhelming desire to punch something surged through me. All along, I'd thought Mom the problem. The cavern that had developed between us, her animosity toward Dad, I'd misread it and blamed her.

"Sorry for what? Sorry you did it or sorry you were caught? How did you get caught anyway?"

"You wouldn't understand," he said.

"Oh, yeah? Try me."

"It was one time. She was a business associate, and I haven't seen her since."

"A business associate? Seriously, Dad?"

"I regretted it. That's why I confessed everything to your mother. I went to her and told her about it."

"But why? Why would you do it in the first place?"

He stared at me a while. "I don't know. I've gone over it a thousand times. Your mother was always busy, working all the time, shopping and rubbing shoulders with the executives at her office; you were growing up, getting your own life. It's a pathetic excuse, but I suppose I felt left out.

"Your mother and I had fought before I went to meet a company rep that night." He paused and briefly cupped his hand over his mouth. "I had too much to drink, and—and it happened. I know it sounds sleazy, and I'm not making excuses." He touched the screen. "You're crying. Don't cry. It breaks my heart. You know I can't stand it when you cry."

I wiped the tears from my eyes, rubbed my nose with my sleeve, and glowered at the monitor while he continued.

"I can't tell you how many times I've regretted it. It cost me my wife, my home, and now my daughter."

When I shifted uncomfortably in my chair, he begged, "Please, Christine, give me a chance. I know it may be too late with your mother, but please don't shut me out, too."

A throbbing started behind my eyes and shot to the back of my head. I groaned and pinched the bridge of my nose to staunch it, and when I lowered my hand, he was staring at me, waiting for my verdict.

"I don't know what to say, Dad. I don't know if I even want you to come home anymore," I snapped. Then I hit the End Call button.

Chapter Thirty Eight

Burrowed under my bed covers, I was still crying when Mom came home and entered my room.

"I went to Whole Foods and bought that pineapple yogurt you like."

She saw my tears then and hurried to the bed. "What's wrong? Why are you crying?" Pulling me to sit up, she pushed my hair back, and searched my face. "Are you hurt?"

My mouth felt filled with sand but I managed to mumble, "Dad told me about his one-night-stand."

"He told you? Oh, no. Why would he do that? We didn't want you to know."

"Why not, Mom? Why would you keep it from me?"

She pressed her lips together and hesitated. "That's not exactly a topic you want to discuss with your teenage daughter. How was I supposed to bring it up? 'Oh, hey, Chris, your dad is a low-life cheating SOB, but we're going to trudge on and pretend it never happened'."

To my knowledge, my mother had never called my father a name, but she'd obviously harbored her anger for a while.

"Plus," she sighed, "I know how much he loves you and you him. He's still your father, no matter what happens. I would never want anything to come between the two of you. Not even this."

"I owe you an apology." I sniffed.

"Me? Whatever for?"

"I thought you were cheating with Cooper Nance, and I told Dad to try to get him to come home."

She made a nervous twittering sound.

"You find that funny?"

"It's not that it's funny, it's...I don't know...I guess I did find Cooper's attention appealing, and the idea of your father hearing a younger man thinks me attractive is a bit of a balm to my bruised ego, but it's okay that you told him. You're not to blame for any of this."

Her eyes grew watery and she lightly dabbed a tear balancing on her lower lid. Then she pulled me into her arms and we cried together, her rubbing my back and cooing comforting declarations in my ear.

When we'd run out of tears, she held me at arm's length. "Better?"

I nodded.

"We'll be okay. I promise." Then she stood. "I'm going to put the groceries away, but I'm in the kitchen if you need me."

After she'd gone, I got up and strolled to Dad's theater room. My original shock had turned to sorrow, and I still wanted to feel his presence there, to smell the leather and any of his cologne that lingered.

Alone in the dark for a long time, I thought of calling Jenna or chatting with Marisol, but I couldn't bring myself to do it. It hurt too much to let either of them in yet.

Around four, I got hungry and went to the kitchen for

some of the yogurt. After grabbing a spoon and popping the top into the trash, I headed for my room. The sound of Mom's elevated voice caught my attention, so I tiptoed down the hall to her bedroom door. There was a tiny crack in it, enough for me to hear she was on the phone with Dad.

"Benjamin, it was not my idea for you to go over there. You did that. And you're the one who told her why you went." She was quiet a moment. "I don't know. She's okay now, but I don't think we should tell her about the divorce yet."

Divorce. They were going to divorce. I looked down at the yogurt cup in my hand and lost my appetite.

"Yes, I know what time it is there," Mom snapped, "but I felt this was too important to wait. Fine. Yeah, yeah, I'll be here at ten tomorrow. Okay—I said okay. I'll talk to you then."

She'd obviously hung up the phone, and I contemplated going to her, but I didn't know what to say. They'd hidden so much from me already.

When she began to cry, I backed quietly down the hall, careful not to draw her attention. In my room, I set the yogurt and spoon on the side table and picked up my phone. The only way to get rid of the oppressive weight sitting on my chest was to go to the theater and dance until I didn't feel it anymore.

Chapter Thirty Nine

"Are you there?" I called into the theater shadows. "Erik?" I'd sent him a text but wasn't certain he'd received it.

Several seconds passed and the curtains shuddered.

"I'm here."

"I want to dance."

"Then let's get to work," he said.

Warming up, I strove to push Mom and Dad out of my mind, but the months of dead-end conversations with Mom, and the devastating talk with Dad, played like a video clip on repeat in my thoughts. After I'd blundered through several steps, Erik finally stopped me.

"No, no, no. There's no fluidity. Where is your head tonight?"

I fell out of position and slapped my hands on my thighs. "I don't know what you want. Without seeing my instructor, how am I supposed to gage my performance, to know what you're thinking? It's like dancing blind."

"That's not an entirely bad thing, Christine. You rely too much on your instructor's facial expression and body language."

He didn't sound the least bit sympathetic. And when he started the music and called out a command, I whirled around, throwing my hands in the air to link my fingers behind my head. Several seconds passed as the arrangement played on. Still, I stood like that fighting the tears threatening to take over. I refused to give into them, though, and dropped my hands again to gather myself. Taking a deep breath, I did an about-face and lifted my chin.

"I'm sorry. Start the music over—let me do it again."

The music stopped all together then, and after a beat, he spoke and he'd moved from the back curtain to the left side of the stage, very near me now.

"Something's happened. What's bothering you?"

I struggled with my composure, afraid to speak, and burst into a bout of crying. Getting a grip, I drew from years of training to stand in first position and lock eyes on a focal point.

"I'm ready. Start the music again."

The curtain swayed and to my surprise, his long pale, fine-boned fingers slipped from behind the curtain to curl around the edge of the fabric, and I wondered if he was going to step out. But he merely held it in his hand.

"Are you going to tell me?" he asked. "I thought we'd established a level of trust."

He was right. He'd certainly trusted me with his story.

"My family is falling apart," I choked. "My parents are separated and they're planning to divorce."

"I'm sorry," he whispered.

"My dad lied to us. He let me believe...I...I don't know what he let me believe, but it wasn't the truth."

Everything pressed in on me then and I couldn't take it

anymore. The tears came.

"I should leave," I sniveled at last. "This isn't working tonight."

"Wait," he pleaded, and his hand disappeared. "I have an idea. Stay there. I'll be right back."

"Huh?"

"Just promise me you'll stay there."

"Okay, I'll stay."

His footsteps echoed behind the curtain. He was leaving the backstage area, and I couldn't imagine why."

After pacing a while, I went to the edge of the stage to sit down, hang my legs over the side, and look out on the pencil-straight rows of burgundy theater seats.

Several minutes passed when I heard, "Christine—I'm over here."

I whipped my head to the left and my mouth fell open. Erik was standing on the stage for me to see, dressed in black warm-ups and arrayed in an elaborate costume mask that concealed his face.

With effortless grace he approached me, every step revealing his nimble dancer's body. When he stopped he extended his open hand to me and I took it, allowing him pull me to my feet with a strong arm.

Mere inches from me, he waved a hand in front of the mask. "I know this is strange. But it was the only thing I could think of. And it didn't seem right for me to be behind the curtain and you out here crying all by yourself."

Still surprised to see him on stage, I stared open-mouthed at the mask. Full-faced, it was white with angular, almond shaped eyes. The upper half was stippled gold, with raised filigree swirling across the forehead and down the sides of each cheek. The lips were of a softer, more buttery, shade of gold. The face-piece connected to a length of black knit that was swathed in an Arabian style across the top of the mask, draped under his chin and wrapped back up to be pinned high on the other side. It was stunning.

"Are you afraid?" he asked.

I closed my mouth and shook my head.

He was still holding my hand in his, and lifting it between us, he placed his other on top so that he held my hand warmly between his, and asked, "Then will you let me dance with you?"

Chapter Forty

*I*t was impossible to tell his age with so much of him covered up, but I thought of Cooper Nance and figured Erik younger than him. But the baritone register of his voice led me to believe him older than Raoul, no longer a teenager.

"We're going to use this—your pain," he said, "to transform your dancing. You'll learn to channel your pain, your love, your hate, everything you're passionate about into your art."

Curling my bottom lip in, I held it between my teeth.

"You don't believe me, but you'll see."

He released my hand to glide behind me. Then gently, he took each of my wrists and lifted my arms straight out into second position.

"Now tell me how you feel."

"I...I..."

"Tell me how you feel," he pressed, never releasing his hold on my arms. "Remember it. The moment pain pierced you. What did you feel?"

My thoughts went back to the video chat with Dad. The revelation had been piercing.

"Betrayal."

"Betrayal," he echoed in my ear. "So you are Giselle. See it?"

I closed my eyes and nodded.

Then he shifted and brought his face around to the other side, and the mask brushed against my hair.

"You are Giselle. The man you love, Prince Albrecht, has betrayed you. He wooed you and stole your affection from the gamekeeper Hilarion. You thought him a simple peasant, someone with whom you could grow old, but he kept the truth from you."

My eyes flew open as I thought about Dad keeping the truth from me.

"When you learned he was royalty and already promised to another, you were so devastated it drove you mad, and you died from a broken heart.

I visualized it, me in a medieval village falling in love with Prince Albrecht, and then the grief of his duplicity, which ultimately led to my demise.

"When Albrecht learns of your death," he paused and lifted my right hand in the air over my head while bringing the left in front to pose in fourth position, "when he discovers you've died, he brings flowers to the grave. He doesn't know the Wilis, the spirits of women who died despondent over lost love, lie in wait. He doesn't know you've been pressed into becoming one of them and the vengeful Wilis plan to force him to dance until he dies of exhaustion."

He lowered my right hand so it was even with my left in front of me. Then he released both my wrists but didn't step away.

"He doesn't know his only hope for survival is for you, Giselle, to dance with him until the sun comes up."

He paused and his breath stirred beneath the confines of the mask. Then he asked, "Will you dance the *grand pas de deux* from Act II of Giselle with me?"

I nodded vigorously. Never had I wanted to dance as keenly as I did right then.

"Y-yes."

My back still to him, the music started. Then we danced as if it wasn't our first time but our one thousand and first. His grip was powerful, and I never feared he would drop me or lose his hold in the middle of a lift. With every swish of the air around us, the scent of fresh soap wafted about. And only once did I come close to losing concentration and breaking character, when my hand brushed over a patch of gnarled threadlike skin beneath his sleeve, and I remembered I was dancing with Erik.

We performed the complete *grand pas de deux*, and when we'd taken the last step, done the last lift, and he'd placed me back on my feet *en pointe*, I started to worry. His breathing sounded arduous and there was a tight wheezing in his chest. Perhaps the mask had been too much for him. I turned to face him and was about to suggest he take it off when he spoke.

"I'd like to give you something," he said. Then he circled his arms around his neck and worried with the cloth hanging from the back of the headpiece. When he lowered them, he held the ends of a necklace in each hand.

"Will you wear it?" he asked.

"It's beautiful, but..."

"Please," he interrupted. "It belonged to someone special

to me, and tonight you've given me something special. After the fire—when I finally danced again—I always danced alone. For the first time in years, tonight, I danced with a partner. It's a moment I'll treasure and may never have again. Please take this as a symbol of my gratitude."

He extended the necklace, a silver chain with a heart locket, toward me. As it hung suspended in the air, I felt uncomfortable at the idea of taking such a valuable gift from him. Here he was telling me I'd helped him when he was the one who'd donned a mask to come on stage to comfort me.

"I don't know, Erik. It looks expensive."

"Please," he said. And without waiting for a response he stepped behind me, raised the necklace over my head, and fastened it around my neck.

When he moved back before me, I stared at the mask, wishing I could see the face beneath. The Arabian style headgear made the experience surreal, a mystical dream. He seemed otherworldly.

Without thinking, my hand went to the locket, still warm from where it had been next to his skin.

"Thank you," I said.

Bending a knee, he bowed deeply and murmured, "No. Thank you, ballerina." Then he strolled back into the shadows, leaving me alone on the stage once more.

Chapter Forty One

I slept until two o'clock the next day. It seemed impossible, but when my stomach growled, I knew it was true.

Throwing back the cover, I placed my feet on the floor next to the dance clothes I'd shed the night before, and everything came back to me. Immediately, my hand went to the necklace and I grasped the locket. In the stark light of day, I regretted taking it. It didn't seem quite right somehow. But I hadn't had the courage to refuse Erik the night before, and if I tried to give it back now it might hurt him all the more.

My stomach protested again, so I slipped the necklace under my T-shirt and headed for the kitchen.

"Hey, sleepy-head," Mom said from where she sat on the sofa, her feet tucked under her and iPad in her lap. "Yesterday was pretty rough. I didn't want to wake you. I thought you could use the sleep. Do you want some lunch?"

Part of me still wanted to be angry with her. She and Dad had lied to me, and even now, by not telling me they planned to divorce, in a way they still were. But I didn't have it in me anymore.

"Don't bother," I told her. "I'll find something."

After I'd gone to the kitchen for a glass of juice and a protein bar, I took it back to the living room to sit beside her on the sofa.

"I still don't understand why Dad had to go to the other side of the world to get away from us."

Mom sighed. "My guess would be shame, or cowardice."

It hurt to hear her call Dad a coward, and the bite of protein bar I'd swallowed lodged in my throat.

"Did you want to split up?" I asked. "Did you want him to leave?"

"Oh, yeah, I wanted him gone."

My heart dropped. I'd hoped for some sign that she still loved him.

"But I'd also wanted certain parts of his body to fall off, and oozing boils to develop all over his flesh." She paused to smirk. "But then there was grief, followed by self-pity, anger, and loneliness."

I marveled at how she'd kept all this to herself. Then again, it explained a lot about her mood swings and her growing need for approval.

"I'd spent almost twenty years of my life with your dad," she mused. "I didn't know how to act without him. At the same time, I hated the sight of him. Crazy, right?"

Though uncomfortable, at least we were talking. We were actually on the same page, surviving Dad's betrayal together.

"You still love him?" I asked.

She looked at me. "It's not that simple, Chris."

"Why can't it be? He's sorry. He said so yesterday. He even asked me if you were home. I think he wanted to talk to you."

It was strange, me defending him, but I did. I wanted things to go back to the way they were before the move to Houston—back when I was still blissfully naïve.

"If he came home maybe you could start over—we could start over," I said.

She was silent for a while.

"This is a one-day-at-a-time thing," she finally said. "I can only take it one day at a time, and today your father is still in Norway."

She was shutting down. It was in her eyes and tone of voice. And even though she was raising her defenses again, she still hadn't completely ruled out the possibility of their reconciling.

Exhaling, I got to my feet to take my glass back to the kitchen, but she placed a hand on my arm to stop me.

"I love you, honey."

I smiled. "I love you, too."

Chapter Forty Two

*A*fter I'd eaten something more substantial than a protein bar, I went back to my room and found I'd missed a call from Jenna and two from Raoul. I returned Jenna's call first because she'd also sent me a text with enough exclamation marks to give my fifth grade grammar teacher heart failure.

"You're not going to freaking believe this," she exploded the instant she picked up on the other end of the line.

"Believe what?" I said, wondering why the drama.

"Mom was at the Memorial City Mall and saw Deirdre's mother. According to her, Mrs. Hahn is talking to Mr. Darby about Deirdre. Atilla is trying to get Deirdre a spot in the second company without her even auditioning."

"What! She can't do that, can she? I mean—I know she can—but she can't. It's not right." Resentment flooded me. I was working my tail off just for the chance to audition, and Deirdre wouldn't even have to try out? How was that fair?

"I don't know," Jenna said. "Look what they did with Van."

"Yeah, but Van is different. He's a true prodigy. Deirdre's simply a suck up."

"It's crap like this that makes me think about quitting," Jenna grumbled.

"Seriously?"

"Yeah. Sometimes I wonder if it's worth it. You know?"

I did know. The same thing crossed my mind a lot lately.

"Eh, don't listen to me," she muttered. "It's probably the ice cream deprivation talking."

"My mother would wig-out if I said anything about quitting. Especially, since the Rousseau Academy was the whole reason we moved to Houston, and Houston is where her marriage fell apart."

"You can't blame yourself for your parents splitting up," Jenna said. "That's on them."

The image of Dad with some faceless hoochie popped into my head, and I almost told Jenna about it, but it was too embarrassing. I'd already looked like the naïve ninny when she was the one who had to tell me Dad was out of the country because he'd left my mother.

"Maybe not," I said, "but when I see stuff like this, I wonder if I'm doing the right thing."

We'd dissed Deirdre a good five minutes, when I got a text from Raoul. I told Jenna he'd called a couple of times so I needed to return his call.

I dialed his number and my heart skipped a beat when he answered.

"Hey, I was beginning to think you were ignoring me."

Like with Jenna, it crossed my mind to tell him about what had happened with Dad, explain my distraction. His parents were divorced. He knew what it was like. He even had stepsisters. But snippets of conversations I'd had with him floated forward. He'd said he couldn't see any weakness in me. And he'd referred to what I do at the football classes as shining. I wanted him to continue to think of me in that way.

"I'm sorry. I haven't been feeling well," I said. "I think I ate some bad yogurt."

"Oh, I was going to ask if you wanted to hang out, but if you're sick..."

My pulse sped up at the idea of seeing him, but then I glanced in the mirror across the room. My eyes were red and swollen, my hair tangled and dirty, and my trig book lay on my desk, staring at me."

"I'd love to, but it's not a good time. Bad yogurt and hanging out—not an appealing combination. Plus, I have a ton of trig to get done."

"Yeah, sure," he agreed, "maybe next weekend."

He was quiet a moment. Then he said, "Listen, I was kinda thinking of asking my mother if I could stay a few days with Dad. If I do, maybe I could drive you home after our classes together."

I smiled. He was too amazing, and this was why I wanted him to keep viewing me as shining.

"That would be cool," I said.

We talked a while longer, making plans for me to catch another of his games, and the possibility of our attending a ballet together. Then we got off the phone for me to get to my homework.

Seated at my desk, I opened the trig book and the previous night skittered into my thoughts. Erik's ability to help me take my anger and disappointment in Dad and infuse it into my dancing was beyond anything I'd ever experienced. I've had some great ballet teachers, but he had a gift the others didn't. And as we'd danced, I'd completely forgotten about the mask. It was as if it wasn't there.

In my heart, I felt Erik could help me choreograph a routine that would get me into the second company, but I wondered if I should tell him about my panic attacks and the epic-fail of an audition last year. It didn't seem fitting not to. He deserved to know what he was up against. He also deserved to know how I'd gotten into the Rousseau Academy in the first place.

Closing the trig book, I opened the bottom drawer of my desk and looked in. Shoving aside recent magazines, old jewelry, and a broken cell phone, I dug out the plastic baggy I'd buried deep in the back. Holding it up, I examined the contents—Xanax—the method for my getting through the Academy entry audition.

I'd stolen the anti-anxiety medication from the medicine cabinet at Marisol's house. They'd belonged to her mother, and I'd copped two of them. It was after I'd attended the summer intensive at Rousseau almost two years ago. Mom and Dad had gotten the call that I'd been invited to audition for an opening at the Academy. But I was terrified by the prospect. More than anything, I wanted to join the school, but the panic attacks had increased, and Mom thought I was faking. And to her credit, I had faked it when I was younger and didn't want to go to class. I'd pretended to be ill, using the phantom pains as an excuse to skip. She caught on to me and unfortunately, I lost credibility in that area.

But as time went by, and the importance of my training grew, so did the anxiety. I wished that I could go back now and undo those phony episodes because the real deal was so distressful that I'd never play around with something like that again.

So I'd stolen the pills. I only took half of one the day of the Academy interview, and my conscience almost ate me alive because of it. It seemed the coward's way out, not to mention the whole stealing drugs thing.

Then, when it came time for the audition for Rousseau II, the junior company, I'd considered taking the other half, but I couldn't bring myself to do it. But I'd kept what remained and stuffed them in the drawer. After my horrendous meltdown in front of Ms. Zaborov and Mrs. Hahn, though, I'd wondered if I shouldn't have used it after all. Even if I had, though, what would happen when I ran out? I couldn't exactlyl drive across Texas to Marisol's and say, "Excuse me while I use your mother's bathroom," to get more. No, I had to learn to deal with this myself if I was going to advance. And with Erik's help, maybe I could try-out without the medication.

Chapter Forty Three

*T*he next week was a blur, filled with class every day, lessons with the Diamondbacks, time with Raoul, and then the theater with Erik at night. I was on autopilot. But it was worth it when on Friday Ms. Zaborov asked me to her office.

Gracefully, she extracted herself from behind her desk when I entered the room and glided over to stand before me. "I am seeing some encouraging things in your work, Christine. If you keep this up, I will be bringing it before Director Darby for consideration. Perhaps we can reassess."

Casting aside restraint, I squealed and threw my arms around the woman's neck. Then I released her and backed up. "I'm sorry. Ms. Zaborov that was a—oops."

She laughed and shook it off. "Well, it is good news, is it not?"

"It's excellent news!" I replied.

Leaving her office, I rushed to the cafeteria where Jenna and Van hunched at a table in a heated discussion.

"Hush, you two," I commanded, not caring what they argued about. "I just came from Ms. Zaborov, and she thinks I'm improving enough that she's considering intervening with Mr. Darby."

"Great!" Jenna said.

"So what are you doing different?" Van asked.

"She has a secret tutor," Jenna replied.

"Jenna!" I kicked her under the table.

"Ouch." She recoiled and rubbed her shin.

"A secret tutor," Van said. "Princess, if you wanted tutoring, you know you could have come to me."

Jenna rolled her eyes and Van said to her, "What? I could teach you a few moves, too."

"You couldn't teach a pig to oink," Jenna teased.

"Where'd you get that?" Van asked me, shifting the topic of conversation.

"Get what?" I followed the trail of his pointing finger to the locket that had worked its way out from under my leotard.

"That's nice," Jenna said, leaning in to lift it for closer inspection. "Looks expensive."

It had been my intention to show it to her and ask her opinion on whether or not I should risk hurting Erik's feelings to give it back. But after she'd spilled her guts about my tutor I thought better of it now.

"I've had it," I replied, retrieving it from Jenna's grasp to tuck it back under my leotard. "I forgot to take it off before class."

Jenna eyed me with what I thought was skepticism, but it may have been my imagination. Van went back to his favorite topic then, himself, and bragged about how he planned to wow the crowd at Sunday's recital.

Shortly before the end of lunch, Liam joined us, his face flushed and obviously distressed.

Motioning for us to draw closer, he leaned in and whispered, "It happened again."

"What happened again?" Jenna asked.

"Someone broke into the Wakefield last week and took a bunch of stuff from the offices."

"You're kidding," Jenna said and we both turned our gazes to Van.

"Don't look at me," he said. "My phantom doesn't take stuff, he leaves it."

"What was taken?" I asked.

"Computer equipment, money, even some junk from the Lost and Found."

"The Lost and Found? Why would anyone want to steal from the Lost and Found?" Van asked.

"Beats me," Liam replied. "But there's definitely something freaky going on around here."

It was time to return to class then, so we dropped the matter and went on to our respective studios.

That night I shot a text to Erik to meet for lessons. When I arrived at the theater, Erik wasn't there yet, so I warmed up. While I stretched, I thought about how compartmentalized my life had become, and how each segment had its own little set of lies, or half-truths.

Marisol knew little about Erik and nothing about my stealing her mother's meds, Jenna knew more about Erik than Marisol did, but only what I'd been comfortable doling out. Raoul, well, I kept him in the dark about everything. And my parents were entirely clueless when it came to my life anymore. Erik seemed to be the only person I felt free to tell everything to. There was no agenda—for him or me—so I had no reason to hold back.

When time had passed and there was no sign of Erik, I readied to leave, thinking something must have held him up. Then the entrance door at the far end of the theater opened and surprised me. I froze because I knew Erik would not be coming through there. He always arrived from backstage, never from the guest entrance.

Someone began making his way down the side aisle, and I squinted into the dark. It didn't take long for me to recognize the man in the Wakefield janitor's uniform. It was Mr. Sims.

Chapter Forty Four

*H*ow was I going to explain my presence to Mr. Sims?

"H-hi," I stammered. "I was uuuh, I came to...,"

"It's okay." He cut me off. "I'm here to see you."

"I beg your pardon?"

"Erik sent me. Come down here, and I'll explain."

Bewildered, I moved slowly to the stage exit and went down and through the usher doors to where he waited.

"You know Erik? You know that—we've been meeting here?"

He didn't answer but asked, "Can we sit?" He indicated the front row, and I followed him over, where we unfolded seats and sat down.

We waited quietly for a moment and Mr. Sims's knee bounced nervously. He didn't appear to be going to speak, so I asked again, "You know Erik?"

Taking a breath, he cupped his hand on his knee to stop the fidgeting and nodded. "Yeah, and he wanted me to let you know he couldn't come. He's not feeling well. But he was worried about you being here alone."

"He's not well? What's wrong? Has he gone to a doctor? Do we need to help him?"

Mr. Sims shook his head. "No, he won't see a doctor." Then he raised a hand to his brow and massaged his temple. "Maybe I should start from the beginning so you'll understand."

Swiveling, he looked back over the seats as if he expected to see someone there.

"Mr. Sims? You were saying?"

He faced me again. "A few months ago I was working the late shift, taking trash down to the dumpsters in the parking garage. On my way back, I heard something. We've had kids sneak down there to do drugs before, so I investigated. That's when I found him lying under the stairwell."

"You found Erik there?"

He nodded dismally. "He was curled up under the stairs, moaning and coughing."

"Omigod," I gasped.

"He was sick. At first, he wouldn't let me get close to him, but I could tell he was in bad shape. So I pulled out my phone to call for an ambulance, but he stopped me, slapped the phone out of my hand. Shocked me that he was able to do anything the shape he was in, but he said if I called any one he'd run."

"What did you do?"

"At first, I couldn't get close enough to examine him, but he was coughing, not just coughing—hacking. Sounded like a dying man. I thought he had pneumonia. I begged him to let me get help, but he wouldn't hear of it. He tried to leave, but I convinced him I wouldn't call anyone if he'd stay put. It was freezing outside, and I was afraid if he went back out, he might die.

"Eventually, he let me get near enough to discover he was

running a fever. After a lot of cajoling, I convinced him to move inside to the boiler room where it was warmer."

"So, you've seen his face," I said.

Mr. Sims nodded. "That was the only time. Since then he keeps it hidden. He wears a bulky jacket with a hood, shrouds himself in it."

Mr. Sims's knee was jerking again. "The problem is his lungs. The heat and smoke from the fire damaged them, and now they're weak. I've tried to tell him staying in that boiler room is only going to make it worse."

"Wait a minute, are you telling me he's in the boiler room, still? He lives there?"

"I'm afraid so," Mr. Sims replied. "I didn't have the heart to throw him out while he was on the mend, and honestly I think he was homeless. He was like a wounded animal and, well, now he's sort of stayed."

"And he has problems with his lungs right now?"

I recalled our dancing the other night, and the tight wheezing in his chest. Had I caused him to become ill again?

"Poor Erik," I mumbled. "You have to take me to him, to help him."

Mr. Sims shook his head. "He won't let you see him like this."

My stomach rolled as I pictured him in a dark room, ailing and needing medical attention.

"I'm not sure about his state of mind when he has these spells," Mr. Sims confided. "There are some things about him that are, well, they're strange. I think he's a genius. Anytime something around here breaks, he tells me how to fix it; and I know he's supposed to be some kind expert dancer." He stopped and appeared troubled. "But sometimes I think he's not operating with a full deck either. I can't figure it out. I didn't tell anyone around here about him because I thought after a while he'd move on. Now I don't know what to do. I've been here thirty years and have two girls in college. I can't afford to lose my job, so I keep my mouth shut."

"I wish he would let us help him," I said. Then feeling a heaviness in my chest, I rose to my feet. "Thanks for coming and telling me. Please let him know if there's anything I can do to help, all he has to do is ask."

Mr. Sims nodded and stood, and as I made to leave, he placed a hand on my arm to stop me. "I think you should be careful with him, Christine. Be very careful."

Chapter Forty Five

*I*t was impossible to fall asleep that night. Racked with guilt, I worried it was Erik's dancing with me that had made him sick. If his lungs were weak, he shouldn't have done it. The lifts alone required an enormous amount of energy. On top of that, he wouldn't allow anyone to help him.

Finally, I slept, but it was fitful. Then the next morning, Mom's cursing from somewhere in the apartment roused me. I slipped out of bed to see what was happening and was surprised to see her dressed in work clothes and bustling around the living room, cramming papers into her brief case.

"What's up?" I yawned.

"I have to go into the office this morning. I'm not sure what time I'll be home."

"M-kay," I said and shuffled toward the kitchen.

The doorbell rang. Who could that be?

I heard Mom in the foyer. "Let me grab my bag."

"No problem," a man replied. Then he said, "Listen, I thought we'd have lunch after we're done." Recognition rolled over me. I knew the voice.

I whirled about and rushed into the foyer and discovered Cooper Nance standing in the open doorway. Dressed like he'd just come from a what-every-young-stylish-metropolitan-man should wear fashion show, he smiled like his presence was an everyday occurrence.

"Hi, Chris."

"Christine," I corrected. "Mom, what's he doing here?"

"I told you I have to work today."

"But why is he here?"

"We're carpooling," he said.

I gave him a dirty look.

Then he suggested, "Why don't I wait downstairs?"

When he'd left, I prodded Mom. "What the hell!"

"I'm going to work. If Cooper wants to take me to lunch afterward, I don't see anything wrong with having a nice lunch with a handsome, young man."

"But—Mom."

"Dammit, Christine. It's only lunch. Now I'll see you later." Then she grabbed her purse and briefcase and went out the door.

I ground my teeth together. What was she thinking? He was probably ten years younger than her. It would have been more plausible for me to date him.

Having lost my appetite, I skipped breakfast and sat in front of the TV. Mindlessly watching some cooking channel, I heard the video chat notification from the laptop in my bedroom. I ignored it. It was time for my regular chat with Dad, but I didn't want to talk to him. When my phone rang, I walked to my room to get it. If it was him, I wasn't going to answer it. Happily, it was Raoul.

"Hey," I said and sat on the side of my bed thinking the day just improved.

"Hey, what's up?"

"Nothing—vegging in front of the TV."

"I'm downstairs at Dad's. Can I come up?"

The request propelled me to my feet. I hadn't even brushed my hair.

"Umm, yeah. Can you give me 'bout half an hour?"

"Sure. See you in thirty."

I tossed my phone on the bed, hurried to my closet, and found the best thing I had clean. Then I ran to the bathroom, and in less than thirty minutes my mouth was minty, my hair brushed, and I had on my sexiest jeans and tee. By the time he rang the doorbell, I was already in the foyer waiting. Counting to five and taking a deep breath, I opened the door.

"Hey," he said as he stepped across the threshold and leaned down to kiss me.

The familiar warm, fuzzy feeling came over me and before he could pull away, I wrapped my arms around his neck and let myself enjoy the kiss. When he drew away he looked surprised by my enthusiasm. I smiled at him and said, "Hey." Then I closed the door and took him by the hand, leading him through the apartment.

"Is your mom home?"

"Nope."

"So where are you taking me?"

"My bedroom."

Chapter Forty Six

"Whoa," Raoul yelped. "Your bedroom? You trying to get me killed?"

"Relax." I laughed. "Mom went to work this morning. She won't be home for hours."

I had no idea what I was doing. The things coming out of my mouth sounded mature and cool, but I was terrified. Still, Mom and Dad were moving on. Why shouldn't I?

Raoul sat on the edge of the bed while I picked up the remote to my iPod station and turned on some music.

"Is there something you want to listen to?" I asked.

"That's good," he said as he glanced around my room.

I looked about as he did and became a little embarrassed by the sheer girliness of it. Leotards and ruffled tutus hung on the closet door. My dance bag lay on the floor, *pointe* shoes and tights spilling out of it, not to mention my first pair of slippers Mom had bronzed sitting on the dresser.

"Wow," he observed, "You really are serious about this ballet stuff, aren't you?"

"Kinda weird, huh?" I moaned.

"No, not at all. I think it's cool you know what you want to do with your life. How do you do it though," he asked, bending down to pick up a *pointe* shoe. "It's gotta be hard on your toes."

I smiled and stepped closer to take the shoe from him. "No harder than getting plowed by those bulldozers you call football players."

"Touché," he said, reaching out to take my hand.

I dropped the shoe and let him pull me down beside him. With feathery fingertips, he pushed my hair off my shoulder and leaned in to kiss my neck. It tingled to my toes and I snickered.

"Can't say that I've ever made a girl laugh when I kissed her."

"No, it was nice. It's just that it tickled."

"Mmm," he sighed and did it again. Slowly and deliberately, his lips made a trail up my neck to under my ear, giving me a shudder.

Somewhere in my mind a voice warned, *you're alone with a boy on a bed; what are you thinking!* Then I thought *Dad was in Norway doing who knows what, while Mom was out getting herself a boy-toy, so I'm doing exactly what I want.*

When Raoul lifted his head, I tilted mine so my lips met his, and before I knew it, we'd fallen back on the bed, wrapped together so tightly a shaft of light couldn't have come between us. I had no idea how long we made out, but at some point Raoul sat up abruptly.

"Whoa," he exhaled. "If we don't stop now..."

I sat up. "What? Why are we stopping?"

"I can't...we can't..." he stammered breathlessly.

All of a sudden, I wanted to cry. Was he rejecting me? What had I done wrong?

He must have seen my concern because he sputtered

quickly, "It's not you." He took my hand and kissed it. "Believe me, I want to. Man, do I want to." He motioned to where we'd left an indention in my bed. "It's, well, I can't. Not here—in your bed—in your mother's house."

I smiled. He was being chivalrous. With more temptress in me than I knew I had, I raked my hand across his bangs, making them lay properly. "So, no kissing," I teased, planting one on his eyelid. "If you say so." Another to the cheek. "Absolutely no kissing." One more at the corner of his mouth.

"Okay," he growled, "maybe some kissing." And being the gallant football hero he is, that was all we did.

Chapter Forty Seven

*M*om came home to find Raoul and me in the theater room watching a movie. Caught off guard, she didn't know how to respond when she saw the two of us sharing a chair.

"Christine, I didn't know you were having company."

"I'm sorry, Mrs. Dadey." Raoul jumped to his feet, flopping me onto the chair arm as he did. "I was downstairs at my father's and I called to see if I could hang out for a while. I hope it was okay."

"I suppose it's alright. But in the future, I'd prefer to be home when you visit."

"Yes, ma'am," Raoul said.

"I'm going to order pizza for dinner. Will you be staying?"

Raoul looked at me. I nodded, and he said, "Yes, ma'am. Thank you."

When she walked out and Raoul was sure she was gone, he fell into a chair—his own, and I started to laugh. "You don't have to be afraid of her."

"You just stay in your chair," he said.

Since he was spending the weekend at his father's, Raoul didn't have to leave until midnight. Mom hovered a lot. I showed him my schoolwork and explained how I do most of it online, Mom hovered some more, and we watched television. Having him around was nice. The I-could-get-used-to-this kind of nice.

He was back the next morning with a box of donuts, and he stayed around while I worked on math. When he left that afternoon, I found Mom waiting for me on the sofa.

"We need to talk." She pointed for me to sit next to her. "I'm not sure if Raoul being around here so much of the time is a good idea."

"So much of the time!" I sputtered. "He was here yesterday and a couple of hours this morning."

"You know what I mean," she said.

"Let me get this straight. I can't date a perfectly nice boy, have him over occasionally, but you can go to lunch with Cooper Nance."

"I told you I was working yesterday," she countered.

"Riiight, with your carpool buddy."

She took a deep breath before continuing, "You have a lot going on right now. Do you really think you have time for a boy in your life?"

"I think I'd have all the time in the world if I quit ballet."

This sucked the air out of her speech.

"What?"

"I'm thinking of quitting ballet."

"You can't mean that."

"I've considered it. Especially since Mrs. Hahn's been on my case."

"That's your nerves talking. You always get jittery when it gets close to audition time. But this is what you've wanted. You're so close to attaining what you've worked for. Why would you give up now?"

"It's what you've always wanted."

"Don't give me that crap. Of course, I want you to succeed, but you've been given plenty of opportunities to quit along the way. Why now? Why all of a sudden? Is it Raoul?"

"No," I protested. "It's, well, I want something in my life that feels normal. Other kids go to school, attend football games, hang out."

"And haven't you been doing those things?"

"But..." words caught in my throat. I wanted to share my fears, talk about the panic attacks, and even confess to pinching the Xanax. I couldn't muster the courage, though.

"What if I don't make it? What if Mrs. Hahn lets me audition and I don't make it again?" I started to cry. "What if I'm simply not good enough?"

"Oh, baby," Mom murmured and pulled me close. "I have absolutely no doubt you can dance every girl in that school under the table, and if you want in the second company, you'll get in. But you have to want it."

I wondered if she was right, and I wondered if I even really wanted it anymore.

Chapter Forty Eight

*T*hat night, I texted Erick and asked how he felt. He didn't respond and it worried me. Concerned for him, I contemplated going to the theater, to the boiler room, but it would have been intrusive. Erik had made it clear when he sent Mr. Sims that he didn't want any intervention, and I needed to respect his wishes.

Monday morning at school, a crowd of students milled around outside the building's entrance. As I approached, I sensed something was wrong. A few of the young level fives seemed to be crying.

"What's going on?" I asked.

"You haven't heard?" a young girl responded.

"Heard what?"

"Van broke his leg last night."

I gasped. "No way! What happened?"

"Nobody knows," the girl said. "He was here after the recital. They say he fell off the catwalk."

"Omigod!" I exclaimed. "We told him to stay away from there."

I ran into the building in search of Jenna and found her in the dressing room standing near a vanity table, her head sagging low.

"Is it true? Did Van break his leg?"

She dropped into a chair with a loud sigh. Eyes moist, she swallowed hard. "Yeah, it's true."

"Oh, no." I lowered myself into a chair next to her. "What happened?"

"He was on the catwalk. The stupid little fart was probably up there planting his phantom evidence. We should have gone to Ms. Zaborov about that when we first learned of it. But I swear, Chris, I never really thought he'd keep it up, you know? I thought he'd lose interest and move on."

"He's a boy," I said. "Boys do stupid things. Especially boys like Van who believe they're invincible."

"I know, but what if he can't dance anymore?"

Ms. Zaborov popped in the doorway. "Everyone to studio A—right now," she said then moved on.

Grabbing a handful of tissue, I passed them to Jenna. "Let's go see what's up."

I figured since they were gathering us into studio A it had to be about Van because that was the only studio large enough to hold everyone. The school's assistant director Mrs. Crane was already there waiting. Once she'd comforted a couple of crying level fives, she explained to everybody she'd been in contact with Van's mother, and Mrs. Woodruff had assured her Van would be fine. He'd broken his leg, but it was a clean break, and when healed wouldn't affect his dancing. Heartfelt cheers and expressions of relief resonated around the room, and when everyone had settled down again, Mrs. Crane released us to our classes. But before the first person could step out of the studio, Mrs. Hahn stormed in.

"I'd like them to remain, Mrs. Crane," she said sternly.

"Elaina," Ms. Zaborov said, "I do not think now is the time for this."

"Now is the perfect time," Mrs. Hahn snapped. "They're all here."

Jenna looked at me as if to say what is she up to now?

Mrs. Hahn paced in front of us, taking time to let her gaze linger on several different students. She came so close to a few I feared she might come down on a foot with her cane.

"My office has been broken into again," she said. "And some of my personal property has been taken. In light of what has happened to Evander Woodruff I can't help think someone here knows about this. All these robberies—you people are bound to be aware of what's going on." She raised her cane and pounded the air with it, punctuating her accusations.

Murmuring broke out around us, and Jenna was about to speak when I gave a slight shake of my head to discourage her. Even if we needed to share what we knew about Van, this was not the time to do it.

Mrs. Crane spoke up then. "If anyone knows anything about this, you may come directly to me. But for now, I believe you should get to class."

"But I..." Mrs. Hahn sputtered.

"That's enough for now, Elaina," Mrs. Crane said.

For several seconds, Mrs. Hahn glared at some of us and then angrily slammed the cane back down and stomped her way out of the room.

Mrs. Crane and Ms. Zaborov shared a look. Then Mrs. Crane led the youngest group of students back to class, while Ms. Zaborov stoically released the others, one class at a time.

Only the level eight dancers remained, and when Ms. Zaborov stepped into the hall for a moment, Deidre made her opinion known.

"I don't see why they don't have security investigate the lockers and dressing rooms right now." She shot a meaningful expression at Jenna. "No doubt they'd find the missing items."

Gasps rippled through the studio.

"Wow, Deirdre," Jenna snarled, "how original; blame the dancer here on scholarship. Sounds like the plot to a B movie gone straight to DVD to me."

I'd forgotten Jenna was at the Rousseau Academy on a grant. Leave it to Deirdre to remind everyone.

A couple of girls snickered and Deirdre spun and flounced out of the room. Then Jenna postured in a manner that dared anyone else to comment; most either turned their backs to whisper among themselves, or scurried to the other side of the room.

Jenna snorted out a *cha* sound and gave her back to them, as well. "Should we have told them about Van's phony phantom? Do you think tht that had anything to do with this?" she asked in a low voice.

"No, of course not. Why would it?"

"Maybe he and Liam didn't tell us everything."

"Surely they wouldn't have stolen from Mrs. Hahn, though. To what purpose? Not to mention, Liam is afraid of his own shadow. I don't think either of them are the type to steal."

Jenna shrugged. "Who knows what they've been up to. I could choke him. He may be a narcissistic pain in the ass, but a person can't help but love him."

"I know," I replied.

Jenna chewed her lip and shook her head. "I have an idea. Why don't we go see him tomorrow?"

"At the hospital?"

"Sure, why not. I'll see if I can get the car."

"I suppose we could."

"We'll take him something—balloons or flowers—cheer the little guy up. What do you think?"

"Sounds like a great idea."

As soon as her mother arrived to pick her up that afternoon, Jenna asked to use the car for the visit. So before we'd left school, we'd arranged a trip to the hospital the next day to see Van.

Chapter Forty Nine

I was super relieved to receive a reply to the text I sent Erik that night. It had been three days since Mr. Sims had told me Erik was ill. Since then, I'd sent him two texts expressing my well wishes, but he hadn't responded to either of them. Now that he had, it was simple and short.

I'll be there.

Anxious to learn how he was, I could hardly wait until Mom went to bed that night, so I could rush out of the apartment and hurry to the theater.

"Erik? Are you here?" I called the moment I stepped on stage.

"Yes, I am." The curtain stirred. "I apologize for the other night. I'm sorry I was unable to be here."

"Well, of course—you were sick."

"So let's get started then," he said. "I've been thinking about Giselle's entry in Act II. I think we should..."

"Erik." I stopped him, surprised he would just pick up where we'd left off. Especially, since I felt his illness was my fault "Maybe we should postpone my lessons for a while. Until you feel better."

"I'm fine. It was only a cold. No need to delay your

lessons."

"Mr. Sims said you were very sick. He said—" I faltered. "He said you're living in the building's boiler room and the atmosphere down there is bad for your lungs."

His response was slow to come, and when he spoke his voice quavered. "So you know. Sims told you everything. Now you know what a total loser I am—living in the theater's basement. How pathetic I must seem to you."

"No, of course not. I understand you've had a hard time lately. But I feel responsible for you getting sick. You shouldn't have danced with me like that."

Another silent pause before he murmured, "It was worth it."

I couldn't help smiling because his reply held a playful lilt.

"That may be, but I don't understand why you haven't seen a doctor. They might be able to help you. There could be medications or treatments. They may even be able to help with your face." I regretted that last statement the moment it was out.

"Ah, I see. Your concern—your pity—is for my appearance. Well, don't bother. My face is what it is. But if you find it to be too much for you then we can consider this our last encounter."

"No!" Embarrassment flooded me. "That's not what I meant. Not at all. I only wanted to help. I'm concerned for your health. That's why I thought you should see a doctor. Not because of your appearance."

A hush fell between us then, and I listened intently to determine if he was walking away. All I heard was the swishing of my tights as I shifted my legs nervously.

At last, a low murmur drew my attention to where he was

on the right side of the stage now. "You really do care," he said. Then the curtain fluttered, and like the night we'd danced together, I saw him grip the velvety edge.

"Yes." I sighed with relief. "That's what I've been trying to tell you. If you're unwell, we can skip the lessons. I'll get by without them. Your health is more important."

His fingers worked the curtain then he pulled it aside and loomed out of the darkness. He wore jeans and a tee tonight, and the captivating mask and headpiece concealed his face and head as before.

"I think you're really sincere," he said.

"Of course, I'm sincere."

"I promise you, I'm well enough to put you through your paces, so don't think I'll go easier on you because you're being kind."

I laughed. "Oh, no, I'm well aware what a taskmaster you are."

"But maybe you're right," he said. "We should take it easy tonight."

In four smooth strides, he'd made it to me, but he kept walking until he got to the edge of the stage where he sat down, tossing his legs over the side as I had.

"Let's have a different sort of lesson tonight." He tilted his head upward, the mask covering any emotion he might be expressing, and patted the floor for me to join him.

Smiling, I moved to sit down beside him, and we spent the remainder of our time talking about all things ballet. We discussed choreographers Jorma Elo and Christopher Wheeldon and their methods. I was surprised to learn he'd even danced at the Bolshoi. I was envious and told him so.

"No need for jealousy, you'll get there. You're learning

what it takes to make a role believable. Facial gymnastics just aren't enough. The body has to act. And I've seen you do it."

Though he said some of the same things Ms. Zaborov had, coming from him it hit me differently. It was so easy to talk to him. There was no judgment in his assessment of my skills. There was no ulterior motive. He wasn't being paid so he owed no one anything, not the school, not my parents, not even me. And maybe it was wishful thinking on my part, but it seemed like I was helping him, too. We were helping each other.

Chapter Fifty

On Tuesday, Raoul drove me home after the Diamondbacks' lesson. I knew we'd gotten a tad carried away with the goodbye kiss when a car passing by honked its horn and the driver stuck his head out to whoop.

When I'd peeled myself away from him with the promise of letting him drive me home again after Thursday's lesson, I went upstairs and showered for the trip to the hospital. I was apprehensive about it, unsure what to expect upon seeing Van for the first time. Injury was a constant threat to a dancer. Prevention was always in the back of the mind, but a broken leg was everyone's worst nightmare.

Jenna, appeared on edge, too, because we talked little as she navigated the traffic on the drive over, and she was silent on the ride up in the elevator, except to curse at the enormous bundle of balloons she struggled to control.

When the elevator stopped on Van's floor, we located his room and knocked gently on the door.

"Come in," someone said.

Jenna pushed the heavy door aside and we walked in, the balloons trailing behind us. A woman in jeans and a green blouse sat in a chair near Van's bed, and I recognized her as his mother. They had the same creamy brown skin and bright, sparkling eyes.

"Can I help you?" she asked.

"We're here to see Van," I said.

"We go to the Rousseau Academy with him," Jenna added.

"Oh, of course, I've seen you. Please, sit down." Getting to her feet, she motioned for one of us to take the chair, but we both declined.

I noticed Van hadn't moved. He had his back to us, which wasn't easy with a cast holding his right leg stiff, so I wondered if he was asleep.

"Is this a bad time?" I asked. "Is he sleeping?"

"No," Mrs. Woodruff replied. "He's a little down this afternoon, though. You've come at a good time. He could use cheering up."

Jenna slipped to the foot of the bed, swinging the balloons out for Van to see. "Hey, dude, if you're up for an escape we can tie these around your waist and slip you out the window. The landing might be a little rough, though."

When he didn't respond, Jenna's brow tightened, and we both looked at his mother.

She moved close to his bed, and placed a hand on his shoulder. "I'm going downstairs for a while. Since the girls are here, maybe they can stay while I grab a bite."

"Sure, Mrs. Woodruff," I replied. "We'll hang out."

When she'd gone, I moved around the bed to see Van's face. He didn't acknowledge me, only stared absently at the wall.

"C'mon, Van, it's not that bad," I said lightly. "Your little level five girls will drool over you even more. There won't be room enough on your cast to hold the signatures."

"I can't dance," he muttered under his breath.

"It's not forever, Van," Jenna said. "You'll dance again. You'll be back to torture us in no time."

He continued to stare.

"Mrs. Crane told us your doctor says it won't hinder your dancing in any way," I reiterated.

Jenna fumbled with the balloons, tying them to his bed table, and the Mylar squeaked and screeched so I couldn't hear his response.

"What'd you say?" I asked.

"It wasn't an accident."

"Of course it was. You shouldn't have been up there, but it was an accident nonetheless."

"No it wasn't," he said emphatically. "I was pushed."

Jenna's head snapped back as if he'd spit on her. "What are they putting in your IV, dude, because you're delusional."

"It's not funny," Van grumbled and swerved to look at us. "Someone pushed me off the catwalk stairs. And I saw him."

Jenna's eyes were huge. I was sure mine were, too.

"It was dark," Van explained, "and he came up behind me and shoved me."

Jenna's voice went up in alarm. "Did you tell your mother?"

"Yeah, but she doesn't believe me."

"Why not?" I asked.

"She thinks it was my imagination because of the pain medication. She thinks I dreamed it."

"Oh, well, she's probably right. Pain killers can make a person hallucinate," I said, knowing firsthand what high fevers, pain meds, and hospitals can do to the imagination.

"I wasn't hallucinating. I saw him plain as day!"

In a flash, Van's hand shot to his face and he flattened his palm over his cheek and eye. "It was like a Halloween mask— mangled up like Leatherface. It was a phantom, Jenna. A phantom!"

Chapter Fifty One

*T*he ride home was dismal. Neither of us could find anything to say. Although Jenna and I recovered enough from Van's outburst to tease him into a better mood, I couldn't stop thinking about his rant now.

His comments rattled around in my head. He'd been adamant about seeing a deformed phantom and that the phantom had pushed him down the stairs. It couldn't be Erik. It couldn't. I suppose it was possible that when Van fell he saw Erik in the shadows and it had all run together in the aftermath, but surely Erik wasn't responsible.

The car idled at a red light and Jenna broke the silence. "Well, that was weird."

"I know. He's really shook up."

"What do you think of the phantom pushing him story?" she asked.

I flicked my gaze toward her.

"You don't think he's started to believe his own lies, do you?" she said.

"No. I think his mother was right. The pain killers caused him to imagine it."

Glancing out the window, I watched the streets go by as

Jenna navigated toward the apartment. I had to talk to Erik. He would have an explanation, I was sure of it. Restless, I couldn't wait until I got home to contact him, so I pulled out my phone and texted him to meet me later that night, and I added that it was important.

"Who's that?" Jenna asked.

"Just Raoul," I replied and shoved the phone back into my pocket.

By the time we arrived at Templeton Towers, I was glad to climb out of the car. Saying a quick good-bye, I hurried upstairs. Mom wanted to know about Van, and after I'd given her an update, I went straight to my room. Apprehension coursed through me like static electricity, and I paced my bedroom floor. Every minute that ticked by I worried Erik could be in trouble. There was no way I could rest until I'd spoken to him. I refused to believe he would do anything to hurt Van, but he needed to know what Van was saying. When Mom finally turned in, I left and practically ran to the Wakefield Center.

Throwing the curtains aside, I bound onto the stage where I found Erik sitting and hurried over to him. Smoothly, he boosted himself up and under the stage lighting the gold on the mask glowed like smoldering embers.

"Why aren't you dressed?" he asked.

I was still in sandals and the clothes I'd worn to the hospital earlier that day.

"I'm not here to dance. I told you, we need to talk."

"Is there a problem with your family again?"

"No, it's not that. It's about Van."

"Who?"

"Evander Woodruff. He's a student at the academy."

He lowered his head a moment then said, "Go on."

"He's a level seven dancer. Do you know him?"

"You mean the little nuisance who runs around causing trouble?"

His response flustered me. "He's not a nuisance. He's a nice kid, and he's in the hospital with a broken leg."

"If you're not here to dance then why are you here?"

"Erik? Did you hear what I said?"

"I heard you. But I don't see what it has to do with you and me."

Mouth open, I stared at him.

"Erik, Van is telling people he was pushed down the catwalk stairs. I'm afraid you might be blamed if anyone finds out you're living here."

He pulled his hands from the pockets of the hoodie he wore and took a step away from me. "So that's why you're here? Because you're worried for me?"

"Well, yes. He says a man with a leather-face shoved him down the stairs." Immediately, I regretted my choice of words. It was what Van had said, but the term leather-face conjured pictures of gory horror movies with psychopathic killers who never died.

I noticed his hands at his sides clenching into fists, and he reeled back around. "So, that's what you think. I'm a leather-face?"

"No, of course not. I'm trying to tell you Van thinks you pushed him down the stairs and broke his leg." Again, a poor choice of words. Everything I was trying to say had jumbled together and come out wrong.

"He should have known better than to creep around here after hours. If I'm not mistaken, Sims warned him."

I sucked in a breath. "What are you saying?"

"Does it matter what I say? You already think me a monster, a leather-faced phantom."

"Stop it!" I cried. "That's not fair."

"Fair!" he bellowed. "Don't talk to me about fair. You and your friends come and go; you play at being ballerinas like children playing Barbie dolls."

I inhaled sharply at the scathing insult.

"Why don't you just go," he demanded, not giving me a chance to counter. "We're done."

For several seconds, I paused there as anger festered inside me.

"How dare you accuse me of playing!" I cried. "I have worked my tail off for you. I came here because I care for you—and Van!"

"Just go," he said again. "And you will pay *révérence*."

My eyes widened and my mouth dropped at not only his command that I treat him like a teacher and bow before him, but the superior tone in which he'd said it.

"You want me to pay you reverence?"

He dipped his head in affirmation and the mask raked over the hoodie collar.

I've never been so hurt, so angry. Only years of keeping my mouth shut while an instructor berated me kept me in control of my tongue now. Defiantly, I took a couple of deep breaths. Then in my most condescending manner, I dipped into a deep, pompous curtsy, but I refused to lower my head. I kept my gaze on the mask's almond shaped eyes. When I was certain I'd made my point, I stood and stomped off the stage.

Chapter Fifty Two

I didn't text or try to see Erik the rest of the week. I was still too hurt. How could he say I played at ballet? I worked as hard as anyone in the school did. And I'd gone there to warn him, to help him, and he'd taken it wrong. Granted, I'd put my foot in my mouth, but he didn't even give me the opportunity to explain.

During the week, though, my anger cooled and I started to rethink everything. If I were in his shoes, having lost my mother, my looks, and my career to a horrible fire, I would be sensitive about it, too. And aside from Mr. Sims, I was the only person in his life. He had no one, and I had gone and pointed out how pitiable he was.

Then on Thursday night, I dreamed about him. He was somewhere in the theater, calling my name, but I couldn't get to him. And by Friday morning, I regretted the whole matter and wished there was a way I could undo it.

At lunch that day, I picked at my food and Jenna asked, "What's up with you? You seem down."

Chewing a bite of apple, I shrugged.

"What gives? You've moped around all week. Raoul asked me if something was wrong after class yesterday."

"He did?"

I didn't want to push Raoul away. Maybe if I confided in Jenna, I could shake off some of the unease. But would she suspect Erik of pushing Van down the stairs?

"Hey—you remember the tutor I told you about?"

"Um, yeah, Aaron?"

"Erik."

"Yeah, right. What about him?"

"Well, I royally pissed him off, and now I'm afraid he might not forgive me and probably won't work with me anymore."

"Really? What'd you do?"

"I hurt his feelings."

"You hurt his feelings?" Jenna scoffed. "How old is this guy? Ten?"

"There are some things about Erik I haven't told you." I picked a seed from my apple and rolled it between my fingers to give myself time to think about how to proceed. "The reason Erik doesn't have a studio, or even go out in public, is because he's terribly disfigured. His face is scarred and he's self-conscious about it."

"Whoa, seriously?"

"He's sensitive about it and keeps to himself." I glanced around the lunchroom before continuing. "Then last week we argued, and we both said some things that were hurtful."

"So have you tried apologizing to him?"

"No."

"Look, why don't you lay low for a while. Then go back, grovel, stroke his artistic ego, and get back to work."

She made it sound simple. Maybe she was right. Erik was a dancer; he could be as temperamental as any other artist. I would give it time, go back and apologize, and perhaps we could resume lessons.

I finished my apple and tossed the core onto my tray. The hum of students around me felt oppressive. I didn't want to be here today. The school was suffocating me. I wanted to get out, go somewhere, and do something.

"Hey," I said, "how do you feel about ditching the rest of the day?"

"What?" Jenna's eyes widened.

"It's Friday and I'm sick of this place. How do you feel about ditching?"

"Damn, girl." She popped her head back in surprise. "What's gotten into you?"

"You brought your mom's car to school today, right?"

"Yeaaaah?"

"So what if all of a sudden, I caught a stomach virus?"

"I hear ya," she said and smiled.

"You know how Mrs. Z. loathes germs. If I were in the bathroom throwing up—" I fingered air quotes around throwing up, "—and you had to take me home, she'd never investigate for fear of catching it."

"You sly little devil," she muttered.

"So you're in?"

"Hell yeah!"

We stood at the same time.

"Wait," I said. Then I picked up my half-eaten container of yogurt, stirred in a little green bean juice from Jenna's plate, and said, "I'll dump it in the toilet just in case."

"Christine Dadey, I don't know what's gotten into you, but I like it."

We executed my plan flawlessly. And when we'd climbed

into her car and prepared to leave, Jenna asked, "So where are we going?"

"Ever heard of Urban Honesty?"

"No. What's that?"

"They're a dance crew at a studio called Street Feet in the Montrose area, and I want to check out their studio."

"Cool," Jenna said. "We'll pop the address in the GPS and follow the yellow brick road."

Chapter Fifty Three

*W*e stopped by the apartment to change clothes before heading to the Street Feet Studios.

"Crap, you're skinny," Jenna complained as she tried to squeeze into a pair of my jeans.

"Here, try these. They're big on me." I tossed her another pair from my closet.

"So where did you meet these people?" Jenna asked, zipping up the jeans.

"I saw them performing in an alley once. Then the night Raoul and I went out, they were at Discovery Green for a festival."

"And we're going to see them because...?"

"I don't know. I thought they were cool, and Magdalena invited me to visit some time. And now's the time."

I told her more about the troupe as we traveled across town. Jenna had no trouble finding the studio, but I had second thoughts as we walked to the entryway. How I'd felt that night I'd danced with Dionte came back to me—that hesitation brought on by self-consciousness. How could I feel intimidated by, yet drawn to, these people?

Inside the studio office, a girl with pink spiky hair, a nose ring, and heavy black eyeliner looked up from a desk when we entered.

"Can I help you?" Her smile was wide and sincere.

"We're looking for Magdalena," I said.

"Christine?" I looked beyond the receptionist to see a smiling Magdalena emerging from an office door. "I thought that was you." She moved from behind the desk to give me a hug that smelled like sunshine and citrus.

"Hi," I said then found I didn't know what to say next, so I turned to Jenna. "This is my classmate, Jenna."

"Hi, it's nice to meet you." Magdalena shook her hand. "So what are you doing on this side of town?"

"Nothing. We ditched class and were hanging out, so I thought we'd come see your studio."

"Great. I'll give you the grand tour."

Magdalena led us down a wide hall deeper into the building, an old cinder block structure they'd converted into a dance studio. Colorful murals of dancers lined the walls, and music reverberated from everywhere. I looked at Jenna and she mouthed an excited *sweet* at me.

We passed by a couple of rooms filled with small children in the middle of lessons, some taking tap and others actually dancing flamenco. They were adorable and it took me back to my first dance lessons as a child.

"There's always something going on around here," Magdalena commented. "At the moment, we're preparing a program to take into public schools. Dionte's working on it now. C'mon, I'll show you."

Magdalena guided us away from the children's classes through the building and into a studio filled with the people I now knew to be Urban Honesty. There was no music playing at the time because Dionte was standing before the group, giving instruction and demonstrating steps.

When he whirled around and saw us, he called across the room, "Hey, it's the ballerina! You're just in time." Then he motioned with his hand. "Get in here, girl; we'll turn you into a real dancer."

I froze, feeling plain and ordinary among these wildly talented dancers. It was one thing to dance with them at a festival, but here, on their territory, was something altogether different. I looked at Jenna.

"You don't have to ask me twice," she said and hurried over to join the group.

Jenna picked up Dionte's direction naturally. In no time, she could pop, lock, and drop it as well as they could. Shaking her booty like Jell-O, a person would have thought Jenna a charter member of the group. It made me jealous. I marveled at how she could relax in whatever scenario she found herself. I wished I felt that comfortable in my own skin.

Magdalena sidled up closer to speak over the music. "Whatcha really doin' here, love? You're a little out of your element, aren't you?"

I laughed. "I don't really know. Lately I...Well, you all seem so confident. I'm amazed by it. You don't even think about it when you dance."

"Oh, trust me, we think about it," Magdalena said. "It's hard work. But you know that."

"Yeah, but it doesn't look like it's hard for you."

"Listen, momma, I know what you're thinking, and this ain't for you." I glanced at her. I wasn't sure if she was making fun of me.

"To find what you're looking for you've got to get out of here—" she tapped her index finger to the side of my head, "—and get in here." And then she touched it to my chest above my heart.

I smiled at her. She did get it. Even if I didn't.

Chapter Fifty Four

*W*e got back to the apartment shortly before five. I'd sent Mom a text earlier, telling her the same story we'd told Ms. Zaborov, so I had to be home sick when she got there. Jenna stuck around for a while, and she couldn't stop chattering about our visit to Street Feet.

"That place is awesome. Why haven't you told me about them before?"

"I don't know. I wasn't exactly keeping it a secret."

"I wanna go again. When can we go back?"

"Go back? What for?"

"Not sure. I just wanna go again."

My phone buzzed. It was a text from Raoul. He was on his way to the football stadium, but he was letting me know he would be staying the weekend at his father's again.

"Aw," I said and smiled, "it's awesome to have my boyfriend practically living in the same building with me."

Jenna rolled her eyes. "You two are way too cutesy."

"You're just jealous. By the way, what happened between you and Troy? I haven't heard you say anything about him in a while."

"I don't know. It's not really working out. I guess I'm not

as into him as I thought I was."

It occurred to me that our problems weren't that different. Jenna was unhappy with her dating situation but couldn't see how to fix it in the same way I was unhappy with my dancing career.

When Mom came home, Jenna left. I was supposed to be convalescing, so I stayed in my room. But before the night was over, I told her I was feeling better. I had to be well if Raoul was going to visit tomorrow.

The next morning, I dressed and put on make-up, readying to see Raoul. My chat alert went off as I styled my hair, but I ignored it. Dad and I hadn't chatted since the day he'd told me he'd cheated on Mom. And I still didn't want to talk to him. He'd even sent Mom an email to ask her to intervene, but I refused to talk to him. There was nothing to say anymore.

Mom answered the door when Raoul showed up. She was surprised to see him because I didn't tell her he was coming. Why put myself through one of her diatribes.

We stayed around the apartment for a while, playing video games and watching TV, and that afternoon, I managed to convince her I was well enough to go to a matinee with him.

The movie was tremendously boring, but I didn't care. I spent the hour and thirty-nine minutes teasing Raoul, tugging on his hair and kissing him senseless. Best movie ever.

When it was over, he still had time before curfew so he came upstairs with me again. The apartment was dark, and I saw a light on under Mom's door. She was probably reading. Taking him by the hand, I put my finger to my lips and pulled him behind me like a train car to my bedroom.

"You really are determined to get me killed, aren't you," he whispered as I closed the door to my bedroom.

I switched on the bedside lamp. "She's never said you couldn't come in here, so until she says you can't, I'm taking it as a green light."

"You are bad," he teased and pulled me into him to plant a delicious kiss on my lips. As I wiggled my fingers into his hair, he groaned and pushed me away. "Wait, I have something for you. I was going to give this to you earlier, but there never seemed to be a good time."

He pulled a small box from his pocket.

"It's no big deal," he said. "I thought of you when I saw it."

I hesitated and he pushed the box toward me. There was little doubt it was a jewelry box.

"Raoul?"

"Just open it," he said and blushed.

My fingers shaky, I took the cardboard lid off the small box. Inside was a silver chain. I looked at Raoul. He appeared anxious, expectant.

Lifting the chain from the cotton it lay nestled in, I murmured, "You shouldn't have."

"Do you like it?"

I stared at the delicate sterling silver chain with its ballet slippers charm, and my breath caught in my throat. It was so sweet. Too sweet for words. I didn't have the heart to tell him that over the years I'd received dozens of such pieces. They were go-to gifts for any ballerina. But never had one ever meant so much to me as this one did.

Tossing the box on my bed, I handed the necklace to him. "Here, hold it a minute."

My fingers trembled as I reached to unfasten Erik's

necklace. His probably cost much, much more, but Raoul's was the one I wanted to wear. Linking the ends of the locket together again, I opened my jewelry box and dropped it in. If Erik ever spoke to me again, I would return it to him.

Then I swirled around, lifted my hair, and said, "Will you do it?"

When he'd draped the chain around my neck and snapped the clasp in place, he leaned forward and kissed the back of my neck, sending shivers down my spine. I pivoted about to face him, and he took both my hands in his. We stared at each other, until we heard, "Christine, is that you?"

Chapter Fifty Five

*M*om wasn't too freaked out about finding Raoul in my room. After all, we were standing when she waltzed in, but after he left, I got the don't-know-if-you-should-have-a-boy-in-your-room speech.

She was even less thrilled when he came back the next day, as he had the weekend before, and stayed until he absolutely had to go home. I got the impression she wanted to complain, but kept it to herself.

The following week, I worked doubly hard for Ms. Zaborov. Without Erik, she was my only hope. Time was running out. It was already the middle of October, and only six months remained until the auditions.

Tuesday, right before lunch, I came out of the dressing room to see Van and his mother walking down the hall. He was on crutches, wearing a pair of sweatpants altered to fit over the cast on his right leg. The light blue, fiberglass cast already had signatures and short notes scrawled across it.

Excited, I squealed his name and ran toward them. I knew if I hugged him, I could knock him down, so I did a couple of exaggerated air kisses.

"Easy, princess, I know you missed me, but please, not in

front of my mother."

Mrs. Woodruff pinched her lips together in a sideways smile and shook her head as if to say he was beyond hope.

"Man, I've missed you," I said. "It isn't the same here without you."

"Well, look what the cat dragged in," Jenna cried, coming out of a nearby studio.

"I had to come," Van said to her. "I knew you couldn't carry on without me."

Jenna and I led them to the kitchen so Van could get off his feet. As word got around the school he was there, young dancers began pouring into see him. He was in heaven—everyone made a fuss over him, signing his cast, and telling him how much he'd been missed.

Eventually, the room cleared and only Jenna, Ms. Zaborov, assistant director Mrs. Crane, and I stayed behind. Jenna and I sat at a table where Van had his casted leg propped in a chair, while Mrs. Woodruff talked with the two women at another table.

"So, listen," Van said, towing himself forward to lean in secretively. "You didn't tell anyone about what happened at the hospital, did you? You know—what I said about the phantom?"

"No, shrimp, we didn't tell anyone," Jenna replied.

"Why?" I asked.

Van shrugged. "I've been thinkin' about it. Maybe it was like Momma said, trauma. I could have imagined it. I'm not sure anymore. When I try to remember it now, it's blurry, and I don't want everybody around here thinkin' I'm a wuss."

"Don't sweat it, buddy. We got your back," Jenna said and gave him a playful punch on the arm. "We're the only ones around here allowed to give you a hard time. Anybody else tries, and Christine and I will be all over 'em."

"Thanks, Jenna," he said sheepishly.

When they'd left, I couldn't get Van's confession out of my mind. He'd admitted he'd imagined the leather-face incident. I'd let a frightened, injured little boy come between Erik and me. What kind of friend was I? The only thing Erik had ever asked of me was trust. I couldn't stand it anymore. That night I would go to the theater to apologize, even if I had to grovel.

Two hours before Mom's usual week night bedtime, I sent a text and crossed my fingers Erik wouldn't ignore it. I didn't bother dressing in my dance clothes, as I was only going to talk to him.

Once there, I called his name repeatedly and walked the stage, weaving in and out of the curtains, and waited. Staying for more than two hours, I even went down and paced the theater aisles. But he never showed. Fleetingly, I considered going to the boiler room. Somehow, it seemed like an invasion of his privacy, though. There was no getting around it. I'd royally screwed up, and I hoped that one day he would forgive me.

Chapter Fifty Six

*I*tried to push Erik out of my thoughts. He was gone, and I still had the auditions coming up. But first I had to get past Mrs. Hahn. Wednesday after class, I went to her office to talk to her.

"Mrs. Hahn?" I tapped on the doorframe. "May I come in?"

"Yes, Christine."

Taking off her glasses, she laid them on the desk. "What can I do for you?"

"Well..." I was so nervous my voice cracked. "I was wondering...has Ms. Zaborov talked to you—about me?"

She scrutinized me as I stood before her, fighting the compulsion to say never mind and run out of the room.

"She has, but I'm afraid I haven't seen much reason to change my mind."

I raised a hand to my throat and gripped it. Suddenly I couldn't breathe.

"Christine, it's nothing to be ashamed of. If you're not ready, you can always try again next year. Honestly, I think you'd benefit from taking some acting classes. Technically, you're flawless, but if you can't convince the audience you are that character, they're not going to give a flying fig about your technique."

"But...but I'm improving. Ask Ms. Z."

"I'm sure Ms. Zaborov has seen improvement in your performance, but I'm not convinced. And as I am the one who counts..." She let her meaning hang in the air. Then she picked up her glasses and set them on the bridge of her nose. "Now, if that's all, I have work to do."

"No. I mean, yes, ma'am. That's all." I curtsied and backed out of the room.

I cried on the walk home. People on the street looked at me like I was crazy. If Mom knew I was blubbering my way down the streets of Houston, she'd have a cow. But I didn't care. I'd foolishly let Mrs. Hahn see my weakness. It was a power struggle and she made it clear she had the control. She was wrong, though. I had improved. Erik had helped me and I knew it.

To assuage my miserable failure with Elaina Hahn, I stopped at the corner store and bought extra-cheesy cheese puffs, a bag of bite-sized chocolate bars, and a two-liter bottle of soda. I'd deal with the zits later.

With my comfort foods gathered around me in my room, I called Jenna.

"Wow, Attila really seems to have it out for you."

"I know! That's what I've been saying." I crammed a handful of cheese puffs into my mouth. "What has she said to you?" I asked. "Is she going to let you audition?"

"Yeah, I dropped the five pounds."

I shoved more chips in and mumbled, "I think I'm gaining them." Then I tossed the bag aside and lamented, "Why can't some other school come along and recruit her? Let her go to

New York and teach at the American Ballet."

"If only," Jenna said.

"No, seriously. Sometimes I wish she'd leave. At least until the auditions are over."

"Unfortunately," Jenna surmised, "that's not going to happen. You've got to find another way around her."

"There is no other way around Attila the Hahn."

Chapter Fifty Seven

I regretted the junk food the next day. My stomach was upset and I was lethargic. I had a processed foods hangover. Raoul was the one bright spot in the day. He drove me home Thursday night, rode up in the elevator with me, and walked me to the door, trying to encourage me the whole time.

He surprised me when he asked, "Do you want me to talk to my uncle for you?"

"What?"

"I'll talk to Uncle Mark. He has pull on the board. Maybe he could get the old crone to lay off."

"That's so sweet, but if I can't do it on my own, I don't want to do it at all."

His text alert went off, and he pulled the phone from his pocket to read the message. "I gotta go. Mom's looking for me." His mouth curled into a naughty smile. "But I think I can make you feel better before I leave."

Lightly, he pushed me against the apartment door and kissed me until I thought my hair would curl. After several seconds, he lifted his head, more than satisfied with himself he teased, "Told ya."

I gave him a playful shove and unlocked the door to go inside. As much as I liked kissing Raoul, it really only served as a temporary distraction. Mrs. Hahn would still be there tomorrow. It—she—was a problem that wasn't going away.

At lunch on Friday, Jenna and I toyed with the idea of skipping again, but we both knew we'd never get away with it so soon after the first time. It was a lie to be used sparingly, so we stuck it out the rest of the day, and I ended up glad I did.

Classes had been dismissed and kids were piling out of the building to their waiting rides outside when I walked into the kitchen and discovered Mr. Sims tinkering under the sink. When he scooted out and saw me he said, "Hello."

"Hi, Mr. Sims."

Bearing himself up, he continued, "Sink's plugged. Kids pouring stuff down it they shouldn't."

Listening to his small talk about coffee grounds blocking the drain, I realized the answer to my problem was standing in front of me with a wrench in his hand.

"Mr. Sims," I interrupted, "have you seen Erik lately?"

His gaze darted to the door.

"There's no one here but me. Have you seen him?"

"I may have," he responded vaguely.

"Did he say anything—about me?"

"No."

"Can you get a message to him for me?"

"I don't know 'bout that. I'm not sure that's a good idea."

"Please. I'm afraid I said some unkind things, and I really hurt him."

Turning away from me, he tossed the wrench into his toolbox.

"Will you tell him I'm sorry? That I was wrong and I'll be at the theater tonight. If he's there, I'll know he's forgiven me, but if he's not, I'll never bother him again."

Mr. Sims stared at the floor, and I held my breath awaiting his answer. "I think that's a mistake. I think you should stay away from him. There's something about him that's not right."

"He can't help what happened to him," I said. "You have to understand what it means for a dancer to lose his career like that. No one will ever pay the price of a ticket to see someone like him dance. Box office receipts are made off pretty people. I'm grateful for what he's done to help me, and I won't turn my back on him just because he's eccentric. So if you don't tell him for me, I'll be forced to go to the boiler room to find him." When he didn't say anything, I went on. "I only want to talk to him one last time. After tonight, when I'm sure he's forgiven me, I won't bother him again."

"If you promise me you'll stay away from him after that."

He sounded so ominous that I was sure he was overreacting, but I knew if I didn't agree he wouldn't help me.

"I promise. After tonight, I won't see Erik anymore."

Chapter Fifty Eight

*M*y stomach swirled all evening. Nervous and unable to eat, I knew if Erik didn't show this time, I'd never see him again. And I didn't want to live with the knowledge that I'd added insult to his injury.

Around nine o'clock, I decided to call and chat with Marisol until it was time to leave for the theater. Lately, we hadn't talked much. We were growing apart—the thing that had concerned me most when I knew we were moving. So much had happened in my life and less and less of it had I shared with her.

Marisol's face appeared onscreen and we'd barely said hello when she set off on a tangent about Inez stealing the teacher's test key in her math class, and her mother, wasted out of her mind, showing up at school to deal with it.

"That sucks," I said, trying to sound sympathetic, all the while selfishly concerned with my own problems.

When it finally seemed appropriate, I told her everything, recounting Van's broken leg, his nonsensical version of the accident, and my argument with Erik. For the first time in a while, I told her everything on my mind.

"What should I do?" I asked.

"I don't know. This whole thing is sounding pretty wacked out. What do you think happened to that kid? Do you believe he was pushed down the stairs?"

"No, of course not."

"Then what are you getting at?" she asked.

Looking away, I shrugged. "I don't know. I feel bad about how it went down. Erik was offended. And I don't know what to do to fix it."

"I dunno what to tell you, *mija*, but you should be careful—just in case. Ya know?"

"What do you mean?"

"Well, you really don't know this guy. What if he is a mental case?"

"That's rude," I grumbled.

"Still, I think you should watch yourself. Just because he's a good dancer doesn't mean he's not a creeper."

"Marisol, that's coldhearted."

"I'm just sayin'."

Suddenly, I regretted contacting her. She'd called Erik a mental case and a creeper and she didn't even know him.

"Well, I'm going there tonight to apologize. I have to."

She opened her mouth to respond or protest, but I cut in. "I'll call you and let you know how it goes. I have to get off now. Talk to you later." I pushed End.

When Mom went to bed, I slipped out of the apartment and headed to the Wakefield Center. I wasted no time getting inside to walk briskly down the hall toward the Griffith Theater. To my surprise, the smell of hot wax hit me as I neared the stage entrance.

My hands sweaty, I made an opening in the curtains and stepped through onto the stage. I smiled and my heart filled with relief when I spotted Erik seated on the ledge like the last time we'd been here together, before the argument. His back to me, the headpiece's black fabric was sleek and inky in the dim light. A blanket lay spread on the floor next to him, and in its center were the candles I'd smelled. A tray of fruit and cheese, a bottle of wine, and a vase filled with lively pink flowers were on it, as well. I smiled because the flowers were like the one I'd taken from Claudette Sunderland's dressing room. The one he'd caught me with.

"Erik?" My voice sounded feeble in the cavernous theater. He'd heard me, though, because he stiffened in response. Slowly, he twisted toward me. The rigid, unyielding features of the mask made it impossible for me to guess what he might be thinking. He could have been either frowning or smiling for all I knew.

Diving into my apology, I took a tentative step. "I'm so sorry. I was wrong. The whole thing was a big misunderstanding."

Some of the tension left me when he waved his hand in the air as though something minor had passed between us.

"I'm the one who's sorry," he said. "My ego got the better of me. But I don't want to talk about it anymore." Then he held out an open hand. "Will you sit down?"

I sprinted across the stage to settle on the blanket next to him. He adjusted the mask, securing it in place, and I apologized again. "I'm truly sorry."

"Shhh." Airily, he placed a finger to the mask's golden, inert lips. "It's over. Really" Then he picked one of the flowers from the vase, broke off its stem, and placed the bud in my hair. "For the ballerina," he said.

My fingertips fluttered over the feathery petal lodged

behind my ear. "Thank you."

"Do you know what these are?" he asked, gesturing toward the bouquet.

"No, but they're lovely." I looked at the vase overflowing with the pink blossoms.

"They're dahlias. They symbolize hope and everlasting union between two people."

His statement amped up my guilt-ridden conscience, and I groveled again. "I can't believe what happened. I've seen Van and he told me it was all a mistake. I came one night to explain—I wanted to tell you—but you weren't here."

"Don't sweat it. It's over. Let's talk about what's next."

"What are you saying? Will you tutor me again?"

He nodded. "Only a fool would walk away from a dancer like you. And now that I know you're loyal, nothing will get in our way again."

I was surprised how easy it had been. I'd been so concerned—both dreading and dying to have this conversation—but everything had turned out fine.

Motioning to the blanket and the picnic arranged across it, I asked, "What's this?"

"I thought we would celebrate. It's a special occasion."

The candle light flickered off the gilded facemask, and again, I wondered if he'd been a handsome man before the fire. As a principal dancer, many girls—and women—would have fawned over Erik. How many hearts had he broken? I envisioned Raoul, how gorgeous he was, how lucky I was to have him, and the grief for what Erik had lost squeezed my heart.

"Please help yourself." He dipped his head in the blanket's direction.

Taking his cue, I picked up a piece of cheese and nibbled on it, but I was acutely aware that he couldn't join me.

"You don't have to be uncomfortable," I said. "If you want to eat something, it would be okay."

He picked at the seam of his jeans, and it frustrated me that I couldn't see his face. Then he murmured, "No, I don't suppose I do. But maybe some other time."

While I ate a few grapes, he poured the wine, and I grew uneasy as the blood-red liquid sloshed into the single glass. I've never had anything remotely alcoholic before. I didn't want to sputter and choke like I'd seen people on TV do.

"Here you are." He passed the glass to me.

Stalling, I asked, "You're not having any?"

He chuckled and fanned his hand before the hard exterior of the mask. "I would look ridiculous drinking wine through a straw."

"Oh, yeah, right." My face heated with embarrassment.

Then, after raising the glass in a mock toast, I sipped the scarlet liquid carefully. It was strangely bitter, but I assumed that that's the way it was supposed to taste.

After more of the food, I finished the wine. Quite relaxed now, I placed the glass back on the blanket, and licking my lips a few times, I noticed my tongue tingled from the alcohol and apparently, it had loosened it as well.

"I hate ballet," I groaned, swinging my legs like a toddler along the stage's drop-off.

"No you don't." Erik sniggered. "You hate the bull shit that goes with it, but you love the dance, and you know it."

I nodded and got serious then. "There's something I have to tell you. A confession."

"Oh, yeah? That sounds intriguing."

Shaking my head, I frowned. "You're probably going to think I'm scum when I tell you."

"Well, now I have to know."

"I took drugs before auditioning to get into the Academy." I held up my hand, my thumb and forefinger centimeters apart. "It was only a half a sedative, but if I hadn't taken it I would have had a panic attack and never gotten in. I'm ashamed of it now, and I wanted you to know. It's not fair for you to help me without you knowing."

Bit by bit, I relayed my story from the first visit to the ER, missing the recital I so badly wanted to perform in, my appendectomy and subsequent infection, and even the phantom pains that ultimately led to the panic attacks. When I'd finished, I waited for his response.

Beneath the mask, he took a breath and stared off into the empty theater. Then propping his hands on his thighs, he addressed me. "That explains a lot, Chrissy. But there's more, isn't there."

Sucking in a breath, my eyes widened. Chrissy. He'd called me Chrissy.

I nodded and tried not to cry. Why was I being so emotional about this? It had happened so long ago, but I couldn't get free of it.

"Tell me," he pressed.

"Why'd you call me that? Only my grandmother called me Chrissy."

"Called?"

"She's dead now. But she always called me Prissy Chrissy." I swallowed hard. "She was supposed to come to my recital— the one I missed because of my appendix, but she'd been sick, too. That's why I didn't want my parents to know I was ill. They were so stressed dealing with her in and out of the hospital, chemo, and radiation. She wanted to come, though, so Dad made special arrangements. I remember hearing him talk about her pain meds, hoping it would be enough to get her through. She was determined to be there. And I—I blew it."

"You didn't blow it," Erick said. "You could have died."

Dropping my gaze to my hands in my lap, I chewed the inside of my lip. "She did die—while I was in the hospital. My dad was the only one to go to her funeral. It was his mother."

The theater was silent then, as silent as the tears that slipped down my cheeks.

Never trying to stop me, he let me weep until air hitched in my throat, and I eventually breathed easy again.

When I was finally able to lift my head and look at him, he lightly daubed a tear from my cheek. "I had no idea," he whispered. "It makes sense now. But you don't have to let this define you anymore. Leave it here—" he indicated the stage "—where it can fuel rather than fell you."

I nodded, inhaled deeply, and palmed another tear.

"That was hard for you. Telling me about your grandmother. Thanks for trusting me." He adjusted the angle of the mask and said, "I have something I'd like to show you. Maybe it will make you feel better."

"Oh?" I snorted and dragged my sleeve across my nose.

"Will you come with me?"

"You mean it's not here?" I pointed a finger at nothing in particular.

"No. It's in my room."

Chapter Fifty Nine

*A*t first, I was reluctant to go with him. Marisol's warning suddenly popped to the fore, and I wondered if I shouldn't find a way to politely decline. But it was absurd. After what had just passed between us, and all he'd done—the food, the flowers—how could I say no?

"Sure. What is it you want to show me?"

He blew out the candles then got to his feet, hauling me with him. "Follow me."

Still holding my hand, he led me purposefully down the stage stairs, out of the Griffith Theater, and into the main hall of the Wakefield Building. It was strange. We'd never been anywhere together outside of the stage.

"I can't tell you how happy I am that you came back to me," he said, as we navigated the grand foyer separating the Griffith and Werner theaters. "I live for our time together."

This seemed an odd thing for him to say, but something else bothered me more. My feet felt heavy and slow, as if I wore ankle weights. It must be the wine, I thought, since I've never had it before. Still, I didn't think a single glass could make me tipsy.

We took the service stairs down to the main floor, missing

the security guard at the front entrance, all the way to the passage leading to the parking garage.

When we stepped through the glass doors into the underground facility, stale exhaust fumes, damp mildew, and the smell of urine blasted us, and I thought how horrible it must be to live in such conditions.

Our footsteps echoed throughout the concrete structure, as we traversed the lot and stopped in front of a door labeled Employees Only. Erik glanced around the vacant garage. Then he reached above the doorframe, where he retrieved a key. After unlocking the door, he returned the key to its hiding place and we entered the room.

When he closed the door behind us and I heard the bolt click into place, I shuddered and started to tell him I would be more comfortable with the door open, but my surroundings caught my attention. Around us, fat white pipes and copper colored tubing formed lattice walls that made me think of a jail cell. And to one side were a couple of steel tanks, large enough for two people to stand in, and a wall covered with luminous gauges. Steampunk creepy.

"Over here," Erik said and pulled me along until we were at the rear of the dismal room. Reality hit me then. I'd had no idea how Erick truly lived. I mean I knew, but I didn't know. I let my eyes rove, taking it all in. There was a pallet of old blankets on the floor in the corner, and a table and chair were against the wall across from it. To my surprise, a computer sat atop the table, along with several other electronic gadgets.

"It's here." His breaths were short and rapid from the long walk.

Releasing my hand, he gently propelled me toward the

table and pointed to something on it. I blinked to adjust my sight in the dim light, and saw there were charcoal sketches, dozens of them, splayed across the tabletop. I picked one up. It was me. They were sketches of me, in street clothes, in costume and in various positions of dance.

Lifting my gaze, I brandished a piece of paper before him. "What is this?"

"It's you."

"Yes, but why?"

"Don't you like them?"

I stared at the sketch in my hand. Then I replaced it and shuffled through the others. There were so many. How long had it taken to create them? Hours—days—weeks?

"I don't understand," I said, confused.

"Wait, that's not all." He reached out and punched several keys on the computer keyboard. "Watch this."

Scrunching my eyes together, I struggled to focus on the screen. What was wrong with my vision?

Through heavy lids, I stared at the monitor. The words For Christine materialized and the score to Giselle began to play. Then my graphite likeness appeared on the screen. Erik had made a stop-motion video of the sketches, and I was dancing to the musical score of Giselle.

I watched in horror as the harmony progressed, and the graphics of me moved haltingly across the screen. It was terribly unsettling. It was wrong. So wrong.

As I stood there, glued to the monitor, he moved close behind me.

"Do you like my art?" he asked.

I closed my eyes tightly and thought this is not art. This is an invasion of my privacy.

Chapter Sixty

*F*og rolled across my brain, and I grew so dizzy I had to grab the back of the chair, while my digitized counterpart floated across the screen.

"Erik," I croaked. "What? Why?"

"For you, ballerina."

My stomach lurched and I pressed my fist into it. "I don't feel so good."

"Steady," he murmured and gripped my elbow to keep me from swaying.

"It must be the wine. I'm not used to drinking."

One hand still on the chair, I rubbed my eyelids and blinked several times. "I think I should go home, before it gets worse."

"Oh, no, I'm afraid that would be impossible." He was close enough behind me now for his leg to bump against mine. "You have to stay."

"But this is not why I came here. I shouldn't be here."

Casually, he placed his hand on my arm and grazed it up and down. "This is precisely why you're here, Chrissy. You wouldn't have come back if you didn't want to be here."

Everything was so fuzzy. I needed to do something. To get

out, to scream. Anything but stand there.

Trailing his fingers up my arm and shoulder, he took the length of my hair in both hands and combed his fingers through it. On a breezy exhalation that vibrated beneath the mask, he let it cascade from one palm to the other. Then he leaned in, drew a handful near, and inhaled, and I stiffened and swallowed my rising fear.

"Erik, what's wrong with me? I'm so...disoriented."

"Don't worry. It was only a little something to help you relax."

"You drugged me?"

"Just a little. It was necessary."

Necessary for what? I thought, and alarms rang inside my head.

Still clutching my hair in one hand, he fingered the clasp of my necklace with the other. "You know you can't wear this anymore. You can't wear something that belongs to him when you're with me."

His voice sounded like he was in a tunnel, and every word grew more edgy, menacing, until I grasped the tiny, silver slippers and muttered, "Raoul."

Swiftly, he released my hair to snake his arm around my waist and jerk me back against his chest. Then he clamped his other hand over mine, squeezing it tightly so that the charm beneath it bit into the skin of my palm.

Pushing his head close to mine, he growled and the sound vibrated beneath the mask. "Do not say his name to me." He shoved my hand away then and seized Raoul's necklace. "What a gaudy bauble—probably came from a vending machine." Forcefully, he wrapped the chain around his fist, winding it tighter up my throat. "Do you have any idea how much the locket I gave you cost? The trouble I went through to get it for you? And you wear this cheap piece of shit." He ripped the necklace from me then, and launched it across the room. In a quick swoop, his hand was back at my throat where he slipped his fingers around my neck and, tightening his grip, he forced my head up at an angle.

"Say my name," he whispered. When I didn't respond, he squeezed tighter and brought his head around so that the mask pressed into my ear. "Say my name," he demanded.

Tears started to roll down my cheeks and with my head tilted awkwardly, they pooled in my ears. "E—Erik," I choked, and immediately he freed me. I gasped and sputtered to get a full breath as I rubbed the chafed skin on my neck.

"Never say his name again. You belong to me."

"I want to go home," I sobbed.

"Don't be ridiculous. After all those texts you sent, begging and pleading for my forgiveness. You said you'd do anything to make it up to me. Remember?"

I whipped my head from side to side in denial. "I only wanted to be your friend, Erik."

His arm was still lassoed tightly around my middle, pinning me tightly to him. And ignoring my protests, he took a strand of my hair again and rolled it between two fingers. "Stay with me, Giselle," he implored. "Stay and dance with me all night that I might live."

Gulping back tears, I struggled to understand his meaning. Things were happening so fast, coming at me quicker than I could process. My mind felt numb as I remembered the night he'd stepped from behind the curtain, when he'd first worn the mask, and we'd danced the *grand pas de deux.* Did he want to dance the piece again?

Suddenly, he turned me loose and moved away, and for a moment, I thought I'd gotten through to him, that he was allowing me leave.

Gazing back through the room's pipes, tanks, and humming engines, the door seemed so far away now, and I wondered if I could make it. My body was heavy, cumbersome, so I used the desk to balance and maneuver myself about. With his back to me, this was my chance to get away. I had to try.

With all my strength, I shoved off the desk and lunged forward. It was a pathetic, futile attempt. All I did was stumble into Erik's back.

He caught me, sharply digging his long, slender feelings into my arm. "Knock off the melodramatics, Christine. You're not going anywhere."

Then locking onto my shoulders, he hauled me close, and hobbled us to his makeshift bed, where he lowered me to the floor. After propping me against the wall, he went to his knees beside me. I squinted into the mask's abysmal eye sockets trying to see him, and flinched when he unexpectedly raised the back of his hand to my face.

"Don't be afraid, Chrissy," he cooed, gingerly stroking his knuckles over my cheek. "You said yourself there's no need for us to be uncomfortable together."

Panic shot through me like flare guns firing, while my heart pounded and every breath seemed coated in sludge.

"Erik, I—I'm scared." My tongue was thick and my voice slurred. "I wanna go home."

With unnerving familiarity, he swept my hair off my neck. "You don't really mean that. You wanted to come here.

Remember? You are the only one to see past this." He gestured to the mask. "You wanted to be with me."

In my head, I was screaming no, yet nothing but throaty groans came out. Frustrated, I mustered what strength I had and threw my hand out to grab the headpiece and jerk it off, slinging it to the floor beside me.

Violently, he recoiled, cursing and ducking his head away from me. Beastly grunting noises emitted from his chest as he threw an arm over his head to shield himself from my view. For a moment, his shoulders rose and fell with his labored breathing, and every exhalation sizzled and hissed like droplets of water in a hot pan.

Unwilling to turn where I could see him, he groped about, blindly trying to lay hands on the headpiece. When he couldn't find it, he gave up and bellowed, "Why did you do that?"

I swallowed the lump in my throat and struggled to speak. "I...have a right to see."

The droning of the machinery around us closed in on me and synchronized with my nausea, ebbing and flowing with the horrible whirring.

"Very well," he snarled and hammered his fist vigorously on the floor. "If that's what you want. Then you shall have it!" And he whipped about for me to see.

For a split second, I was six years old, running a raging fever, nestled in my father's arms in the middle of an ER waiting room. Like then, the face before me appeared to have melted. Maybe it, too, was from the fever. But I didn't have a fever now. I wasn't in a hospital. So I waited for the face to return to normal, just like the nurse's had. But this face, with its molten skin and jagged scars, remained a lumpy, wax-like figure.

"Now, are you happy?" he demanded.

"Erik," I muttered and whirled away as something tightened in my chest.

With a strong hand, he gripped my chin and forced me to look at him again. "This is your leather-face," he spat. "This is what you wanted to see."

I wanted to close my eyes, to not see anymore. At the same time, I couldn't help staring at the phantom in front of me. Like a relief map, lines and crags of pallid, gray flesh covered the left side of Erik's face. A concave segment at the top of his skull held my attention until I followed a blistery fissure from it to his eye—his opaque, lifeless eye. Something sour in my stomach worked its way up my throat and I gagged.

"That's what I thought," he growled and pushed my face away.

Whatever he'd drugged me with was quickly sucking me under. My vision swam and my mouth went dry. Unable to hold my eyes open, I closed them for a second, just a second, and then forced them open again. If I surrendered to the blackness tugging at my senses, I'd never get out of there. Feebly, I clutched his gray sweatshirt in both fists. "Please—I want to go home."

Without a word, he pulled my hands away and eased me down onto the pallet, crushing the pink dahlia in my hair.

"What are you doing?" I croaked. "Erik, I don't want to..."

"It's okay, Chrissy, I love you. And you love me."

Chapter Sixty One

Standing on the corner across the street from the Wakefield Center, I couldn't remember leaving the underground garage. Orange rays of sunlight peeked over the city skyline, and I wondered what time it was. My clothes were wrinkled, so I brushed out some of the creases and noticed my reflection in a storefront window. My hair was a wreck, so I raked my fingers through it, and when I pulled my hand away, there was a single, tiny, pink dahlia petal on one of my fingertips. Suddenly, I became nauseated and knew I needed to get home before I got sick right there on the street.

Since it was early on a Saturday morning, there was little traffic, which was a good thing because I was oblivious to crosswalk signs and red lights. In a zombie-like state, I just wanted to be home.

On the ride up in the elevator, I prayed it wouldn't stop on the third floor. I didn't want Raoul to be visiting his father and see me in my present state.

There was a dull thud in my head that simply walking intensified, and I held my breath with every other step to numb the pain. When I got off the elevator and slipped into the apartment, Mom was there waiting for me.

"Christine Alysse Dadey, where the hell have you been? I was worried sick. I called Jenna and she said you were probably with some guy named Erik."

I stared at her as she ranted, unable to respond because my head was about to explode. "Mom," I croaked, "I need something for a headache." I walked past her into the kitchen where I poured myself a glass of water and pulled the aspirin bottle from the cabinet.

"Here," she fussed, snatching the bottle from my hand when I couldn't open it. "Let me do it." She waited until I'd had time to swallow the pill before starting on me again. "I want to know where you've been."

"Can I sit down?" I asked.

She pressed her lips into a white line. Then she whirled about and led the way to the living room, where we sat on the sofa.

"Well?" she prodded.

I took a sip from the glass of water again and set it on the table, mostly to give myself time to think. I couldn't remember what had happened. I'd gone to meet Erik to apologize for accusing him of hurting Van, and I remember there'd been a picnic of fruit and cheese, but I couldn't recall much beyond that.

"Christine, were you with this boy Jenna told me about?"

"Yes," I replied.

She released a pent-up breath and fell back on the sofa with a disappointed grunt. Shutting her eyes, she pinched the bridge of her nose. "Help me understand. I thought you were dating Raoul, but now you're sneaking out to see someone else. How long have you been doing this?"

I shrugged. "I don't know—maybe a month."

"A month!" She bolted upright again. "You've been sneaking out for a month?"

"Mom, please don't shout. My head is killing me."

"So you're going out with two boys at the same time, and one of them you've been sneaking out of the house to see?"

I shook my head—big mistake—then I squeezed my temple between the heels of my palms. "No, I'm not dating Erik."

"Then what are you doing?"

Bone tired, I couldn't track well, so I got to my feet. "I'm going to bed. I don't want to talk about this right now."

"You don't want to talk about this right now!" she screeched and jumped up. "Well, too damn bad. You don't have a choice. Now sit down."

Gingerly, so as not to jostle my brain, I did as she said and she joined me.

"Tell me who this Erik is."

"He's a dancer—was a dancer—and I've been taking lessons from him. He's been helping me with my acting— characterization and affectations."

"Helping you? Is this something Ms. Zaborov initiated? Why is it in the middle of the night?"

"Ms. Zaborov doesn't know. No one does."

"Then where did you meet him?"

"At the theater. When I went to see Romeo and Juliet."

"So this has nothing to do with school? Is he a member of the main company then?"

"No, he's not a member of any company anymore."

"So let me get this straight. You've been leaving here at night to meet some guy you claim is teaching you acting, yet you've told no one. You realize how that sounds don't you. And if I think it's suspicious, how do you think it would look to your teachers, or even Mr. Darby, if it were to get back to them?"

Hot anger pulsed behind my eyes, and I pulled up to the edge of the sofa to stare at her. "That's where you want to go with this? The how-will-it-freaking-look thing? Is that seriously all you care about? Well, I don't give a crap how it looks, Mom, because I'm done."

Inhaling sharply, she snapped her head as if I'd thrown ice water in her face. "What do you mean?"

"I've spent more of my life in ballet slippers than sneakers, and I'm sick to death of it. I'm through trying to please everybody. I am finished with Erik, the Rousseau Academy, and with ballet. As soon as I can, I'm moving to Norway with Dad."

Chapter Sixty Two

Surprisingly, Mom didn't follow me to my room. I think she was too stunned. Wearily, I turned down the bed, slipped out of my shoes and jeans, and crawled in as I was. Dead tired, I sensed I should be doing something, sorting things out, but my brain felt too large for my skull and thinking hurt. All I wanted to do was sleep, and I was out by the time my head hit the pillow.

My dreams were fretful, filled with shadowy images and unsettling emotions. By the time I awoke later, those images and emotions had coalesced into a truth I hadn't been sure of before—I had been with Erik. And although parts of the night remained a blur, I had no doubt now that Erik and I'd had sex.

Disgust and shame swept through me, and I didn't want to think about what had happened, so I tunneled under my covers, rolled over, and went back to sleep, where I didn't have to deal with it now.

Hours later, a knock on my bedroom door roused me. I lay there thinking if I pretended to be asleep, Mom might go away. I was surprised to learn it wasn't her.

"Chris, can I come in?"

It was Jenna.

Tossing back the covers, I shimmied into my jeans and went to the door. When I opened it, Jenna stood there, eyes wide with unspoken questions.

"Come in." I stepped aside for her to enter, and we went to my bed and sat down together. As I gazed across the room at a spot on the wallpaper, I sensed her eyes on me. Finally, I attempted a smile.

"What the hell, Christine? You look like shit."

"Thanks."

"Well, you do. Your mom called me super early this morning. I'm sorry I panicked and narced on you like that, but I didn't know what else to do."

"I wish you hadn't been caught in the middle," I said

She waved a hand dismissively. "She thought you were with Raoul. I had to tell her about Erik because she threatened to go to Raoul's dad."

"Oh, no," I groaned.

"She didn't believe me right away. She couldn't wrap her head around you having a secret tutor and thought I was making it up."

"Don't worry about it. She was bound to find out sooner or later."

"Yeah, but she called again this afternoon, practically wiggin' out. She said you were threatening to leave school and move to Norway."

I laughed derisively. "She's worried because her little Tina Ballerina isn't following the rules anymore."

"That's not the half of it," Jenna said. "She thinks you're hooking up with this guy. But I told her that's not true, right?"

I dropped my gaze to the floor because I didn't want to see her reaction.

"Oh. My. God. You slept with him. When? Why didn't you tell me? I thought you said he was ugly."

"Jenna!" I barked.

"Oh, yeah—no, I didn't mean it that way. But you said his face was burned, and I..." Her voice trailed off and we sat there a moment, while I resisted a strong desire to cry.

Finally, I said, "I'm not sure how it happened."

"What do you mean?"

"I went to apologize—to grovel like you said. He'd arranged this beautiful picnic for us, right there in the theater. It was nice. We talked, and he said we should let it go." I paused and took a breath. "We had this wine. Well, I did. He couldn't drink any because of the mask."

"The mask!" Jenna's voice went up a notch. "What were you two doing?"

My bottom lip quivered, and I couldn't speak as my eyes watered.

Jenna noticed my discomfort and scooted closer to me on the bed. "This is bad isn't it," she observed. "Something went down. Tell me everything."

I spilled my guts. Going back to the beginning, I recounted our sessions together, his promising career and the choreographers he knew, and the fire that ruined everything for him. I even divulged how Mr. Sims found him and the fact that he was homeless and living in the Wakefield's boiler room. Lastly, I told her about the mask he'd worn when we'd danced together.

"Wow, he wore a mask to come from behind the curtain," she repeated, as if my saying it hadn't convinced her, and she had to form the words for herself to believe them. "This is some weird crap," she added. "Like something out of a movie."

I nodded and continued, "He said he wanted to show me something. I started not to go, but I followed him downstairs to the room he's been living in."

When I hesitated, she pressed, "Then what happened?"

My hands clasped in my lap, I twisted my fingers into knots so tight that my knuckles paled. "I remember feeling weird on our way downstairs, kind of tired and woozy. Then he had these pictures of me."

"He's been taking pictures of you?"

"No." I shook my head. "They were sketches, charcoals. And he'd made a video out of them and put it to music."

"Whoa, seriously? That's messed up stalker business."

"Everything gets hazy after that. It's blurry, but I remember feeling queasy and telling him I needed to go home before I got sick."

"What do you mean? Were you drunk? Did you pass out?"

"No. I don't think so. I don't know. I didn't think I'd drunk that much wine, but I can't remember everything now."

Jenna blinked several times and her jaw clenched. "Wait a minute. You said he didn't drink the wine."

I nodded.

"Son of a bitch. He drugged you."

As she said this, I recalled Erik saying it was necessary.

"He didn't drink any of it," she said, "because he laced it with something."

"But why would he do that? He's helped me. He was helping me prepare for the second company auditions." I denied the obvious, refusing to admit it out loud.

"No he wasn't. He was helping himself. Think about, Chris." Her hazel eyes bore meaningfully into mine. "You were raped. He drugged you and forced himself on you, and you have to call the police."

Chapter Sixty Three

*T*hankfully, there was a trashcan near my bed because Jenna's words forced me to face the truth, and I barely had time to get to it before vomiting. Then I fell to the floor in a heap and bawled uncontrollably.

Jenna swooped down and held me close, saying things meant to be reassuring, but overcome with shame and humiliation, it was all gibberish to me. After a while, only the tremors remained, and I was able to get a steady breath.

"You need to tell your mother," Jenna said. "Call the police and bust this bastard."

"No!" I yelped, and then lowered my voice. "I can't tell my mother. She'd completely freak out. You see how she's acting now. Can you imagine what she'd do if she learned what a fool I've been."

Our backs against the bed, we sat silently on the floor for a while. Then Jenna pulled her legs up and wrapped her arms around her knees. "I get that you don't want to tell your mom. But you're not a fool, Chris, and you can't blame yourself. Not even for a minute. You were duped. I think this guy knew exactly what he was doing, and he's played you all along."

"How could I have been so blind?"

"You could only see what he revealed. And the dude sounds totally twisted—Jekyll and Hyde-ish."

I dropped my head back to stare up at the ceiling. "Promise me you won't tell anyone about this. Swear."

When she didn't reply, I picked up my head and looked at her. "Jenna."

"All, right. All, right." She threw her hands up in surrender. "I want to go on record, though, as saying I think you should nail his ass to wall. But I get it. I won't tell anyone."

"Thanks." I let my head sag onto the bed again, and we sat quietly until she finally had to go home.

When she'd left, I sat on my bed gazing across the room at the blank monitor on my open laptop. Snippets of the night were still coming back to me, and the more they did the more revolted I felt. Eventually, I dragged myself out of bed and took a long shower.

On my way back from the bathroom, Mom called my name from the kitchen. She was at the stove, stirring something in a pot.

"I'm preparing soup for dinner."

She was trying to make peace, probably even hoping to get me to talk, but I wasn't ready for that. There was no way I was going to tell her what had happened, and even though my threat to live with Dad was just that, a threat, I didn't have it in me to go another round with her right now.

"No thanks." I kept walking. "I'm not hungry."

In my room, I turned on some music and noticed the message light on my phone blinking. There were several texts from Raoul. The first one simply said the

Diamondbacks had won their game last night. The next asked if I was awake. And the third one teasingly called me a sleepy head. Lowering myself into the desk chair, tears trickled quietly down my face, and my heart felt like it would implode. It hurt so intensely that I ached all over.

Phone in hand, I went to the bed to lie down, and morosely, I thumbed through the photos taken the night we'd gone to the Frozen Tundra. Then, when I couldn't take the pain anymore, I buried my face in a pillow and cried, and screamed, and cried some more. How had I screwed things up so badly? If only there were some way I could go back to the night Erik had told me about his mother's death. I'd wish him the best for his life and go on with mine.

It was too late for that, though, and I had to find a way to deal with Raoul now. I had to break up with him. I couldn't bear for him to learn about Erik—what had occurred between us.

Then, as if he knew I was thinking about him, I received a text from him.

Hey, babe, wanna hang out tonight? Thought I'd stay the weekend at Dad's.

Every nerve ending in my body longed to say yes, come over. But through wet eyelashes, I reread the text, and the only thing I could think to do to prevent him from showing up at my door was to lie. So I told him the first thing that popped into my head.

Sorry. Grounded. Failed a couple of classes. Mom put the brakes on my social life.

I waited for his response.

No prob. Miss me. Cuz I'll miss you.

Right when I believed it couldn't hurt any more than it

already did, he had to say something so utterly sweet. Yeah, I had to find a way to break it off. It was the honorable thing to do.

On Sunday, I kept to my room all day, not coming out until Mom called me for lunch. She sneaked glances my direction as we sat beside each other at the breakfast bar, and what conversation we had was stilted.

Finally, when I couldn't eat the food on my plate and went to the sink to wash it down the disposal, she said, "I've tried to give you some space, hoping you'd come to me and we could discuss whatever it is that you've been doing. But since you haven't, the issue has to be addressed. I don't want you going around this Erik again. There's obviously more to this than you're telling me, and frankly, it scares the hell out of me. But I can't force you to talk to me. Still, I want to know who he is. The school needs to be made aware that a former dancer is skulking around, hitting on some of the students."

"No!" I cried, circling around to face her as a myriad of scenarios flashed through my mind, pictures of Deirdre and the other girls whispering behind my back, Ms. Zaborov giving me pitying glances, and I didn't even want to think about the disapproval I'd receive from Mrs. Hahn. Not to mention if I told her who he was, could I get in trouble for knowing he was living in the boiler room and not reporting him?

"I'm not going to see him again, so just drop it. Please, Mom."

"Chris..."

"I messed up, but I won't do it again. Can't you keep it between us?"

She placed her fork on her plate to perch her elbows on

the table. Lowering her face into her hands a moment, she exhaled. "Tell me—have you been sleeping with this man?"

"No. I was seeing him for ballet. That's all. So see, there's no reason for you to go to anyone at the school. I promise I will not see him again—ever."

She wavered. "If you promise."

I tipped my head in agreement.

Chapter Sixty Four

*T*he next morning, I told Mom I had a headache and stayed home from school. Recalling Jenna's advice, I considered telling Mom what Erik had done, but I couldn't bring myself to. I was too ashamed at the thought of her knowing my part in it.

By midmorning, I wished I'd gone to class. Being alone in the apartment was unsettling. I tried watching television, reading, catching up homework, but my mind inevitably ended up on Erik. Every detail of that night was clear in my memory now. I tried to understand how it could have happened. Had I somehow led him on? All I'd done was dance for him. I'd never hinted at wanting anything more than to be his friend.

When my phone rang at five-fifteen that evening, it was Jenna, and I'd made a decision.

"I need you to break up with Raoul for me," I told her. "It's cowardly, but it's better than doing it in a text."

"Oh, no, are you sure you want to do that? He's a great guy. Believe me, I know what I'm talking about, I've dated enough losers, and I'm telling you you're making a mistake."

"How can I not? There's no way in hell, I'm telling him

about Erik. And I couldn't pull off that level of deception—to go on like nothing has changed. My conscience would eat me alive. Plus, even if I wanted to, I wouldn't know how to go about telling him. I can't do it." I choked back a sob.

"This really blows," Jenna sighed. "Seriously blows."

"Will you help me or not?"

"Yeah, but are you sure you don't want to talk to him first."

"No, I can't. Please, just do this for me."

"If that's what you want."

"It's what has to be done."

Tuesday morning I went to Ms. Zaborov to ask her to let me out of working with the Diamondbacks. Seeing Raoul at class after Jenna had given him the news would be agonizing. When Ms. Z. asked for an explanation, I told her it interfered with my own practice. She was understanding and promised to find another dancer to take my place.

That afternoon, when it was time for the Diamondbacks to arrive, I stayed behind with Mrs. Hahn to work with the rest of the class. Then, to keep from bumping into Raoul when the day was over, I hurried to the car where Mom waited.

There was no way to determine what might come next, but at least Raoul would never discover the truth, and I'd squashed the possibility of him thinking I was a tramp. But I deeply underestimated Raoul.

Later that night, the doorbell rang and when Mom answered it, I heard his voice. "Hi Mrs. Dadey. Is Christine home?"

"Uh," Mom stammered as I came up behind her. She glanced at me, unsure what to do. Obviously, she hadn't expected Raoul to be in the picture anymore.

"It's okay. Let him in." When he came through the doorway, I said, "Let's go to my room."

He followed me there, and nervously, he stood in the middle of the floor, shifting his weight until I motioned for him to sit down. He took a place on the bed and I settled in the chair at my desk, being so close to him was unnerving. For several strained seconds, neither of us spoke or made eye contact, and he picked up a throw pillow from the bed and plucked at its fringe before flipping it over and eventually tossing it back onto the bed.

Finally, he cleared his throat. "You weren't at practice today. Some guy took your place, and Ms. Zaborov said you wouldn't be back."

"No, I quit. It's interfering with my own practice."

"Jenna stopped me after class was over."

My heart squeezed. This was it. This was where he'd tell me I was a coward and the least I could do was break up in person. But when he lifted his gaze to focus on me, I wasn't prepared for what he said.

"She told me everything."

I opened my mouth, but a beat passed before I could say, "She told you I wanted to break up, right?"

"Yeah, and she also told me why."

Suddenly I felt dirty. My skin crawled and my mouth went bitterly dry. I was sure Erik's handprints lingered on my body and Raoul could see them. I glanced at him certain there would be revulsion on his face.

He scooted to the foot of the bed. "Why didn't you tell me?"

Crushing my bottom lip between my teeth, I willed it to stop quivering. To avoid his gaze, I adjusted my head and stared through the lace window curtains at the high-rises outside. How could I tell him that I couldn't bear for him to know I no longer shined?

"Talk to me," he pleaded. "Do you want to be with this guy? Because if you do..."

"What exactly did Jenna tell you?" I butted in.

He hesitated, ruffling his hair in the way that I loved so much. "She said you were a...that you had an instructor who...well, you know. You could have told me, Chris. I wouldn't have—I don't—blame you. Jenna says he laced your drink, knocked you out. What a dirtbag—I could kill him, but it wasn't your fault."

The compassion in his voice released the aching in my chest, and I sank my face into my hands and burst into tears. In a flash, he was up, coaxing me from the chair and drawing me over to sit beside him. Tenderly, he took my hand, and said, "I'm sorry this happened to you. But you can trust me. I'm not going anywhere."

The tears fell even harder then, and for the first time in days, I felt clean. "I didn't know what else to do," I explained to him. "I didn't have the courage to tell you, so I asked Jenna to break up for me."

He reached for a tissue from the box on the bedside table, and handed it to me.

I blew my nose. "You still want to be with me? You'd go out with again, knowing I was...knowing what he did?"

"My sister's swim coach tried to put his hands on her. He was a freaking college teacher—damn perv. No one blasted her for it, though."

A bond seemed to develop between us then. It was unspoken, but it was there. And if Raoul didn't condemn me maybe I didn't need to condemn myself.

He squeezed my hand and easily moved on. "Have you told your mother? What did she say?"

I shook my head. "No, I haven't told her. She would completely lose it."

"Are you going to report him to the police?"

"Did your sister?"

"Nuh-uh. But look, you have to do what's right for you. If you don't want to tell anyone you don't have to." He paused then said, "I could kick his ass for you. Me and a few of the Diamondbacks could meet him in a dark alley somewhere."

I couldn't help myself. In the middle of the debris of what was left of my life, he made me smile. "No. All I want is to put it behind me and move on."

"You're gonna get through this," he assured me. "We'll get through it together."

Chapter Sixty Five

Raoul stayed for about an hour. I ended up telling him how I'd met Erik in the first place, and I even told him about the fire that scarred Erik's face. Eventually the conversation moved on as we kicked back on my bed, backs against the wall and our feet hanging over the side. It felt more like the night at Discovery Green when we'd danced with Magdalena and her friends. That night seemed so long ago now, but it was as if Raoul and I were there again and our relationship was unfolding now as it had then, gently and naturally. It wasn't going to be easy, but I was convinced I could put Erik's betrayal behind me.

Later, when he'd gone, I went to the kitchen, where Mom readied dinner.

"Leftovers," she said, popping a bowl into the microwave. Then she sat on one of the stools at the island and patted the seat of the other for me to join her.

"I was surprised to see Raoul. I thought you weren't dating him anymore."

Tracing a vein in the granite countertop, I hedged a moment. "We worked it out." A beat passed, and I said, "I'm sorry. I shouldn't have made those threats. I'm not quitting ballet and moving in with Dad."

She smiled ruefully and reached for my hand. "I'm sorry, too. I just snapped when I learned you were sneaking out. I understand you wanting to have extra help, but you should never have met with someone your father or I had not approved of."

"I know. It won't happen again."

The microwave dinged, but she continued to hold my hand and look me in the eye. "You're sure there's nothing more you want to tell me?"

She was no simpleton. Of course, there was more, and she knew I was holding back. But I shook my head nonetheless. And even though we'd made our apologies, she didn't trust me. It would take a while to regain her confidence.

Lying in bed that night, listening to music and thinking about Raoul, my text alert went off. I levered myself up to retrieve the phone from the bedside table and swiped my finger across the screen. Startled, I shot straight out of bed when I saw Erik's name in the message line. Then, as if it had burned me, I tossed the phone on the bed and backed away.

He'd texted me. He'd never been the first to text, only responded to any I'd sent. I didn't know what to do. In all that I'd stressed and worried over since that night, I hadn't once considered having to face him again. I wrapped my arms around myself and debated whether I should delete the text without reading it. Then the alert sounded again.

I crept closer to the bed, eyeing the phone suspiciously. What could he want? Why wouldn't he just go away?

My legs went weak and I trembled until my knees buckled and I dropped onto the bed and opened the first message.

Hello, love, I've missed you.

I had to read it twice for it to sink in. And upon the second reading, I grew angry rather than frightened. He spoke as if nothing had happened. Then I opened the next message.

Don't forget to wear dance clothes. You know I get distracted when you wear those tight jeans.

My hand flew to my mouth. He was insane, delusional, acting as if we'd entered into a mutual relationship.

Throwing the phone down once more, my anger turned to outrage, and bounding to my feet, I paced the room until the phone actually rang and I shrieked. With leaden legs, I approached the bed and looked at the screen. It was him. I waited, ogling the chiming phone like it was a singing alien. Finally, it stopped, and in a matter of seconds, the voicemail notification sounded.

It was like I was in a dream, a slow-motion nightmare. Picking up the phone, my fingers wobbly, I pressed the button to listen to the voicemail.

"Chrissy, why won't you answer my call? You didn't respond to my texts, and now you ignore my call. I suppose if I'm going to speak with you I'll have to phone your house—talk to your mother."

Jenna was right. He was certifiably a Jekyll and Hyde, making the subtlest of threats that he knew would rattle me.

Before I had time to consider what to do, the phone resonated in my hand, and I almost jumped out of my skin. I knew without looking it would be him, and he would follow through with his threat to call my house if I didn't answer. So I hit the green button on the screen. "Hello?"

"Ah, that's better. I knew you'd see things my way."

"What do you want?" I demanded.

"To see you, of course."

"No."

"You sound troubled."

"What did you expect, Erik?"

"You're not upset about Friday night, are you?"

For a moment, I was speechless.

"Yes, I'm upset about Friday night. You drugged me. How could you do that? To think, I'd worried about hurting your feelings, and all along you'd planned to dope and rape me."

"No, no, that's not the way it was." Instantly, his tone changed. Gone was the confident swagger. "I love you, Christine. You have to know that. And you love me, too. I know you do. You came back for me. Surely, you understand. I never meant to hurt you. The drug—it was to make it easier for you. Why you said yourself you had to take a sedative before the Academy audition."

"Don't even compare what you did to my situation with the audition. Besides, you'd had the wine planned before I ever told you about my panic attacks. You weren't making things easy for anyone but yourself."

"You have to give me another chance," he begged. "We belong together. We have to stay together."

"Stop right there. We're not a couple. I'm not in love with you, and I never want to see you again."

"But, Chrissy," he bellowed, "I can't live without you. I will die without you. I'll die, Christine, and it will be your fault."

Chapter Sixty Six

*W*as he threatening suicide? I stared at a painting on the wall, contemplating the implication. Ultimately, I believed Erik loved himself too much to commit suicide. His threat was an attempt to manipulate me.

"I let you close enough to deceive me, once," I said into the phone. "But never again. You're not going to make me feel responsible for your life." I said this not thoroughly confident he wouldn't do it. But I couldn't allow him to exploit my sympathies anymore, and his response proved me right.

"You ungrateful bitch!" His voice sliced through the phone, sending runners of ice up my spine, and reminding me of how he'd destroyed Raoul's necklace and choked me. "You're nothing without me. I've made you what you are now. None of the instructors in that stupid school could have done it. Certainly not Elaina Hahn."

"You're right," I agreed. "You have helped me. But what happened between us—what you did—was wrong."

"But I love you, Christine. Don't you believe me?" Once more, his voice turned pathetic and mewling.

"I trusted you with the one thing that meant the most to me," I said. "My dancing. It's always been about dancing for me. I've never thought of you as anything but a teacher. A brilliant, gifted teacher, but that's all."

"No. No." He sputtered. "You love me. I know you do. You wouldn't have come back to the leather-faced monster if you didn't."

"What makes you a monster is not what's on the outside, but what's on the inside. And, I felt sorry for you, but I never loved you. I love Raoul."

He howled then, and I had to pull the phone away from my ear. When I pressed it close again, I heard huffing and puffing, punctuated by sharp hisses. "Ehhh!" he yelled. "I told you to never say his name to me! I hate him. Raoul! Raoul! Raoul! You don't seriously think I'll let you go back to him, do you? You belong to me."

"I don't belong to you or Raoul. I don't belong to anyone. I'm just me, and I'm okay with that."

"But you need me."

"No, I don't, and I told you, I never want to see you again."

"I should have known. You're a slut—just like her."

The word was like a slap to the face.

"She never appreciated what I did for her either," he went on. "She used me—the same way you did. And then she pushed me aside for another."

"What are you talking about? Who is she?"

"Elaina Hahn."

I gasped then pressed my fist to my mouth. He stormed on, but stunned by his revelation, I couldn't hear him. He'd had a relationship with Mrs. Hahn. What had I allowed myself to be pulled into? My thoughts scrambled for something that made sense. Had he slept with her to be promoted? Maybe she found out he was mentally unstable and dismissed him from the school. Whatever the case, the whole thing was revolting.

"You'll see," he said, breaking into my reasoning. "Just wait. When you realize what I can do, you'll come crawling, begging me to take you back."

"No, I won't. And if you keep calling and texting me, I'll call the police."

"Oh, really." My blood went cold at the tone in his voice. All at once, it had veered both daring and threatening. "Does this mean you plan to turn yourself in for the stolen Xanax you keep hidden in your room? Because I know you're not going to show them all the texts you've sent me. There are probably, what, a dozen of you scheduling our midnight meetings. Then there are the ones you sent begging me to see you again, with promises of doing anything to make it up to me. Hell, you even sent old man Sims to intervene on your behalf. And let us not forget that you came to me. Every. Single. Time. So go ahead. Call the police."

Tentacles of fear wrapped around my stomach and squeezed it into a hard ball. He was right. I'd initiated every encounter. There was no way anyone, let alone the police, would believe that he'd raped me.

"Aw, what's the matter?" he teased chillingly. "Cat got your tongue." Then he chuckled derisively. "Don't worry, Chrissy. You can go on with your little Barbie doll world and forget about the monster you stepped over to get to the top. But the time will come when you regret turning your back on the phantom. You, Hahn, the whole damn school. You'll all regret it."

That was when I pushed the End button and turned off my phone.

Chapter Sixty Seven

I waited until Mom had gone to bed and retrieved the house phone from the dock in the kitchen. Because I'd powered off my cell, I didn't want Erik to call and Mom answer it. And I wanted to phone Jenna.

When I'd rehashed Erik's phone call to her, she said, "This guy had a fling with Atilla? That's creepy. He is clearly out of his mind."

"What do I do? I can't notify the police because I have nothing to prove my side of the story."

"I don't think there's anything you can do. But watch your back, at least until this blows over."

"Do you think it will—blow over, that is."

"Maybe. Obviously, whatever he had with Hahn blew over because we've never heard anything about it. And you know it's nearly impossible to keep secrets at the Rousseau. Look, if he texts you again, ignore it. And leave your house phone off the hook for the next few days. I doubt your mother will notice, and if he can't get through, after a while he'll give up."

"Yeah, you're probably right."

More than anything, I wanted to believe she was anyway. So I did as she suggested, keeping the cordless phone line open, and leaving it in the closet so Mom wouldn't find it. And I didn't reboot my cell again until the next day. By then, I'd pushed away some of the doubts and fears. In the light of day, I was less frightened, and I could view things more logically. And when he'd cooled down, I doubted Erik would really carry out any of his threats. At some point, he'd realize I was not coming back and he'd move on.

Wednesday morning I went to school, feeling optimistic. I was even able to laugh when Jenna made a snide comment about never being able to look at Mrs. Hahn the same way again. And I steeled myself for that very thing when we went to repertoire that afternoon, but she wasn't there. Admittedly, my first thoughts were of Erik, but I dismissed it and clung to my earlier hope that he'd move on. Then when she wasn't there again on Thursday, I began to worry in earnest that Erik had followed through with his threats. But I felt silly on Friday, when Mrs. Hahn was there, stern as ever.

And that was why, when Raoul asked me to his mother's house for lunch on Saturday, I really thought my life was moving forward. At least until I climbed into his car in front of Templeton Towers that morning.

"I am super nervous about this," I told him as I buckled my seatbelt. "What if your mother doesn't like me?"

"Of course, she'll like you." Looking out the driver's side window, he was checking the oncoming traffic, waiting for an opening to slip into. "What's not to like?"

That was when I noticed his knuckles gripping the steering wheel. They were red and splotchy and dotted with tiny cuts. Without thinking, I reached out and tugged his hand free of the steering wheel to examine it. "What did you do to your hand?" He turned to face me then, and I gasped.

"Oh, my God, what happened to your face?" Beneath his left eye was a purply-black, crescent shaped bruise, its edges already turning yellow-green. Concerned, I released his hand to skim my fingertips gingerly over the ugly bump. "Does it hurt?"

He slid away from my touch to look out the window again. "Nah, it's no big deal."

"But what happened?"

Bearing down hard on the gas pedal, he shot out in front of a honking car. "It's nothing—almost gone now."

"Was it football practice? Did you get hit without your helmet on?"

He watched the car in front of us and shook his head, and an uneasy feeling crept over me. He was avoiding my questions. Why wouldn't he tell me what had happened?

"Raoul, answer me."

Glancing briefly my way, he pressed his lips together then said, "I didn't want to upset you. I got into a fight. Erik jumped me and we fought."

I inhaled sharply. "What? How? When?" My thoughts splintered a thousand different directions with all the possibilities.

"The other night. He ambushed me after the team's lesson with Ms. Zaborov."

My mouth fell open, but I couldn't form words as fear and dread filled me like ice water being poured into a glass. Erik had attacked Raoul. The thought of it caused my heart to race, and I broke out in a cold sweat as the familiar panic returned. But this was worse than before. The panic attacks I'd suffered so far were a result of fears of my own making. There had never been a real threat. Now, there was reason to freak out. The threat was a living, breathing man, and he'd attacked Raoul.

"Chris—Christine?" Raoul's voice elevated and he seized my hand. "Hey, are you okay? I started not to tell you. I should have let you believe it happened at football practice, but I'm no good at lying."

He squeezed my hand as if expecting a response, but when all I could do was shake my head and gulp for air, he let go and cut across traffic to whip into a small parking lot behind a building. Slamming the car into park, he unfastened his belt, then mine, and forced me to face him. "Take a breath," he commanded. "In—out. In—out. Focus on me. In—out." He bobbed his head as my pace slowed to match his. "Good. Now look at me. I'm fine. You're fine. We're both fine— okay?"

Slowly, I floated back down from the heights of soul splitting fear, and nodded to let him know my composure was returning. "I—I'm all right."

He rubbed his hands up and down my arms as if trying to warm frozen limbs, and at last I spoke. "Tell me what happened." My voice was so weak I was surprised he could hear me.

"On Thursday after the team's ballet class, I decided to hang out with some of the guys. I left my car in the parking garage and we drove to the paintball field. When we came back, Troy dropped me off by my car, but I didn't notice until he'd gone that I had a flat tire. When I walked to the trunk for the spare and the jack, Erik rose up from where he'd crouched on the other side." I slapped my hand over my mouth, and Raoul continued. "I'm sure he flattened the tire because my trunk had been popped open and it was my tire iron he came at me with."

"He hit you with a tire iron?"

Raoul shook his head. "I've dodged enough linebackers to know how to get the hell out of the way when someone's coming at me like that, so when he lunged, and the blow didn't connect, it threw him off balance and I took the iron away from him."

"Did you hit him with it?"

"No, of course not. If I'm gonna fight someone it'll be *mano a mano*."

"So what happened?"

"I beat the crap out of him, that's what happened." A satisfied smirk crossed his lips. "Stupid son of bitch should have known he'd need more than some fancy dance steps to take me down."

Again, my fingers went to the semi-circle bruise on his cheekbone. "You're sure you're all right, though?"

He took my hand in his and kissed the inside of my wrist. "Never better."

Drawing my hand away, I stared out the front window. "You're certain it was him? I mean, it could have been someone else, a mugger maybe."

"I saw his face, Christine. It was him."

"We have to call the police then."

"Why? I told you, I handled it."

I looked at him again and pointed at the bruise. "What did you tell your mother—about your face?"

"That I head-butted someone on the field."

"And she believed you?"

"Sure. She's seen me in worse shape than this."

"But what if he comes after you again?"

"He won't."

"How can you be so sure?"

"Because he ran."

"I don't understand."

"He was wearing a big hoody, and in the scuffle we got tangled up in it. I flipped it inside out and yanked it over his head, which is how I got this"—he indicated the blackened eye—"the idiot flung an elbow in my face as he tried to get free. When he peeled out of the hoody, I went sailing backward and landed flat on my back. It took me a second to catch my breath, get the jacket out of my face, and get back on my feet, and by the time I did, the damn coward was haulin' ass for the garage exit. I yelled after him, told him what I'd do if he ever came near you again."

I let my head fall back against the seat's headrest. I wanted, really, really wanted to believe Raoul was right, that Erik was gone, and would never come back.

"How can you be so sure?" I asked again. "He's crazy. He may still come back for one, or both, of us."

Raoul placed a hand on my arm, "Chris, I pounded the pavement with the guy. Trust me, he's not coming back."

Covering my eyes with my cupped hand, I wanted to shut everything out, but it only made matters worse as visions of Raoul and Erik throwing punches and battering one another filled the dark behind my eyes.

"Tell me you're not mad," Raoul said. "I had no choice. He came at me, and instinct kicked in."

Dropping my hand, I looked at him. "I couldn't possibly be mad at you. I'm only sorry that it happened. I feel like it's my fault."

"Don't even go there again. If anything, this proves it

wasn't your fault. It's all on that crazy S.O.B. But it's over now."

"I hope so," I mumbled.

Shifting around in the seat again, he gripped the steering wheel. "So we're good? You're okay with coming to my house now?"

We buckled our belts simultaneously. "Yeah, we're good," I said, hoping he was right and the nightmare was truly over.

The car was quiet on the rest of the trip. But by the time we pulled into his driveway in River Oaks, I'd gotten over the initial shock. And even though I worried his mother would sense something was wrong, Ms. Raeburn turned out to be a delightful person, putting me at ease. She was kind and considerate, and I could see how she'd had a strong influence on Raoul's life. There was only one sticky moment when Ms. Raeburn left us to go to the kitchen, and Raoul took me by the hand and led me upstairs.

"Where are we going?" I asked.

"To my bedroom." He smiled and the dimple in his chin shone.

"Are you trying to get me killed?" I teased, parroting the words he'd said the day I'd taken him to my bedroom. Then we spent the better part of an hour in his room listening to music and him showing me his school pictures and trophies—not just in football, but baseball too—and in spite of the neon welt on Raoul's face, I forgot about Erik and enjoyed my time at his home.

On Sunday, Jenna came over to help me do my homework. With everything that had happened, I was more than a little behind. As soon as she arrived, I told her about Erik attacking Raoul.

"Holy cow. You're kidding me."

I shook my head. "Raoul believes he's gone now—that he scared him off."

"I would think so, after getting his ass handed to him like that."

"Let's hope ," I said. Then we got to work.

We'd studied at the dining table, where we set up my laptop, books, and binders, for a couple of hours, when Jenna slammed her book shut and sighed heavily. "Enough. I need a break. How about some ice cream?"

I lifted my brow. "What about Mrs. Hahn?"

"Oh, one scoop won't hurt."

"Sounds like a plan to me."

So we walked to the Marble Slab Creamery several blocks from the apartment and sat in a booth, gabbing over our ice cream.

"Thank you," I said.

"Sure. Wait. What for?"

"Being there for me."

She blushed. "Forget about it."

"No, seriously, if you hadn't spoken to Raoul the way you did, I don't think we'd be together now."

"He's a great guy. I couldn't stand to see you split up."

"Thanks," I said again, and she smiled and nodded.

"I suppose, since we're being serious and everything, now's as good a time as any to tell you my news."

"Hmm?" I mumbled around a mouthful of ice cream.

"I'm sort of dating Dionte."

I swallowed and craned my neck forward. "Come again."

"Dionte Wells, from Urban Honesty. We're going out."

"No way!"

"Yeah, we exchanged numbers that day at the studio. I didn't want to tell you until I saw how it went, and then you know, well, all hell broke loose."

I skimmed over her reference to my assault to keep us on the happier conversation. "Wow, you and Dionte."

"That's not all."

"What?" I smiled and taunted her. "You luuuv him."

"Real mature. But no, I'm leaving the Rousseau Academy."

I stared at her then, spoon floating before my open mouth, and blinked a few times. "You're leaving the school?"

"I've been miserable for a while. I'm tired of the crazy schedule and constant criticism—and never getting to eat ice cream." She shoveled a spoonful of butter pecan into her mouth as if her life depended on it. "Ever since we went to the Street Feet Studios, I've known I wanted out. If I'm going to dance, I'll dance the way I want to."

"Have you told your parents?"

"Yeah, they want me to wait a month and think it over because once I let go of the scholarship, I won't be able to get it back. But I know what I'm going to do. When this month is up, I'm leaving school."

Chapter Sixty Eight

*W*hen we returned to Templeton Towers, Jenna decided to go home. Standing on the street, I watched her car pull away and thought about what she was doing—leaving the Rousseau. How many times had I considered the same thing? It was right for her. She'd been unhappy for some time. But somewhere along the way, I'd changed my mind. I loved ballet. I wanted to dance more than anything in the world, and I would not walk away. Even if I weren't allowed to audition for the second company this year, I'd stay, work harder, and try again, and again, until I made it.

Upstairs, I stepped off the elevator, unlocked the apartment door, and froze when I heard a familiar voice streaming from the living room. It couldn't be him. Then he spoke again, and I knew there was no mistaking his that voice. Slowly, I walked into the room. "Dad?"

Sitting on the sofa, my father whipped his head up to look at me. Then he bounded to his feet and hurried around the coffee table. Scooping me into his arms, he crushed me to his chest and kissed the top of my head.

When I mumbled into his suit jacket, "I can't breathe," he released me and held me out in front of him.

"You've grown, Tina Ballerina," he observed.

"When did you get here?" I asked.

"Today. Your mother called me a few days ago and told me what was going on, and I tied up everything in Norway so I could come home as soon as possible."

My gaze went to Mom seated on the sofa. Her eyes were red and she held a tissue in her hand.

"What are you talking about?" I asked.

"Sit down," Dad instructed, and moved aside for me to take a place next to Mom. Then he shoved a stack of magazines out of his way and settled on the coffee table in front of us.

"Your mother says you've been sneaking out at night to meet a man named Erik."

I whipped my head sideways to gape at her. "You told him? We had a deal. I promised not see him again, and I haven't. I kept my part of the bargain." My last words were stinging, meant to point out her breaking of our agreement."

"That was concerning the school and your teachers. I had called your father the night you didn't come home. He's the one who suggested I give you some space for a few days."

I clenched my hands at my side. Dad had known what I did from the beginning.

"And I'm glad I did now," Mom continued. "After reading the text this man sent you."

"You went through my phone!"

"You wouldn't tell me what was going on. I had to do something. I, we, need to know what we're dealing with. You're under age, and according to the texts, it's obvious the two of you were doing more than dancing."

"I was not! I only went for lessons. He was the one..." My

denial fell away in a garble of unintelligible nonsense because I still couldn't bring myself to say it to them.

"Anyone could tell by reading those emails you've been intimate with him."

Humiliation swept over me, leaving me in a cold sweat. I looked away from them both and swallowed the bolder sized stones in my throat. Without responding, I rose and moved to the French doors at the balcony. Staring blankly out the window, I understood how foolish I'd been to believe this would merely go away.

Dad came up behind me, gently turned me around, and placed his hands on my shoulders. "If you say you only went for lessons then we believe you. But that leads to another question. Did he force himself on you?"

"I don't want to talk about it. Please don't make me. I'm never seeing him again, okay."

"Listen to me, baby." He paused, and looked back at Mom. "Your mother and I cannot let this go. If he assaulted you, the man has to be dealt with. The authorities have to be notified."

"Honey," Mom spoke up and left the sofa to come stand beside Dad, "you're too young to comprehend how men like this operate. They stalk their prey and victimize young innocents."

Images of the picnic, the sketches and stop-motion video, and the drugged wine, loomed from my subconscious. Images I wanted erased from my memory, wiped clean, and the idea of Dad bringing the police into it was more than I could cope with.

"I can't. Please don't make me. The police, everyone at school finding out, it's too much. I can't handle it."

Curling his arms around me, he bundled me close, and I wept as Mom stroked my back and reassured me. When my crying ran its course, they ushered me to the sofa again.

The two of them remained standing, hovering over me as if to keep me from fleeing. Then Dad said, "Sharon, can I talk to you?" And he walked into the kitchen.

Giving me a reassuring touch before leaving, Mom followed him. They stayed there for several minutes, murmuring and conferring with one another before emerging. After resuming their seats, Dad took my hand in his. "We understand this is upsetting for you, and we aren't going to press the issue with the police right now." He surprised me then by taking Mom's hand in his free one. "But we've decided you need to see someone—a doctor, a counselor, someone who specializes in this kind of thing."

"Mom?" I croaked, panic thundering in my chest.

"Don't worry, baby. We'll be with you the whole time."

Chapter Sixty Nine

*D*ad and I sat together alone on the sofa that night while Mom showered. Despite the circumstances that had brought him home, it was comforting to have him here. With my head on his shoulder, I rested there, his presence making me feel safe.

"I've been selfish," he said as he picked lint off his slacks.

"Dad..."

"Shhh." He patted my hand. "It's true, and I'm going to do everything in my power to make up for the past year."

"So are you coming home?"

He sighed. "Not exactly. I've come home to Houston, but I'm going to stay at a hotel for a while. That's part of the reason for the counseling. We need it as much as you do."

"And the divorce?"

"How did you know about that?" He leaned his head outward to look down at me.

"I overheard Mom on the phone with you."

"We're putting it on hold for now."

I sat up straight. "That's great!"

"Don't get your hopes up. It's—we're—a work in progress."

Reclining against his arm again, I inhaled the familiar

smell of his cologne and thought, the key word is progress.

The next morning, Mom left for the office and I stayed behind. Dad and I had made plans to go to breakfast together, and then he'd take me to school. Stuffing my things into my dance bag, I noticed my phone hadn't charged because the cord was loose at the USB port, so I went to the desk to find an old one.

Pilfering through the drawer, I ran across my old phone, but had to keep digging for its cord. In the shuffle, the bag containing the Xanax managed its way to the top of the heap. That's when something struck me.

Lifting the bag out of the drawer, I recalled Erik's taunting concerning the police. He'd said, "Does this mean you plan to turn yourself in for the stolen Xanax you keep hidden in your room?" How had he known I'd kept them hidden in my room?

I glanced at the clock by the bed. There wasn't much time before Dad would arrive. Hastily, I slammed the desk drawer and hurried to the bathroom. Ripping the bag open, I dumped its contents into the toilet. Watching the bar and a half of Xanax swish around in the swirling water, I tried to recollect if I'd told Erik where the pills were. I remembered telling him about taking the half one, but wasn't sure about the others.

Tossing the empty bag in the trashcan, I headed back to my room and sat on the edge of my bed. I kept asking myself, did I tell him where the pills were hidden? Then, like a bolt of lightning, something else hit me. He knew about Raoul. When he'd torn off Raoul's necklace, he'd told me I couldn't wear something that belonged to him. How had he known the necklace came from Raoul? I knew I'd never talked about

Raoul with him.

"Chris, are you ready?" Dad's voice cut into my pondering. He'd entered the apartment.

"Yeah, I'm coming."

I picked up my bag, hoping that these two things were isolated incidences. After all, there was the possibility I had revealed the pills were in my room, seeing as my memory of that night were chaotic. Plus, wouldn't it stand to reason that I would hide them there?

Brushing aside the questions, I wanted to enjoy my time with Dad. It was nice to be with him, no longer angry about what he'd done. With all that had transpired my hurt feelings toward him had simply disintegrated.

After breakfast, we were caught in traffic on the way to the Academy, so I was late arriving. Everyone was already in the studio warming up. Tossing my bag onto a dressing table, I slipped out of the dance skirt and sweater I'd worn over my workout clothes and hurried to join them. I smiled to myself as I recalled the last time I'd been late for Ms. Zaborov's class. It had brought Raoul into my life. I was prepared this time. I had a note from Dad.

As expected, the instant I walked in the door, eyes turned my way. But almost immediately, I sensed something more was at hand. They were conducting floor barre exercises, and the entire class stopped and ogled me, even though the music continued.

Jenna was close to me on the floor, and I looked at her quizzically. Vaulting to her feet she whispered, "Let's get you out of here." Then she hauled me out the door and down the passageway to the dressing room.

"Jenna," I complained, and she released her grip on my

wrist, "what's going on? Why did everyone stare at me like I'd grown another head?"

"Mrs. Hahn was found in the garage last night. She'd been attacked."

"Huh!" I gasped.

"She's in the hospital. There's all kind of talk going on about it." She lowered her voice then and asked, "Are you thinking what I'm thinking?"

"Erik," I mumbled.

"Exactly." She glanced around her and continued in the whispered tone. "The police have been here since early this morning. And that's not the worst of it."

I frowned and had a sinking feeling I didn't want to know anymore.

"Some of the girls said they heard your name mentioned. There's a rumor spreading that you were involved."

"No. No way. This cannot be happening." I tread a path back and forth in front of our dressing tables, flapping my hands at my sides. "Erik did this. I know he did." I rambled, not giving Jenna an opportunity to respond. "But how have they connected me? What exactly are they saying?"

"I don't really know. I've only heard bits and pieces of con..."

Jenna faltered when we heard, "There you are," and we glanced around to see Ms. Zaborov had entered the room. "Jenna, I must speak with Christine."

We exchanged looks, and I was sure Jenna's face mirrored my alarm.

"But I..." Jenna stammered.

"Now," Ms. Zaborov commanded.

"Yes, ma'am." And Jenna bobbed a quick curtsy and

hurried out of the room.

"We have been waiting for you to arrive," Ms. Zaborov said. "Put something on." I glanced down at my leotard and tights. "You will need to come with me."

My pulse quickening, I pulled on the skirt and sweater I'd only moments earlier taken off. "Where are we going?"

"There is someone who wishes to speak with you."

I swallowed my dread and followed Ms. Zaborov to Assistant Director Crane's office. Seated at her desk conversing with two people occupying the chairs in front of her, Mrs. Crane glanced up at us. "Here she is now. Come in, Christine. Thank you for locating her, Lena. You may go."

"No," I yelped and then cleared my throat. "I'd like Ms. Zaborov to stay with me, please."

Mrs. Crane looked to her guests, and one of them nodded assent. "Very well," she said. "Please, close the door behind you."

We stepped into the room and Ms. Zaborov quietly shut the door and moved to stand poised and imperial in a corner. I couldn't say why, but I felt better having her there.

"Christine, these are Detectives Arnold and Ortiz. You've probably heard about what happened to Elaina Hahn." I nodded. "Well, there here to determine what may have happened."

A man stood and offered me his chair. "Please, sit down."

My legs quivered like gelatin, as I moved to lower myself into the seat.

"Don't be scared," the woman sitting next to me said. "We have a few simple questions. It's no big deal."

I assumed she was Detective Ortiz, with biscuit-colored skin, black hair, and the Rs rolling subtly off her tongue.

Dressed in a gray business suit, her long hair was in a bun like mine. She smiled kindly and dragged herself forward to perch on the edge of her seat. Then she pilfered through a jacket pocket and pulled out a small recorder, pressed a button on its side, and placed it on the desk.

My stomach knotted and started to burn, and before she could speak I blurted, "I want my mother to be here."

She smiled and glanced up at her partner. Then Mrs. Crane said, "We've been trying to contact your mother. Her assistant is tracking her down now."

"What about my dad? He's in Houston. Can I call him?"

The detective placed her hand on my arm. "We only have a couple of questions. We'll be speaking with your parents at another time."

I glanced at Ms. Zaborov, who gave me a reassuring nod.

"Okay. What do you want to know?"

Chapter Seventy

*D*etective Ortiz was patient. She would ask a question and give me time to think about my answer. How long had I been attending the Rousseau Academy? Did I know Elaina Hahn, and how long had I been taking lessons under her. Those were easy enough to answer, but when she asked, "Where were you around eleven-thirty last night?" I wanted to hurl myself out of the chair and run for the door.

"I was at home with my parents," I said. "Why? You don't think I had anything to do with the attack on Mrs. Hahn, do you?"

"We're only trying to piece some things together," the male detective said.

I looked around the room to Mrs. Crane, Ms. Zaborov, and then at the two police detectives. Fleetingly, I considered telling them about Erik, what he had done—tried to do—to Raoul. But I was terrified to reveal that I knew him and possibly implicate myself.

Detective Ortiz scribbled in her notepad the entire time, and after a few more questions, strange ones about my goals as a dancer and the second company audition, I was told I could go back to class. Standing and heading for the door, I paused. "Is Mrs. Hahn going to be okay?"

"I believe so," Detective Ortiz replied.

"Come, Christine. You must get to class." Ms. Zaborov had stepped out the door and beckoned me to join her. With one last look over my shoulder, I left Detectives Arnold and Ortiz in Mrs. Crane's office.

By the time we made it back to the studio, classes were changing and the hall filled with students. Jenna spotted me and pushed her way through them to get to me.

"Are you alright?" she asked.

"Yeah, but they asked me where I was last night."

"Shh." Jenna whipped her head about furtively, as several of the girls around us tried to eavesdrop. "C'mon, let's get outta here." Taking me by the hand, she parted the crowd and steered us out of the school where we stepped around the building to talk privately. "Tell me everything," she said, and by the time I finished, I was numb.

"I don't know what to do," I moaned.

"Do you think he did it?" Jenna asked.

I rubbed the heels of my palms into my eyes and moaned, "I have no idea. After what he did to Raoul, and the whole split personality thing, I just don't know. Maybe I should have told them about him. I'm so confused I don't know what to do."

"Calm down. They're fishing. They don't have anything."

"But what made them question me?"

Jenna pinched her lips together and shrugged. "I don't know. It is weird."

Dazed, I tugged my sweater tightly around me, and leaned my back against the side of the building. "Something made them connect me to Mrs. Hahn. I just can't figure out what that was."

"He's so twisted," Jenna said, "maybe he gave them an anonymous tip—to cause you trouble."

"Possibly."

I pushed off the building's wall then gasped when something occurred to me. "The sketches of me in the boiler room, and the stop-motion video on Erik's computer. What if the police find them? Could that be considered incriminating evidence?"

"Ew, I don't know."

"I have to go down there."

"Are you crazy? What if he's there?"

Thinking it over, I weighed my options. "If they find those sketches, the video with my name on it, they're going to know I haven't been truthful. They might never believe I had nothing to do with it then. I have to get those drawings—delete the files. Will you go with me?"

Jenna's eyes bulged wide. "To the boiler room?"

"Please. I can't go alone. Besides, if he did attack Mrs. Hahn, and after Raoul's beating him up, wouldn't he have left? He wouldn't stay in the garage he'd assaulted her in." Grasping both Jenna's forearms in my hands, I squeezed and gave her an imploring look. "Please."

"Oh, all right."

And before she had time to change her mind, I led the way to the garage.

Chapter Seventy One

*I*nside the underground parking lot, we moved as stealthily as possible, staying close to cars and concrete columns to hide behind if necessary. A few feet from the boiler room door, I placed a hand on Jenna's arm to stop her. Now that we were here, I regretted pressuring her to come with me. "You don't have to go any further. I'm okay now. I can handle it." I may have sounded bold, but on the inside, it felt like my bones were melting and oozing into my bloodstream.

"I said I'm in and I'm in. Now let's go." And she started walking again.

The fear of anyone finding those sketches bolstered my resolve, and in a few more steps, we were at the door.

My breathing rapid and unsteady, I tried the doorknob. It was locked. Then I remembered the key on the ledge overhead, and did a *relevé*, rising up on my toes and running my fingers across the doorframe until I found it. Trembling, it took the use of both my hands to guide the key into the lock.

Once inside, Jenna closed the door and we stood and stared at the jail cell wall of pipes. Suddenly, the smells, the droning motors, and the memories they evoked overcame me, and I clutched at Jenna's arm.

"Are you okay?" she whispered.

Swallowing the disgusting taste that had suddenly plugged my mouth, I nodded and took a couple of tentative steps.

"Erik?" I whispered. "Erik? Are you here?"

Edging close to a web of pipes, I peeked through the cracks between them and saw that he was not there. Hovering over my shoulder Jenna said, "C'mon, he's not here. Let's get this done and get outta here."

Darting to the back of the room, Jenna went straight for the sketches. "Whoa," she said as she gathered the pages, "this guy is seriously messed up. He's been after you for a while."

Right then, something in the corner caught my eye. Squinting into the darkness, I crept over and dropped to my knees. It was my ballet slipper necklace, still lying where Erik had thrown it. I picked it up and saw the clasp was broken, but the charm was still there. I closed my hand around it and made a promise to myself before cramming it into the tiny pocket of my sweater. I would get it fixed and never take it off.

"Awww, shit!" Jenna exclaimed.

I jumped to my feet and jerked about, half expecting to see Erik standing there.

"What?" I demanded, when I saw it was just her.

"You need to see this." She motioned for me to join her, and I almost wished I hadn't.

On the floor beside Erik's bed was an upended cardboard box. Displayed across it was an array of my things, my missing purple shrug, the bracelet I'd lost the night Raoul and I'd gone to Discovery Green, and a large frame with one of the better, more elaborate, sketches of me in it.

"It's a shrine," Jenna observed.

"We have to get out of here." I moved to the computer to start deleting the video files. "Grab all that stuff," I instructed. "We can't leave anything behind."

Taking the mouse in hand, I searched for any related files and saw Erik had several windows minimized on the taskbar. I restored the first one I came to. It was the animated sketches video. I deleted it, and then went to Documents and simply deleted everything there. It was the quickest, easiest way to be sure I got anything related to me. Then I cleared out the Recycle Bin.

To be absolutely sure everything was gone, I clicked on another icon on the taskbar, and it took a minute for it to register what I was looking at—a multi-view screen of the entire Rousseau-Wakefield complex. There were shots of the school's halls, outside the theater's exit, and even the parking garage. He'd tapped into the security system. No wonder he could come and go as he pleased without being seen.

"Jenna, you have to see this."

"What?" She scurried up beside me.

I pointed to the screen. "He's been spying on everyone."

She moved in for a closer look. "What the..."

"This must be how he knew Raoul was in the parking garage and went there to wait for him," I said.

"The dude is freaking nuts," Jenna mumbled. Then she shifted to peer at the back of the computer tower. "You know what, I bet this is...yep, this is one of the school's computers. He's the one who broke into the office."

Clicking the mouse to the next screenshot, I gasped and

shrank back. To my horror, I was staring into my own bedroom from Erik's computer. If there was any doubt it was a live shot, it was wiped away when I saw the half-empty glass of orange juice I'd left on the nightstand just that morning. Vaulting to my feet, I shrieked, "Omigod, omigod, omigod!"

"That looks like your..."

"It is!" I cut her off. "He's been watching me, too. Somehow he hacked into my laptop and has been watching everything I do."

Jenna clicked through the different screens then. "You have to tell the police."

"That's how he knew I was still with Raoul," I said. "And the Xanax. Everything."

Fixed to the floor, I stared at the computer, and Jenna said again, "You have to tell the police."

"Yeah—yeah, I will." I turned to her then. She had wadded the sketches and everything from the deranged shrine into the purple shrug. I snatched the bundle from her and said, "Go back to class. Make some excuse for me."

"Why? Where are you going?"

"I'm taking this stuff home, calling Mom and Dad, and then the police. I have to do this, but I don't want it to be here at the school."

Jenna nodded her understanding.

We hurried out of the room then, not. When we reached the outside again, Jenna said, "Good luck. Call me if you need me." And she took off jogging for the school entry.

Looking down at the stolen pieces of my life wrapped in a piece of my clothing, I tucked them under my arm, started running, and didn't stop until I reached Templeton Towers.

Chapter Seventy Two

Since I'd left my bag at the school, I had to ask the concierge for help to get into the apartment. When he'd unlocked the door, I sputtered a quick thank you and practically slammed the door in his face. I ran to my room, coming to a dead stop at the threshold. The realization of Erik watching me there in the most intimate of places made my skin crawl, the times I'd undressed, Raoul and me making out, Raoul visiting after I'd tried to break up with him, and then it hit me. My laptop must have been open that day and probably why he went after Raoul like he did. There was no way to determine how much of my life he'd seen through that monitor because there was simply no telling when it was open or closed.

Stumbling into the room, I collapsed into the chair in front of it. Then without warning, the video chat alert sounded and I jolted. "Please let it be Marisol, please let it be Marisol," I muttered, knowing she would be at school at this time of day. When I clicked the answer button, Erik's battered face appeared, and I gave a startled yelp.

"If I had known you were coming, Chrissy, I would have been here to greet you."

He knew I'd been to the boiler room. I stared at the laptop and contemplated closing it and shutting him out, but that wouldn't make him go away.

"Do you realize what you've done?" I demanded.

"What I've done? You are the one who has destroyed me. They're up there now, organizing searches to ferret out the leather-faced phantom haunting the theater."

"I didn't tell anyone about you. It's what you did to Mrs. Hahn. That's why the police are looking for you."

"Ha!" He leaned in to the screen, making his bulbous eye appear even more distorted. "You lie! You're just like her, always shoving me aside for another."

"I don't know what your twisted relationship with Elaina Hahn is, but I never wanted this to happen. I never used you, and I hadn't told anyone about you—yet. But I will. I'm going to tell my parents, the police. And I'm going to tell them what you did to Raoul, too."

Nonchalantly, he settled back in his seat, snapped his head, and tossed his long, unkempt hair out of his face to reveal patches of scaly, bald scalp. Not bothering to conceal the scars anymore, he snarled, "You are the one who sent that boy down here to spy on me. I had to defend myself from his fit of jealousy. The police would understand that it was self-defense." He took a wheezing breath. "It's too late to worry about it now, though. It'll be over soon enough. You won't be able to hurt me anymore, Chrissy."

My mind raced, trying to track everything he said. "What are you talking about? Are you accusing Raoul of coming after you?"

He raked a hand across the slack side of his mouth where saliva had pooled, and a conniving grin split his lopsided face. "I had a surprise for the quarterback—to finish him off—but unfortunately, circumstances have forced my hand."

Dread turned my insides frigid. Raoul had been mistaken to think a simple scuffle was enough to frighten Erick away. He was insane, and I had to notify the police and warn Raoul as soon as I could.

Slouching forward then, he gripped the sides of his monitor and whimpered, "We could have been so good together, ballerina. You would have been a star—my star." For a split second, he seemed to soften, some of the anger abated, but then he blustered, "But no, you couldn't be with the freak. So it's over, or it will be when I've hurt you the way you've hurt me."

A grenade of fear exploded in my stomach as a thousand different scenarios tore through my mind. His threat wasn't against just me, but everyone who meant anything to me.

"Don't do something you'll regret, Erik," I pleaded. "We need to get you help. You can see a doctor."

"Again with the doctor. Can't you see? There's no hope for this monster." He gestured to his face.

"What are you going to do? Please don't hurt Raoul."

"Don't worry. I won't harm him. But this"—he arced an arm out across the spans of the boiler room—"this will be the end of the school, the theater, and the leather-faced phantom."

Sweeping to his feet, he angled the computer so I would see his next moves. Then he tramped across the room to stand before a row of pipes. Glancing back at the monitor once, he then proceeded to kick one of the pipes. Grunting and howling, he kicked it several times until it gave way and broke free, splitting open and making a chilling hissing sound.

Gas.

"Erik!" I pitched forward and grabbed my laptop. "What are you doing?"

Strutting back, he leaned into the webcam. "This is the end, my love. I refuse to live without you."

"Get out of there," I yelled.

"You will always know that I loved you. I died for you."

Backing up a step then, he pulled a book of matches from his pocket. And before I could utter another word, I saw a tiny flash followed by an enormous explosion, and the screen went black.

Chapter Seventy Three

*I*bolted for the kitchen, grabbed the cordless phone, because I'd left mine in my bag at school, and dialed nine-one-one. Leaving the apartment, I took the phone into the hallway with me, where I punched the elevator button repeatedly.

When the emergency operator came on I sputtered, "There's been an explosion in the underground garage at the Wakefield Center. You have to get the kids out of the school and anyone who might be in the theater."

"Ma'am," the operator tried to interrupt.

"Hurry. There's no time." I hung up and tossed the phone next to our apartment door. Then, giving up on the elevator, I took the stairs, skipping two and three steps at a time.

On the street, I sprinted toward the school. I'd made it a few blocks when I heard sirens and said a quick thank you prayer. Maybe they would get everyone out safely.

Rounding the corner, I saw smoke billowing from the parking garage. Fire trucks, ambulances, and police cars lined the street. A stitch had formed in my side, but I ignored it and raced by the garage, pushing on for the school. I almost fainted with relief when I saw everyone outside, across the street, a safe distance from the school and theater. No one noticed as I joined them and began searching the crowd for Jenna.

"Christine!" I spun around to see her waving her hand. "Over here."

Zigzagging through the throng, I all but stumbled into her before I stopped.

"Did you hear?" she asked. "There's been a bomb threat."

"It's not a bomb. It was Erik."

"Seriously?"

"He busted a gas pipe and then lit a match—on purpose."

Jenna's hand flew to her mouth and she mumbled through it, "Is he dead?"

"I—I'm sure." I gulped back a sob, still shocked by what he'd done.

"Oh, no."

Right then, another EMS vehicle pulled up, and we stared across the street and watched a dozen firefighters come and go from the school, the theater, and the garage.

Gradually, parents began arriving to take their children home. Some of the younger children were crying, while I noticed older ones talking behind their hands and looking my way.

After a while, I saw an ambulance emerge from the underground garage, and I shuddered, wondering if Erik's charred body was inside.

"This is unbelievable," Jenna commented as the ambulance sped past us. "Why did he do it?"

"He'd threatened suicide before," I said softly, resisting the urge to feel responsible. "But I didn't believe he would actually do it, much less try to harm anyone at the school. I watched him on my laptop at home. He orchestrated the whole thing for my benefit. He wanted to die and he wanted me to see it."

My entire body shook, and I couldn't catch a breath as I recalled it all. Jenna threw her arms around me then, and held me up while I had a meltdown. Clinging to her for strength, I heard my name called, and I pulled out of her grasp. Then I turned to see my parents running toward me. Beyond them, I saw Jenna's mother had arrived and was rushing our direction, as well.

"Are you hurt?" Dad asked, grasping my shoulders and inspecting me.

"No, I'm fine, but I have to talk to the police."

"Why?" Mom asked.

"Because I know who did this."

Chapter Seventy Four

*T*he following week, the city building inspector closed the school and Wakefield Center while they investigated the facilities. During that time, to stay in shape, Jenna and I went to the Street Feet Studios to practice.

One day after she'd dropped me at home, I was surprised to see Mom and Dad sitting at the kitchen table. Dad's visits had become more frequent, but this was a week day afternoon. They should have been at work. Something was up.

"Hey, Tina Ballerina," Dad greeted with a forced pleasantness.

Mom gave me a peculiar look, like she was concerned, and said, "Maybe we should go in the living room."

Something was definitely up.

Tagging behind them, I dropped my bag on the floor and sat on the sofa. "What's going on? Why are you here?" I glanced at the clock. "Shouldn't you be at work?"

"Christine," Dad said, "Mrs. Hahn is on her way here to talk to you—to us."

"She's not coming here to kick me out, is she?"

Ever since her assault, I've worried that the woman

blamed me for what Erik did to her.

"No," Mom replied, "that's not why." Then they exchanged anxious glances. "I think we should wait until she gets here."

Several strained minutes ticked by as we waited. At last, the doorbell rang and Dad went to answer it. I hadn't seen Mrs. Hahn since the last time we'd had class together, and I was ill prepared for how she would look. Not wearing any makeup, her face was smattered with bruises in various stages of healing—purple, yellow-green, and gray. I didn't want to look, but I couldn't tear my eyes away.

Leaning heavily on her walking stick, Mrs. Hahn followed us into the living room. Then after awkward greetings and Mom offering her a drink, we sat down, me between Mom and Dad, and Mrs. Hahn in an armchair.

"I see you're keeping up with your practice," she said, indicating my dance clothes.

"Yes, ma'am. Jenna and I have been going to a studio across town."

"Very good. But that's not why I'm here." She offered me a frail smile. "I came to talk to you about Erik."

My nerve endings snapped to attention. Part of me had known this conversation was inevitable, but now that it was here, I didn't want to go through with it.

"There are things about him—well, there are things you need to be made aware of."

I turned my head to Dad and he patted my knee. "It's okay, honey."

"I'm afraid there's no easy way to say it," Mrs. Hahn continued, "Erik is my son."

Inhaling sharply, I clamped a hand to my mouth and blinked away my shock.

"I was eighteen years old, living and dancing in Paris, when I got pregnant. Erik's father was a choreographer—he was married, just not to me. The man's family was quite wealthy, so they set me up in a house outside the city—that's where Erik spent most of his life. After he was born, I wanted to continue dancing, so his grandparents hired live-in nannies to help. He was a beautiful child, so precocious, and he was a natural dancer. He used to say he was going to grow up to be my dance partner."

If Mom and Dad hadn't been beside me, I might have thought I was dreaming this—Mrs. Hahn sitting in my living room telling me Erik was her son.

She hesitated then, shutting her eyes tightly for a second. "When I moved from the *corps de ballet* to a soloist position, I traveled more. I tried to visit as often as possible, but it was difficult. I was so young and self-absorbed, and I managed to convince myself he was fine. He had everything he needed or wanted, given anything he asked for." Her hand fluttered to the cane and she fiddled with its faux ivory handle. "But, as he grew, it became evident that he was different. He was extremely bright and talented, in not only dance, but also music—he could sit down at a piano and play a tune he'd heard for the first time only moments before, and technology—electronics were like extensions of himself. He was truly a wonder."

She paused, looked down at her wrist, and tugged her silk sleeve down to cover what I now knew to be a burn scar. When she continued her voice was shaky. "As he got older, he began exhibiting signs of cruelty. There were tantrums that escalated, and on occasion, he abused his pets. Eventually, there came a time when he could no longer attend school with other children. He couldn't function—socially, that is.

"Of course, we took him to various doctors, but no matter their course of treatment, whether it was medications or therapy, nothing helped. How could it when he thought himself smarter than they were?

"Ultimately, he directed his malice at me. He resented me being gone so much. He even became jealous of ballet. By the time he was a teenager, he would spiral into violent rages, and I couldn't bear going to see him. I was afraid of him." She pressed her fingertips to her trembling lips.

I spoke up then. "I don't understand. He told me his mother died in a fire. He said he tried to rescue her—you—and that was how he was injured."

Mrs. Hahn shook her head. "He set the fire."

"Oh, my god," Mom whimpered.

"His father and I had started seeing each other again. Erik had always disliked any man I went out with, but he hated his father. And one night, we were together—you understand?"

I nodded.

"Erik had been in a manic state about it for some time, but I'd convinced myself he would get over it, that he'd come to accept his father into our lives. But then he set the fire. It wasn't until we were both in the hospital"—she lifted her cane then and I realized now her injuries were from the fire—"that I discovered what he'd been about. He'd wanted to play the hero, to rescue me, and then I would forever be enamored with him."

"And his father?" Dad asked.

"It was he who died in the fire."

Mom, Dad, and I sat stunned into silence.

"I believed him," I muttered. "Every lie he told, I believed him."

Chapter Seventy Five

"That's how he is," Mrs. Hahn explained to us. "He can be quite persuasive. It's part of his mania."

"If he set the fire," Dad said, "why didn't he go to prison?"

"It became evident the fire was arson, and there was an investigation. We were both questioned while still in the hospital. I suppose Erik realized he might be caught and one night he simply vanished from his hospital bed.

"In the years since then, he's followed me. After my injuries, I left Paris and taught in London for a while. He would leave notes in my home or office—some kind and tender, about how much he missed me, and others angry and threatening. Then when I came here, I knew he was nearby when my office was broken into. Of course, I'd hoped it was some of the students playing a prank, but when my necklace went missing..."

"You're necklace?" I asked.

She nodded. "It was one he'd bought for me, and it was stolen from my purse in my office."

"Is it a heart shaped locket?"

Mrs. Hahn looked surprised. "Yes. How did you know?"

"Excuse me. I'll be right back."

I hurried to my room, opened my jewelry box, and retrieved Erik's necklace I'd taken off the night Raoul gave me his. Back in the living room, I held the necklace out to her. "Is this it?"

With shaking fingers, Mrs. Hahn gently took the necklace from me.

"He gave it to me. Said it belonged to someone special in his life."

Her hands unstable, she opened her purse, pulled out a pocket book, and slipped the necklace into a zippered pouch. "Thank you," she mumbled.

Sitting down again, I said, "Erik told me he'd danced in Paris and at the Bolshoi."

Mrs. Hahn shook her head animatedly. "That was me. I danced there. Erik never visited any of those places. Though he's a gifted, even superior, dancer, he could never master to the personal discipline necessary to dance in a troupe."

My hands in my lap, I stared at a magazine cover on the coffee table and thought, was there anything he told me that was true?

Mrs. Hahn spoke, "I know now I should have called the police when I found the note. I can't tell you how many times I've wished I had."

"The note?" I asked.

"Yes. A few days before he attacked me, I discovered a note from Erik in my car. He hadn't signed it mind you, but I knew it was from him. It said if I didn't allow you to audition for the second company there would be dire consequences."

"That's how the police connected me to you," I surmised.

"I'm sorry, Christine. I tried to handle it myself. I took off a couple of days and hired a private investigator to look for him. I intended to have him confined somewhere where he could receive professional help. Unfortunately, when I didn't respond how he wanted, well, you know what happened next."

The room fell quiet for a moment then Dad sputtered, "This is unacceptable. You should have done something when you first suspected he was near. You put not only our daughter, but also every other student in that school in danger. You might have prevented what happened to Christine had you come forth in the beginning."

"Dad," I muttered.

He sprang to his feet and moved purposefully to stand behind the sofa and place a hand on my shoulder. "Given this man's track record, I think this could have been prevented." His face took on a red hue as he ranted. "Do you have any idea what Christine has been through—all because you wanted to handle it yourself? You had no business even being at that school as long as you suspected he was stalking you."

Mrs. Hahn looked me in the eye then. "He's right, Christine. I should have come forward. I bear the responsibility for what happened to you. You were a pawn in Erik's game of revenge. He wanted to best me by turning you into a better dancer than I could. Can you ever forgive me?"

I swallowed the bitter taste of reality. Dad could be upset and rage on, but what had happened couldn't be undone, and blaming Mrs. Hahn wouldn't make it any better.

"We were all pawns," I told her. "But he's dead now, and I don't hold it against you."

Dad squeezed my shoulder. "That's the problem, and the

reason we let Mrs. Hahn come here to talk to you today. We don't believe Erik is dead."

"What?" I exclaimed, turning to stare up at him. "But I watched him bust that gas pipe, and I saw an explosion. He couldn't have lived through that."

Dad sat back down. "It was all staged, honey. The pipe wasn't filled with gas, but water. What you heard leaking out was steam. Then, like a two-bit magician, he caused a small blast of flame before the computer monitor, which made it appear larger than it was. It was an optical illusion, and in your fear, you ran to the theater believing what you thought you saw."

Incredulously, I shook my head back and forth. "But they said there was a bomb threat."

"That was you," Mom said. "When you called nine-one-one, they thought you were making the bomb threat."

Still disbelieving, I mumbled, "And the ambulance?"

"That's routine in a suspected bomb situation," Dad said. "But no body—Erik's body—was never found."

Unable to sit still anymore, I stood and took a few steps away, only to retrace them and stand before Mrs. Hahn. "So where is he?"

"I wish I knew," she replied. "I still have a private investigator looking for him, and the police have detectives searching, as well."

"You see why we thought you should know about this," Mom said. "We don't want to frighten you anymore than you already have been, but you need to be aware..."

"That he might come back for me," I completed her sentence.

"Personally, I don't believe it's you he would come for,"

Mrs. Hahn said. "It's me he's always been after."

A beat passed while I ruminated on all they'd said. Erik was still alive. The horrible nightmares I'd had reliving the event, and all along, he's been out there somewhere—very much alive.

"That's only part of why I came here today," Mrs. Hahn said. "The other thing is I want you to know I'm leaving the Rousseau Academy. But before I go, I plan to recommend you be allowed to audition for the second company. Ms. Zaborov will see it's done."

How long had I yearned to hear those words? Now they seemed so trivial, so utterly unimportant.

She got to her feet then. "I suppose I should go. But before I do, I want you to know this was not your fault."

I looked her in the eye and whispered, "I know."

Epilogue

*T*rue to her word, Jenna had left school at the end of the semester. She'd started attending public school, spending her spare time at the Street Feet Studios. And now, many months later, she was still seeing Dionte. It was the longest relationship she'd ever had.

After his leg healed, Van came back to school. He'd moved on from his attempts to get a TV show interested in a theater ghost, to auditioning for a reality program about the lives of ballet dancers. Though I never said it to anyone, I believed Erik pushed Van down those stairs. Considering everything I'd learned about him, it wouldn't have surprised me.

As she'd said, Mrs. Hahn never returned. Rumors she'd had a mental breakdown after the attack circulated the school, and only a few of us knew what really happened. Ms. Zaborov, Mr. Darby, and Mrs. Crane committed to protecting me from snooping reporters and blabbering classmates, but only so much could be done to stop teenage girls from gossiping. What they thought didn't bother me, though. I knew what had happened, and so did the people who mattered to me most.

Mom, Dad, and I started seeing a therapist shortly after

Mrs. Hahn's visit. There was family as well as individual counseling. A few months in, Dad gave up his room at the hotel and moved home. I knew it wasn't easy for either of them, but they were trying.

It was a little more difficult for me, though. It took several months for me to stop looking over my shoulder everywhere I went. Finally, I came to believe what Mrs. Hahn had said. It was her Erik had been after. I was merely a tool.

Raoul remained my rock, always there for me. He even applied to the University of Houston so he'd be close to the Rousseau after he graduated. Many times I had nightmares as my vivid imagination toyed with what Erik might have done to Raoul had he had the opportunity, but eventually those dreams faded, too.

In the spring, I auditioned for the second company and was accepted. Though I was grateful for what Erik had taught me, I knew I earned that position and I deserved it. I'd found what was missing, the *je ne sais quoi* that had eluded me, and I had no doubt I got in on my own merit.

Since then, I'd performed with Rousseau II on tour, and I'd received lots of praise from instructors as well as ballet lovers. Mr. Darby even said he'd been told the New York Ballet had their eyes on me. Me! The New York Ballet had their eyes on me!

Tonight's performance was different. It was special because it wasn't with the second company. Tonight, I danced with the main company, the Rousseau Ballet, in La Bayadere, filling out the *corps de ballet* in the Shades scene, which required many female dancers. I was in the back—dancing with the main company! It was a dream come true and reminded me of the evening I sneaked into Claudette

Sunderland's dressing room and imagined the possibilities. Although, I haven't gotten to that level of professionalism— I'm still a long way from my own dressing room—I'm satisfied with my decision to stay in ballet.

And chillingly, I knew I had at least one devoted fan somewhere in the audience at every performance. Because after each show, when I arrived back at the dressing room I shared with the other corps dancers, I found a single, pink dahlia waiting for me on my dressing table.

ABOUT THE AUTHOR

Lesa Howard is the alter ego of author Lesa Boutin. Lesa writes for younger audiences, as well, hence the pen name for her edgier YA and adult writing. Lesa's day job is teaching creative writing to children in inner-city schools. She also conducts writing workshops and author visits to schools and conferences. If you would like to know more about her other books, or arrange a workshop, see her contact information below.

www.lesaboutin.com
lesaboutin@gmail.com
www.facebook.com/lesa.boutin
Other books written by Lesa,
Amanda Noble, Zookeeper Extraordinaire
Amanda Noble, Special Agent

www.ingramcontent.com/pod-product-compliance
Lightning Source LLC
Chambersburg PA
CBHW061324170626
46817CB00001B/307